The Lo__ ___g___

(Matt Drake #10)

By

David Leadbeater

Copyright 2015 by David Leadbeater
ISBN:

All rights reserved. No part of this publication may be reproduced, distributed, or transmitted in any form or by any means, including photocopying, recording, or other electronic or mechanical methods, without the prior written permission of the publisher/author except in the case of brief quotations embodied in critical reviews and certain other non-commercial uses permitted by copyright law.
All characters in this book are fictitious, and any resemblance to actual persons living or dead is purely coincidental.

This ebook is for your personal enjoyment only. This ebook may not be re-sold or given away to other people. If you would like to share this ebook with another person, please purchase any additional copy for each reader. If you're reading this book and did not purchase it, or it was not purchased for your use only, then please return it to Smashwords.com and purchase your own copy. Thank you for respecting the hard work of this author.

Thriller, adventure, action, mystery, suspense, archaeological, military

Other Books by David Leadbeater:

The Matt Drake Series
The Bones of Odin (Matt Drake #1)
The Blood King Conspiracy (Matt Drake #2)
The Gates of Hell (Matt Drake 3)
The Tomb of the Gods (Matt Drake #4)
Brothers in Arms (Matt Drake #5)
The Swords of Babylon (Matt Drake #6)
Blood Vengeance (Matt Drake #7)
Last Man Standing (Matt Drake #8)
The Plagues of Pandora (Matt Drake #9)

The Alicia Myles Series
Aztec Gold (Alicia Myles #1)

The Disavowed Series:
The Razor's Edge (Disavowed #1)
In Harm's Way (Disavowed #2)
Threat Level: Red (Disavowed #3)

The Chosen Few Series
Chosen (The Chosen Trilogy #1)
Guardians (The Chosen Trilogy #2)

Short Stories
Walking with Ghosts (A short story)
A Whispering of Ghosts (A short story)

Connect with the author on Twitter: @dleadbeater2011
Visit the author's website: www.davidleadbeater.com
Follow the author's Blog
http://davidleadbeaternovels.blogspot.co.uk/

All helpful, genuine comments are welcome. I would love to hear from you.
davidleadbeater2011@hotmail.co.uk

Dedication

This one is for my family

CHAPTER ONE

Callan Dudley was the youngest member of the 27-Club—a seven-strong gang of crazy Irishmen whose sanest known act in eight years was to make a blood pact that, when they all finally came together again in Hell, they would dance a healthy jig on the Devil's balls.

His brother, Malachi, at thirty five, was the oldest.

Callan Dudley hadn't seen his crew in about a year. Though they were a gang they didn't exactly run together. At least, not in several years. The members drifted apart, did their own thing for a while, then came together somewhere down the line, in some merciless, dark rat hole of a public house where even the vermin stayed out of the dark corners for fear of being killed and eaten by the patrons. There they partied loud and cursed violently and drank themselves into a rare, dreamless stupor.

Dudley's time with the Pythians had been diverting at least, at times even entertaining. The mercs he ran with were assholes to a man, in the game solely for money and motivated only by their own greed. Every last one of them deserved to die and rot in Purgatory, forgotten even by their own whore-bag, soulless mothers. His enemies, however—now they were a different matter.

Alicia Myles, the female who had beaten him at his own game, sprang to the forefront of his mind. Truth be told she was never far away. And the rest of her comrades. He would be learning more about them very soon.

First things first, however. There was the small matter of his recent incarceration and the imminent transportation to a so-called American 'black site'. Not that they had officially told him anything, but he kept up with the times. If he allowed this to happen the black site would be the least of his worries.

So what to do? *Escape.* Sure, but that wasn't easy when you were clapped in enough iron to take down Tony Stark. Time was his enemy. Not opportunity, you could create those. Not guards, he could destroy those. And not environment, the place didn't matter. It was the precise *when* of it all that would carry the day.

Dudley bunched his muscles when the irons were applied. Stared the guards down as they escorted him along a white-walled corridor. Called their mothers bitches and whores as was expected. None of it mattered. On the surface he was just another dangerous Irish asshole prisoner, seeing the light of day for the last time. Underneath he was as watchful as a starving predator. The corridor led to a low-ceilinged, underground parking lot. Black sedans, SUVs and 4x4s stood everywhere, many of them with engines running and filling the area with their noxious exhaust fumes.

The guard to his right—bright-eyed, young, relatively new to the game since he looked about twenty five and hadn't been knee-deep in mayhem since the age of eight—turned to him.

"Take a last look around, dipshit. This'll be the last thing you ever see that ain't got a set of bars in front of it."

Dudley headbutted him. It was expected.

The guard fell away, his free hand coming up to cup his bloodied nose.

"Be thankful it weren't yer feckin' balls got crushed," Dudley snarled.

Men dragged him further into the parking lot and toward a nondescript SUV. The only thing different about it was the blacked-out windows but sometimes, that one singular feature was more than enough. Dudley held in the smile. Maybe it sported government plates too? No matter, the target was already painted on the roof.

Settling in, Dudley allowed the seat belt to be fastened and two burly guards to flank him in the back. Two more climbed into the front: driver and passenger. The latter, a bearded seasoned individual turned to face him.

"Go along to get along," he said. "If you need to speak address me as Guard Winston. We ain't here to damage you. Nod if you understand."

Dudley nodded, happy to conform. A bag was thrust over his head, making it hard to breathe. The vehicle started and drove up a sharp incline, then out into traffic. Cruising the streets of DC, probably headed up toward Silver Springs or Bethesda. Dudley retained a clear sense of direction, not that it mattered too much at the moment.

Events were out of his hands.

The transport continued in silence until Guard Winston radioed in their progress about an hour into the journey. By then they were navigating country roads, slowing for tight bends and passing no traffic in either direction. Dudley used the time to reflect on what he considered to be a rather storied past. What had led him to this exciting juncture in life?

Family. Of course. His father had been Irish Mob, killed

by the British. Uncles? Still engaged in the fight. Mother? Rotting away in some undisclosed, hateful English town someplace with her new prick of a husband. One day Dudley dreamed of taking the entire 27-Club to visit both of them, just for the night.

Party time.

Dudley was ready, though even he was shocked by the ferocity of it. The distinctly unlikely chance that the Pythians were engineering his escape dissipated to nothing as soon as the first explosion occurred. This was 27-Club discretion and refinement if ever he'd experienced it.

The first explosion rocked the car, sending it up onto two wheels, just as the driver was steering wildly and trying to brake. Dudley was jerked against his seat belt, at the same time trying to wedge himself between the two rear guards to minimize injury. The car flipped, crashing down onto its right-hand side with a crunch of metal and screams from the guards. At forty miles an hour it scraped along the asphalt, rapidly decelerating. Dudley hung on as best he could, still sandwiched. The guards grunted and shifted, well-trained despite their non-Irish affiliations and knowing full well what was coming next.

By the time the second explosion went off, the car was already bouncing. Dudley imagined the mines had been laid in holes dug out of the asphalt, then roughly covered over again until the target vehicle passed over. How had the lads known the route? Well, when all this blew over the Americans would probably find one of their guards was missing, unable to get out of bed because he was strapped down and full of holes.

Dudley crushed the man below him without mercy, trying at the very least to impede his shooting arm. Metal crunched, rasped and grated all around him, fragments of glass lashing at his face. The back end of the vehicle came around, smashing into a hillside verge. All of a sudden the front end whipped around. Dudley was thrown forward, the front of his head leaving the back far behind and seeing stars.

At last, the SUV ground to a halt.

The follow-up assault was instantaneous. Though he couldn't see their faces, or anything at all, Dudley just knew the boots he heard stomping outside belonged to the craziest lads in the business.

The boys are back!

With that thought blasting through his head he began to lurch to and fro within the confines of the seatbelt, smashing between the seat in front and the headrest at back. At least one guard turned their attention toward him.

"The hell you doin', man?"

"Gettin' in the feckin' mood, *man.*"

Dudley smashed his head even harder.

Guard Winston kicked out the windshield with his feet, ensuring his firearm was at the ready. The black boots out there disappeared from sight. The car's driver looked over at Winston.

"Whaddya think?"

"Can't hang around here all day. The distress button's been pressed. Now let's get ourselves free."

Dudley leaned on the guard below as those in the front seats crawled clear of the wreckage. Up on their knees, casting around, they said nothing. The third guard elbowed Dudley.

"I'm gonna crawl into the front. When I do I want you to pull clear of Guard—"

Gunfire rang out, shocking in the silent aftermath of the crash. Dudley saw Guard Winston and the driver fall, faces and eyes staring right at him, now void of life. *And a good riddance to you.* Now the guy next to him was fidgeting like a man on Speed, straining to see in four directions at once.

"I wouldn't bother," Dudley said. "You'll be dead soon too."

That was when the guy got a bright idea. Instead of trying to save himself he grabbed Dudley by the neck, thrust his head down, and shoved a handgun into his ear.

"You want him? Then show yourselves. Or I'll blow his head off!"

"That's our wee brother," a splendid Irish twang rang out. "You hurt him I'll rip yer eyes out."

Dudley's mood soared. *Malachi!* His older brother, reunited at last in bloody murder. His only hope now was that the rest of the 27-Club were here and they could make it a new chapter to be proud of.

"Callan, me wee brother. Yer there?"

"Fire top and bottom," he said. "They got me in the middle."

With not a moment's hesitation, shots rang out. Bullets ripped through the SUV, the lower one coming perilously close to his own forehead. Blood splashed over him, but not his own. The handgun that felt like it had become part of his ear didn't go off in any kind of reflex action.

Score one to the lads for that! Lucky bastards!

Dudley waited patiently for his release. Soon, he heard heavy breathing and the grunting of two men. A pair of hands dug under his belt, releasing it, then the two men helped drag him clear of the wreckage.

No words were spoken. Homecomings weren't made to a man clapped in irons and wearing a mask. When the keys had been located and manacles removed, the hood was whisked away.

"Callan, me fella. How are ye?"

Malachi's grinning visage popped up before his eyes.

"Better for seein' the lads, to be sure. You ready to do some real mischief, lads?"

Six familiar faces surrounded him, all grinning like maniacs now their bloodlust was up. Boyle, Daley, McLain, Byram and Brannan needed no introductions.

"Yer wanna take these Pythian eejits and fill them full of holes?"

Dudley grinned at McLain, the passion in the man's voice igniting his own violent ardor. "Not yet," he growled. "First I want to murder this woman what took me down called Alicia Myles. Then we'll murder her again just for fun, and the team who helped her. We can use the Pythians' help with all that."

"Grand, grand," Malachi said. "Let's get started."

Dudley couldn't help but smile even wider as he kicked the corpses aside and armed himself. "Damn, I'm looking forward to this."

CHAPTER TWO

Mai Kitano awoke to the sound of deep, thrumming engines. Disorientation overcame her for a moment and then the acute stabbing pain in her stomach brought it all back.

The hotel room. The Yakuza. Hikaru shooting her in the stomach; the second bullet slamming into the carpet by her head. The dragging and the lifting, the intense pain. The knowledge that she never should have left the safety of the suite of rooms provided by the Americans. And Matt Drake?

Damn. She had pushed him away, now look where she was.

A plan had been forming in her mind, a plan to revisit Tokyo and seek out the surviving girl from Hayami's family. *Emiko, wasn't it?* That was her name. *Find her and lay all your sins out before her.*

She knew now how ridiculous it all sounded. Yes, her primary motives were selfish—she was doing it for her own peace of mind. But . . . that didn't stop her *needing* to do it.

Then the Yakuza changed all that. Hikaru had grown a set, come to DC and confronted her. Granted, the set he'd grown hadn't allowed him to confront her without an entourage of armed goons, but then why should he?

Mai remembered the agony of being shot in the stomach, the knowledge that such a death was extremely painful. Nevertheless, she would have endured it all night just to keep a certain, special knowledge away from Hikaru.

That Grace had been sleeping in the next room. The

Yakuza never found out.

Now, coming to in the gently rolling, malodorous room with a single bare light bulb and cracked wooden shelves; with a no doubt locked metal door and no windows; with a single desk full of papers and small glass bottles and syringes and tubes, Mai Kitano found she couldn't move more than an inch.

Her arms and legs were strapped to a bed. After a moment she determined that she still wore pants, thankfully, and boots and the tank top she had gone to bed in. The pain of trying to sit up seemed to wrench her stomach apart, making her groan. Somebody had done a decent job down there, removing the bullet and patching her up.

Where the hell am I?

The situation was awkward. Yes, she had been in worse and escaped without a scratch but never with a fresh bullet wound. Ideally, she needed time to heal—even a few days would help.

Not enough.

She knew that and told her inner voice to shut up. The man who had taken her would reveal all, she was confident of that. His egotism ensured it. All she had to do was get better until he did.

Again she lifted her head as much as she was able, fighting the pain. Beyond her feet stood a medicine cabinet and beside that a drinks globe. Interesting set-up. Boxes were piled in one corner of the room, some torn open to reveal such diverse items as bandages, condoms, bottled water and designer aftershave.

The door rattled, opened and a man walked in. Mai saw instantly that he was Japanese, grubby and worn down.

"Ah, you are awake. I will fetch water."

Mai sipped for a while and then said. "Where am I?"

"On board the *Genkai Hida*."

He spoke with such matter-of-factness that Mai wondered if she'd been told before and forgotten.

"And we're bound for . . . ?"

"You are bound for Kobe." Hikaru's strong voice came from somewhere beyond her field of vision. "Where else would the infamous Mai Kitano be going?"

Mai understood immediately. Hikaru belonged to Japan's largest Yakuza organization which, despite being one of the largest criminal entities in the world, had its headquarters in Kobe, Japan. Taking into account Mai's past exploits against the Yakuza it was a no-brainer to expect that she would be afforded a visit to the center of operations. With over forty thousand members, press-covered invitations for their *Kumicho*—their leader—from the police to step in as 'honorary police chief' for the day, and even an in-house magazine, the Kobe based Yakuza family was universally well connected. It was also highly publicized that they had started a large-scale relief effort after the great Kobe earthquake of 1995, helping with the distribution of food and supplies, something that was vital to the local people since official support was non-existent for several days. And again, after the 2011 earthquake and tsunami, the Yakuza opened its offices to the public and sent out supplies to affected areas. Even CNN were quoted as saying the Yakuza "moved quietly and swiftly to provide aid to those most in need". Rather than an attempt at glory-seeking, this was more of an honor-code move by the criminal organization. Their members were well acquainted with having to fend for themselves without government aid or community support, valued justice and duty above anything else, and forbade allowing others to suffer.

Mai knew she would see very little of this honor code. She had wronged the Yakuza. They would make her suffer beyond belief.

Hikaru's face came into view, poised above her. "Doctor Nori here is fixing you up so that we can put you on trial."

"On trial?" Mai repeated, surprised. "I imagined your bosses would prefer something more low key."

"Not at all." Hikaru smiled grimly. "Unfortunately for you and for us, anybody who's *anybody* and most of the world's authorities know how to treat Yakuza." He held up his left little finger, showing her that the tip was missing. "My transgression cost me. But now—now I have truly atoned."

"Not yet you haven't." Mai stared up at the bare bulb.

"You are not in Washington anymore." Hikaru grinned. "And you're wounded. In truth, nobody knows where you are. Do not expect a rescue."

Mai said nothing. Hikaru was right in at least one respect. Until her wound improved she was going nowhere.

"Why a trial? Even for me it seems a little showy."

Hikaru shrugged. "It was not my decision. I would have cut you up and fed you to the pigeons. But a showcase trial . . . and death . . . is required."

Now Mai understood. "And you had me thinking I may stand a chance."

"Make your peace, Mai Kitano. Very soon, the world will see what the Yakuza do to their enemies."

CHAPTER THREE

Matt Drake wanted to break down the door, but hotel policy and the presence of its day manager convinced him otherwise. Still, they lost a precious ten minutes summoning him and allowing him to unlock the door. Drake didn't have a clue what to expect. Last night, their team celebration had gone off without a hitch but still Mai had left early, taking Grace to a new place. This morning, Drake had woken with a thick head, a body still bruised from recent exploits over in Niagara Falls and a nasty feeling.

Phone ringing; early morning; Grace sounding panicked. None of it helped create much of a rosy feeling. Add to that the fact that caffeine had not yet passed his lips, and the man from Yorkshire was presenting a mood that some might call spiky.

Dahl was with him, the big Swede seemingly possessed of some psychic ability to sense danger. The moment Drake had shoved his nose out of the hotel room door, Dahl had happened to glance out.

"All good?"

"*Whoa!*" Drake had been caught off guard, still half asleep. "I don't know."

"Drink too much?"

"Nope. The pint and a half I sank appears to have left me able to stand."

"So . . ."

Drake had motioned the Swede outside and explained

that he'd received a panicked call from Grace. Mai wasn't answering her door or her cell. Some people would have given her several more hours, perhaps allowing Mai to sleep in, but not Grace. Her life currently revolved around panic and stress and nightmares. In truth, Drake was glad she had contacted him so quickly. The way Mai was acting lately it wouldn't surprise him if she'd left town.

That was—if she had taken Grace with her. He sighed in silence. The reality was he hadn't expected any of this—even when she moved out to a nearby hotel, taking Grace with her.

It's not you, she said. And this time he believed her. What the hell was she supposed to do if she couldn't mentally get past something? Different people reacted in different ways but Mai usually confronted problems head on. Drake guessed that if it hadn't been for the severity of the Pandora attacks, Mai would be in Tokyo already.

The hotel manager slid an access card into the door's rectangular slot and pushed the thick, silver handle. Drake pulled him away.

"Best stand back," he said. "Mai's liable to take a stranger's head off."

He didn't add, *if she's in there.*

Once, inside, the appearance of the room didn't immediately start any alarm bells ringing. Only one thing was immediately evident—Mai wasn't in it. Nothing was damaged. The night stand still stood with its dusty alarm clock and much-used TV remote. The work desk looked well ordered, hotel and local brochures lying in a neat little pile. The curtains were closed. Drake borrowed the key card from the manager and inserted it into a little slot, throwing more light on the scene. The bed clothes were rumpled, but that was about it.

He moved further into the room, Dahl at his back. Grace hovered in the doorway.

"What's happening? I can't see."

"She's not here, love." Drake walked around the bed, wondering if perhaps she'd done something even more out of character and headed out to a gym or for an early morning swim. But where were her bags?

Then he saw it.

Drake stopped abruptly. Dahl peered over his shoulder.

"Oh dear, is that—"

Drake squatted. The bedroom carpet was soaked with a dark red substance, and where it ended against the side of the bed someone had drawn three characters. Drake took his phone out to snap a picture.

"Japanese characters?" Dahl asked.

"I think so."

Drake struggled to quell the pounding in his heart. No evidence certainly, but instinct told him that this was Mai's blood. "Try her cellphone," he said with a quiet desperation. "Just once more."

Dahl was about to and then Grace said, "I just did. Nothing. Straight to a stupid answer phone."

Drake backed away. Dahl re-checked the bathroom. Grace was suddenly at his side.

"Oh, no, please no. Is that—"

Drake fought to keep calm. Grace had been going through a worse time than any of them recently with the slow return of her most hated memories. Under Mai's guidance she'd stood up to them with an unfaltering positivity, focusing solely on what lay ahead. Dreams had been achieved and plans made, a hundred things to look forward to. Grace fought the past hard, and though Drake never knew how she coped in the dark watches of the night, he saw her during the day and encouraged everything the plucky youngster said and did. Some people would never recover from a past such as hers, but Grace wasn't one of them.

Especially with the help of someone who had already been through it. With Mai's help.

"We don't know," he said. He heard Dahl in the bathroom, already contacting Hayden. With a great effort he swallowed his own feelings and stared at the picture he'd taken. "Do you know what these characters mean?"

Grace peered over. "No."

Dahl called through. "Hayden says that Karin will have some kind of character recognition software at the office. Send her the photo."

Drake nodded. He sent the picture and then checked the rest of the room, finding exactly what he expected— nothing. Every minute that passed made his blood boil hotter, his jaw set harder.

After everything we've done we're still hot targets. It occurred to him then that if they all stayed in this game there was only one way it was going to end. *Don't think that way!* But what other outcome could there be?

Dahl stopped him near the door. "You remember Whitehall?"

Drake blinked in confusion for a moment, then remembered their most recent adventure. "The terrorist cells that attacked us on the street? What about them?"

"Some guy called Ramses, some kind of terrorist royalty, sent them, yeah? Still had a bee in his bonnet about how we obliterated that arms bazaar." The Swede smiled in grim recognition. "If only we'd known to drop a bomb on the whole bunch of evil bastards."

"You think *Ramses* took Mai? Unlikely, pal. I mean for starters—wouldn't they just blow up the building? Hope for the best?"

"They're not *all* Neanderthals."

"I know, I know." Drake held up his hands, unable to process clearly as Mai's potential fate swirled about his head. "Let's just get back to the office and call everyone in. This is as serious as it gets for us. Personal. Roust the entire team. Now."

CHAPTER FOUR

Tyler Webb studied the walls of his new HQ. Granted, they were further apart than those of the previous one but no way did they hold the same appeal. The view for a start—all he could see out of the eighth-story window was another well-lit office block, and then another, bland and nondescript, but entirely necessary since the Pythians had relinquished their Niagara Falls nerve center.

Washington DC, though?

Webb headed over to the window, angling his neck. To be fair the view did have its charms the lower you looked. The scurrying worker ants were out on the streets and scuttling around their offices, wasting their lives away. How many of them knew his name? How many knew of the Pythians? His guess—a hell of a lot. The smile stretched across his face unbidden, uninhibited.

Yes they had lost the first round, but could life really be any better? This HQ was the second of twelve he'd prepared in this country alone. He stood and watched and ate and slept among his enemies, at their very heart.

Just where he wanted to be.

And even more interestingly . . . three Pythians were dead. Webb couldn't help but giggle. Who would have bet on that? General Stone, Robert Norris and Miranda Le Brun had all met their makers during the Pandora project. And if it wasn't for Beauregard Alain, Webb himself might be in some very sticky substance.

But that wasn't strictly true, he had engineered the Beauregard moment, craved it with all his black heart and decayed soul. That face to face with his enemies? It had been worth all the risk and the deaths that preceded it. *Touché, Drake. And Alicia Myles, Torsten Dahl and Hayden Jaye. I bet I'm already worming my way into your deepest thoughts, aren't I?*

Delicious. Like warm sunshine on a cold day. It heated his entire body to a quiet frenzy.

So how did they find the last HQ? The returning chopper that *he* had intentionally recalled? Or General Stone? Not wanting to take any risks, and still dubious about the General's shady decisions during the Pandora campaign, Webb had used Beauregard to take him out. Nicholas Bell had agreed wholeheartedly to the plan, but then he'd had his fill of the General's vanity. Their other surviving member was Clifford Bay-Dale, the privileged son-of-a-bitch, but also rather fortuitously the only other Pythian with a plan already in motion.

And what a plan! Webb mused. Better even than the Pandora project. If they pulled this one off they would have, without exclusion, access to American military codes and access cards, power utilities and aviation networks, even financial companies. Cyber hacking was the way to shut down the entire US infrastructure.

Excited, he tried to quell the feeling. *A long way to go yet. And mysteries to be unearthed.* He was particularly happy to be hunting for this one—a lost kingdom. It evoked ideas of Atlantis, Hyperborea, even Thule though he held no love for the Nazis and their crusades. It made him wonder

The Lost Kingdom

what else might be out there if they only knew where to look.

A soft chime interrupted his musings. He turned around. Two monitors sprang to life at the appointed hour; two faces stared back at him.

"We are the Pythians," he said.

"We are the Pythians," Nicholas Bell and Clifford Bay-Dale repeated earnestly.

"Good to be back," Webb said, allowing a small laugh to escape. "I trust you are both secure?"

"It was fuckin' hairy there for a while," the wealthy builder said in typical crass style.

Bay-Dale only nodded and winced a little.

Webb continued, "We'll come to you in a moment, Clifford, and your lost kingdom offering. I must say already, though, that I am intrigued by the potential outcome. Our power struggle with the best of the world's governments has only just begun. How nice it would be to end it with but a single stroke."

Bay-Dale again nodded, saying nothing, the supercilious oaf.

Webb ignored the potential affront. "New primary members. Clearly, we are three Pythians short. The balance should be redressed immediately and taken from the First Degree pool. My primary member, Lucas Monroe, should be drafted in along with Zoe Sheers, an offering from Nicholas who has been fully vetted and approved. We need one more candidate."

He stopped, giving Bay-Dale a moment to catch up.

"Oh, you are asking *me?* Well, I haven't given it much

thought. Been busy with all the lost kingdom arrangements, you know?"

"Do you need a pass on this one?"

"A *pass?* Really? Is it that important?"

Webb took an extremely deep breath, turning away for a brief moment. "We can manage with five for now."

"Oh, excellent. That wasn't so difficult. I'll have to take your word on Sheers and Monroe though I'd ideally have preferred to vet them myself," Bay-Dale paused for a breath as if sensing Webb's outrage and rejoicing in it. "And so to the Lost Kingdom. To recap, we know Mu to be an Atlantis-level find, at least to the Chinese, and that is what matters here. Efforts are being redoubled, though very little has come to light as yet."

"Not surprising since it's been lost for eight thousand years," Bell put in.

"Beyond what we already know," Bay-Dale added pointedly. "Now, once the Niven Tablets are found we will have an easier time of it. And that . . . other thing?" He looked steadily toward the screen.

Webb nodded. "Dudley has made contact. He is not only alive, but free and offering what he calls the aid of 'the craziest, nastiest gang of motherfuckers ever to die young'. Seven of them, the 27-Club. They freed him, apparently."

"Can we trust them?" Bay-Dale asked.

Webb almost fell off his chair. *The naivety of this man!* He almost said, "About as much as I'd trust you with my energy bill," but thought better of it. Energy firms and bosses were, quite rightly, taking the brunt of people's anger these days now that the investment bankers had again crawled back into the shadows. Hitting a sore nerve would do nothing to further their cause now.

"No. Not for a second. But, incredibly I've actually *heard* of this crazy gang. Not a single man among them can be called a full shilling and together, they're as potent as Southern Cross Red vodka, 100 percent proof. They're perfect fodder to hit both vaults don't you think?"

"Ah, yes. Killing may be required. And then we can send them to Taiwan for the most dangerous job of all. Assuming Mu ends up being where we think it is."

"Everything points that way," Bell said. "And it's where the US sub was spotted in 1941."

Bay-Dale smiled ruthlessly. "*Spotted?* Ha! But don't forget, Webb, Taiwan will be the trickiest, most delicate operation of all. And I don't necessarily mean the bombs. I mean our careful manufacturing of an outbreak of war between that country and China."

"Yes, you can be sure Dudley won't be involved in that process," Webb said with a smile. "Finding Mu will mean everything to China, it will change its history, and will cement our future even beyond what it is now."

"So we're going straight for the vaults," Bell said. "Will it be known as a Pythian operation? I'm assuming there will be casualties if Dudley's involved."

"Is that a problem for you, Nicholas?" Webb still harbored misgivings as to the builder's total commitment.

"No, no," Bell said hastily. "Just wondering if our name would be gaining even more notoriety."

"The answer is in your own words."

"Of course it is. And the first vault we're robbing—it is the Peking Man, yes?"

"Yes. Vanished in 1941 and one of China's greatest treasures, the Peking Man, an example of *Homo erectus*, was dated to 680-780 thousand years old. He is considered a human ancestor and more specifically the first ancestor to the Chinese people."

"I'd be fascinated to see him."

"You will get the chance. But now, let's get all the balls rolling, hmm? We have much to do."

Bay-Dale looked pleased for the first time. "Indeed. And as soon as the Peking Man is recovered I'd dearly love to get my hands on the Niven Tablets."

"Worry not, Clifford. You're just a few days away."

Webb signed off, happy but still somewhat disgruntled. He wondered if he was making a mistake—recruiting the Pythians from rich and wealthy stock. Such men didn't understand that they were mere puppets, fit only to dance at his whim. But their power and influence was crucial to his plans.

A thorny situation. A double-edged serration.

Happily, the view from the window soon brought his thoughts around to a much more pleasant fantasy. Until now, Webb had stalked faceless, anonymous individuals, content to terrorize and destroy them for a sense of pleasure that bordered on sexual deviance. Choosing a victim at random—the local barista, the youth on the bicycle, the postman, the delivery driver—possessed a certain kind of charm . . .

But constructing a plan that enabled him to stalk his worst enemies, now *that* was engaging. *That* was unadulterated. That was sex to the power of twelve. And, oh the slow sweetness of it all. It would begin, very soon. Steady. Gentle. Rising to a crescendo. A climax. It would satisfy every vilest desire that slithered through his abnormal world.

CHAPTER FIVE

Drake and Dahl, with Grace at their heels, made their way to the SPEAR team's headquarters inside the Pentagon. Hayden and Kinimaka were already present, looking worse the wear from their partying last night. Hayden drank from a two-liter water bottle and Kinimaka held an outsize mug of coffee close, wrapping his huge hands around it.

"Damn, that Claire Collins sure can party." Hayden breathed between gulps.

"Have they left already?" Drake asked.

"Yeah. Caught a case this morning and are on their way back to the West Coast."

"The woman's an animal." Dahl smiled in memory and then slipped back into stoic face. "Where are we with Mai?"

Hayden pointed at the high resolution screen to her right. "Karin is running character recognition software right now."

Karin looked up from where she sat tapping away at a keyboard, Komodo at her side. "Sorry, Matt. Sorry to hear what happened."

"Don't be. We'll have her back by nightfall."

Komodo grinned, the soldier always game to get fully involved.

"Where's the rest of the guys?" Dahl nodded toward empty chairs. "Hangover?"

"Smyth and Lauren are on their way." Karin grimaced when everyone looked straight at her. "Don't ask. Yorgi's awaiting information because they *still* won't give him access to the Pentagon. And, well, Crouch's crew have received some kind of urgent message from a guy called Greg Coker."

Drake shook his head. "Don't know him."

Karin shrugged. "Me neither. Apparently he helped them out on the Aztec gold adventure. His family was threatened by some South African crime lord. Now, Coker's contacted Michael, gibbering about his family being in some kind of trouble. Crouch and crew are already on a plane."

Drake felt a little saddened. "Alicia?"

"I really thought she'd stay to help Mai." Dahl exhaled gloomily.

"Cheer up, Eeyores," a female voice came from behind them, just closing the restroom door. "As if I'd let you get all the kudos for rescuing the Sprite. Bitch would never let me live it down. And of course, now she owes me one."

Drake saw through all the excuses. "Good on ya, love."

Dahl veered toward the more practical side of things. "What of Crouch and his new troubles?"

"Oh, Greg Coker's an arse. Overreacting. Probably got snowed in or something." Alicia moved forward into the room. "What do we have?"

Drake smiled and tried to hide it. *I've missed her style.* Not that he would confess to calling it actual *style*. But the Englishwoman did have a way about her.

Karin spoke up. "Here. The three character symbols Mai drew on the floor are being processed through my program. I don't know how many millions of characters it has to scroll through but it could take a while." At that moment her computer pinged. She looked appropriately startled.

"Works every time." Dahl grinned, leaning over her shoulder, then breathed. "Oh, shit. How can that be?"

Drake could already see the interpretation. Each character was a syllable . . .

ヤクザ

. . . and written in the Japanese writing system known as Katakana. The three syllables, read left to right, spelled out the word: *YAKUZA*.

Grace took a deep breath, slamming her hands over her mouth to stay quiet. Drake was severely taken aback. So this was not Ramses, then? Not any of their old enemies, but one of *Mai's* old enemies. Had they finally taken revenge for the Cosplay humiliations? And what did the blood mean? Was it even Mai's?

Most important of all—where the hell is she now?

Hayden also looked stunned. "All right," she said. "In reality, I'm surprised, but maybe they caught her sleeping."

Dahl snorted. "Not bloody likely. I must say though, Mai has not been herself lately."

Drake caught the hint for information. "Don't ask," he said. "It has something to do with her trip to Tokyo a while back. She killed a guy for the Tsugarai and then the Yakuza killed most of the rest of his family for safekeeping, leaving only a daughter alive. She's been struggling over killing that guy. That's all folks. Talking to Mai sometimes is like talking to a Banyan."

Alicia slapped his shoulder. "Says the Drakester! We all have our secrets, lover boy."

Drake gave her the eye. If there was anyone harboring secrets in this room it was Alicia Myles. "She *has* been off her game," he admitted.

Grace ran fingers through her hair. "And she had been helping me. A lot."

"Well, contrary to some popular opinions the Yakuza are *not* big here in the United States," Kinimaka informed the room. "In our previous roles, Hayden and I barely came across them."

Hayden nodded. "The nearest most of them come is Hawaii."

"You're saying they will have taken her out of the country?" Drake didn't like where this was going.

"That depends entirely on what they're going to do with her. If it was a quick kill then why not dispatch her immediately? It may be personal for the Yakuza or even a contract kidnapping. We simply have too many questions and not enough answers at this point to make a fair assessment."

"I want to help," Grace quickly butted into the lull. "Please, I *so* want to help. Mai has been like a . . . mother to me."

"First, we need to cover all angles." Drake turned away as Smyth and Lauren walked through the door, and swiped his cell out of standby.

Alicia looked over at him but then caught Smyth's eye. "Hello you two."

"Drop it, Myles. Nothing happened."

Alicia studied them both, took in the disheveled appearance. "Can either of you even *remember* last night?"

"Nah, but I woke up soaked but fully clothed in the shower with a new photo of a goat on my phone. Lauren woke fully clothed in bed."

"Same room?"

"Smyth said he wanted to keep me safe," Lauren drawled in her New York accent.

"From a goat?"

"I have no idea where the goat came from," Smyth snapped. "Or where it went. Let's leave it at that."

"Some protection you were," Alicia muttered. "If that goat had been even half-trained it coulda taken you both out."

"It was worth it," Lauren said in a sad voice. "I have to return to hospital today." The doctors were still testing her body after being infected with the Pandora plague.

Drake listened to the banter as his phone connected. When the call was answered it was by a man in weary tones.

"Dude, it's after midnight."

"Is that Dai? Dai Hibiki?"

"Who is this?"

"Matt Drake."

All of a sudden the voice changed. "Oh, hi Matt. Is everything okay?"

Hibiki was a cop, through and through. Even mostly asleep he would regard a phone call from Drake as unusual.

"Not really, no." Drake went through the events of the last few hours, barely believing the facts as he spoke them aloud. Hibiki stayed silent throughout. After a few minutes Drake heard a female voice asking if everything was okay.

Chika. Of course, Hibiki and Mai's sister were seeing each other.

Drake couldn't help that now. It remained imperative that Hibiki be brought up to date. Drake paused when he finished and then said, "I understand if you want to come back to me later."

"I'll do that."

"Good. But don't take all day, mate. If Mai's on her way to Tokyo you need to be ready."

"Not Tokyo, possibly. But Japan, yes. I will not sleep until this matter is dealt with. You should know that. We keep a very close eye on the Yakuza and there has been no talk of any move in *that* direction. Not even a whisper. I will start the squeeze now with everything I have."

Drake ended the call and turned back to address the room. "He's on board."

"Random thought," Komodo put in. "Do you guys think this has anything to do with the Pythians?"

"We can't tell." Hayden sighed. "But I do know we have to move fast. If the Yakuza have Mai they won't keep her alive for long."

CHAPTER SIX

Callan Dudley had no problem projecting the crazy Irishman image. It came naturally to him. He also knew the importance of terror, of bullying and intimidating his prey so harshly they could barely think. Time was, back in Ireland he'd have done it for a free pint. Today, he was working for a boatload of cash and for the Pythian group, and with the greatest set of feckin' arseholes on the planet—the 27-Club.

So they made the mother kneel down on all fours and then covered her in vodka. They bruised the daughter and her boyfriend around the face. When Boyle and Brannan returned to the house looking slightly disappointed and reporting that they'd found no presence of security or bodyguards, Dudley thought it might be time to explain his requirements to their captives.

"Malachi?" He always deferred to his older brother.

"This is yer party, brother. Take it away."

Dudley motioned McLain and Byram to force the aging, gray-haired man to his knees. Their target, a Lawrence Walcott, the Secretary of the Smithsonian Museum, appeared to be around fifty, with salt-and-pepper sideburns and a wispy moustache. His eyes of course were wide, frightened, his knees trembling.

Dudley enjoyed getting up into the old man's face. "I'm gonna ask yer some questions. Yer lie yer daughter and her shagger get a bat? Understand?" Lawrence Walcott wanted to, he really did. Dudley could tell he wanted to. But the Irish accent was too much for him.

As expected. Dudley turned to Malachi. "Show him."

Malachi, grinning, punched first Walcott's daughter and then her boyfriend in the stomach. Their cries were pitiful, making Dudley laugh.

"Yer get me now?"

"Yes, yes. Please . . ."

Dudley took a moment to think. Despite the Irishman's crass violent streak, his penchant toward chaos and brutality, now that his brother and friends had joined the true fight he wanted to prove his worth.

And that meant sometimes having to think.

"Check outside again," he told Boyle and Brannan. "And check the house too. The Smithsonian has its own police force, an Office of Protection Services. Look for a hidden alarm."

"Already on it."

Dudley turned back to Walcott. "So yer want to save time and pain? We're looking for the Peking Man. And we know it's in the museum."

Walcott's face ran through an entire gamut of expressions. Of course the man was no fool. It would occur to him very quickly that there was no point questioning Dudley's knowledge, if only for his family's sake. It would also occur to him that Dudley wasn't swinging in the wind here—the Irishman *knew*. So where did that leave him?

Dudley thought, *Damage*. Quickly, he turned again to Malachi. "The wife now."

Walcott protested. Dudley gave him a slap. Daley,

watching carefully, giggled. Dudley turned to him with a grin. "Yer like that?" He slapped Walcott again, this time reddening his other cheek. Daley burst into laughter. At the same time Malachi was hauling the wife up by the hair and throwing her over the couch.

"The feckin' Irish bastards have yer now." Dudley squeezed Walcott's jaw hard. "If yer want to live you'd better keep yer nose clean and not fib to me."

Walcott nodded, face screwed up in agony. The asshole's wife was groaning too as Malachi worked overtime, practicing his jabs, so Dudley thought this an appropriate time to twist the proverbial knife.

"Yer gonna take us to this Peking Man. And give it over. Then we'll be gone." Dudley explained that Walcott would acquire the long-lost, probably stolen, relic whilst his family remained under Irish guard. Only when the 27-Club walked away with the artefact would Walcott's family be released.

"When? *Now?*" Walcott looked incredulous. "It's the middle of the day. There will be a thousand people wandering around."

"Not in the archives," Dudley said. "It's not like yer have it on show or admit to ever stealing it. An' doing it at night would be even more fierce. As yer know."

Walcott's face fell even further.

"Family or job?" Dudley smiled, a hunter facing his prey. "Choose."

He waited, thinking through what the Pythians had already told him. This lost relic, the Peking Man, would make China sit up and take notice, even beg. Couple to that the knowledge of where the Americans found it in 1945 and what they were actually *doing* there back then, and you had not only China's attention but their complicit support and enduring assistance. Dudley wasn't aware what the Pythians required from the Chinese but he knew it wouldn't be a free tour of the Great Wall. Once the Peking Man was obtained their mission became even more obscure. Something about tablets and Mu. None of it really mattered to Dudley. The Pythians had told him that China might start a war with Taiwan. The war was everything.

Any war.

He grinned, looking over at his brothers. Not only Malachi, but all of them. Brothers in battle. Comrades-in-arms. The 27-Club existed only so its members could live out their ferocious dreams.

Because his oldest brother, Kevan, could not. Dead at twenty seven, killed by the British, Kevan was the reason the 27-Club had been born. Malachi founded it, recruiting his friends to the cause—every one under twenty seven—and then Dudley joined too, already a capable underground brawler at home with violence and unable to reconcile his brother's death. After that, it was pure mayhem. The 27-Club did indeed make waves, bloody gore-filled ones. They wreaked havoc through many a country before Malachi turned twenty seven himself and then they waited. The gang didn't slacken in its cruel dealings. If anything, Malachi took more risks.

One by one, the club members all passed the age Kevan was when he died. All but one.

Dudley turned his attention to Walcott, feeling a surge of hatred and a deep rush of anger. "So what's the decision?

Don't keep me waiting, old man. It's me birthday today. Twenty feckin' seven, I am."

In the end it all went exactly as Dudley expected it to. By the skin of its teeth. But it was a bad situation all around. His mother, the Devil take her, used to say, "Yer can't make a silk purse out of a pig's ear", and that was how he felt right now. Walking the National Mall without weapons he felt naked, exposed. So much space. So much greenery. So much regimented tourism it made him feel sick. He'd taken Byram and McLain with him; extra eyes and ears in case Walcott tried anything. But he needn't have bothered. Walcott was a pure, dyed-in-the-wool family man. He'd do anything to protect them.

Dudley wished he could be there to see them die. But that old bleeder, Malachi, had earned the honor. *No mind, Daley's gonna record it.*

At last the dull red brick façade of the Smithsonian Castle came into view, all spires and arches, windows and a great castle turret. Walcott headed straight up the steps toward the entrance but Dudley held him back.

"Remember now, be a grand fella."

"Sure, sure. I know what's at stake here."

Dudley held out his cellphone, which held a photo of Walcott's wife. "And don't forget."

Inside, they traversed a polished floor along a corridor that gave Dudley the impression it shone with gold. Clearly, it was a lighting trick, but the interior impression of the castle was one of enveloping warmth and security.

Dudley shepherded Walcott past a lone guard who

offered only a flicker of recognition. Further they went, making use of an elevator and then a non-public corridor, this one painted bright white and looking as sparse as a monk's cell. Now, Walcott led them down a clanking spiral staircase, moving deeper into the castle's innards. Dudley had noticed a sign that read *Archives* several minutes ago.

"Yer sure?"

"It's more than a secret. It was never meant to be found. At first a treasure, then secreted away after the tragedy, and now largely forgotten. There are hundreds of old treasures like this around the world, gathering dust, forgotten about by their owners. Who knows if they will ever again see the light of day?"

Dudley thought, *What tragedy?* But Walcott spoke again before he could ask. "Almost there."

The now-familiar white walls surrounded them, the space large and full of rows and rows of shelves, all crammed full with sealed cardboard, wooden and metal boxes of every variety, a mishmash of hundreds of shapes and sizes. Dudley saw two other people wandering the stacks.

He leaned in to Walcott. "They gonna be a problem?"

"No. No. Your problem would really have been getting out once you produce and fill your backpacks. But I have an override card. As I said before, once we leave the building I can't stop the guards challenging us. Even I can only go so far."

Dudley patted him on the head. "Aye, we're countin' on it, old man."

Byram and McLain gave him feral grins.

Walcott pushed further down the rows, entering an area

where the shelves were made of old wood and spaced further apart to accommodate larger items. A fusty smell filled the air, the odor of ancient things. Dust motes spun in the air, visible within the beams of light cast by recessed bulbs in the windowless room. The only sounds were their careful footfalls. Dudley fancied they were way under the red-brick castle by now, possibly even branched out toward the national mall.

"How much further?"

"Not far now."

Walcott walked with hunched shoulders, following the route by memory alone. His shoes started to leave a dusty trail along the floor. When Dudley brushed against a shelf, a bloom of dust puffed out. They walked through the deepest places of the Smithsonian, seemingly untouched for years and even unremembered by many. Dudley understood it now; he saw how easily something might fade away into history, might be allowed to do just that. *Hide it away. Shove it in a box. Place it out of sight, deep, deep in the catacombs.* Essentially it was the same principle as storing a container in an attic. Over the years, you forgot what was there and how important or sentimental it might be to you.

Until you revisited.

Walcott finally halted before a set of uneven shelves, their coating of dust attesting to the fact that nothing nearby had been touched for many years. Dudley saw no trails in the fine coating, no fingerprints.

Walcott hesitated. "This . . . this is ancient history," he said. "Almost a million years old. It is the oldest known form of primitive man."

"And what have yer done with it in fifty years? Shoved it in a museum? Naw, not even that." Dudley gestured angrily. "Hurry up."

"What can you possibly hope to accomplish with it? Make money? At least here, it's safe."

Dudley wasn't a patient man at the best of times. Without any further warnings he punched Walcott hard behind the left ear, sending the man to his knees.

"Yer wife's next, pal."

Walcott struggled upright, reaching out for the skew-whiff shelving. "Help me," he said. "It's this one."

Byram and McLain took hold of a wooden box and lifted it easily to the floor. Walcott bent over, lifting the lid.

"No key?" Dudley asked suspiciously.

"It would only draw attention," Walcott murmured.

Inside the shabby-appearing but surprisingly well-made box was a layer of foam, which Walcott removed, and then the old bones gleamed up at them. Dudley didn't stand on ceremony, just whipped out his backpack and forced several of the bones inside. Byram and McLain did the same. Walcott winced with every clink.

"You should wrap them, at least. Don't you *know* what they—"

Dudley's hand struck as fast as a viper's head, grabbing the Secretary by the collar and drawing him close. "I don't care. I don't give a rat's arse. Shut yer face and do yer job. And yer may get to live."

Walcott tucked his protestations and grimaces away. The three Irishmen filled their backpacks and strapped them on. Walcott then replaced the wooden box and tried to spread a little dust over the shelves to preserve their untouched appearance. Dudley grabbed his arm and threw him ahead.

"Get on with it."

Back through the maze of shelves they went, silence their only companion. Timeworn boxes surrounded them, each one a relic, making Dudley wonder just what other treasures the Smithsonian might have secreted down here. If he had time to make Walcott talk, the 27-Club might be able to find enough valuable "lost" artefacts to fund a few operations of their own.

Later.

He stored that nugget away. Truth be told, it was a good reason to keep Walcott alive. Maybe they should show willing and let the rest of his family live too. It would make coming back in a few months so very much sweeter. *And productive.*

Dudley felt his face creasing into a grin and wiped it clean. This wasn't the time. Motes of dust swirled and eddied around him, micro-hurricanes displaced by the fury of his passing. Walcott stuck faithfully to the center of the passage but the Irishmen brushed against boxes and shelves and caused more than a little damage. Walcott got a move on. At last they reached the more populated area and aimed toward the metal staircase and then an elevator. Walcott attracted little attention and even those who did recognize him only nodded. The Secretary of the Smithsonian Institution was an important man, appointed by the Board of Regents. Probably not the kind of man most employees felt content to stop and discuss their evening plans or crappy commute with.

Dudley was happy with that. Soon, they exited out into the public museum and made their way toward the rear gardens and, beyond that, the street parking. Within minutes Dudley found himself walking in the fresh air, down a straight path toward four large pillars and open gates. Almost disappointed, he glanced to left and right.

Ah...

The guard approached them from behind a bench where he'd been chatting with tourists. Dudley purposely held his gaze, flicking a disparaging glance at the man's paunch. When he reached an audible distance he opened his mouth.

Dudley turned to McLain. "Shut that fat fecker up."

His comrade liked nothing better than to teach security guards what real fighting and real pain was all about. Back in Ulster and an age ago now it had been one of his favorite hobbies. Back then, they had sought out local security guards just for fun, leaving them broken and bleeding, crawling around the floor of the place they were paid to defend. McLain even used to cut his biceps to mark every target they took down.

Back when the 27-Club was young, just finding their feet... Now?

McLain jabbed the guard hard, making the man's eyes bulge and his touristy friends scream. When the guard's hands flew to his throat, McLain used his groin as a punching bag, placing an arm across his upper half and bending him over. When the guard slithered to the floor, incapacitated, McLain lifted a boot over his throat.

"Say goodbye, fat man."

"No!" Walcott's voice was unnecessarily loud. "Don't

kill him. He's done nothing to you. Nothing!"

Dudley grinned. "Aw, come on. McLain here hasn't killed nothing for days."

"Please."

McLain smiled into Walcott's eyes as he brought his boot hard down on the security guard's throat.

Dudley shrugged. "I guess it wasn't the poor bastard's day."

"Bastard! That wasn't necessary. We're free!"

Dudley eyed the scrambling tourists. "Don't be too sure. Letting someone live is always a mistake."

"Do *not* hurt them. Do not! I will raise the alarm. I will—"

Dudley cuffed him. "Ah, at last, you've found a set of bollocks. Let's call yer family and see how long that lasts."

Walcott hung his head as Dudley directed them back to their parked car. Without rushing, his comrades and he deposited their backpacks into the enormous trunk. Then, carefully, they slid into the traffic.

"On second thoughts," Dudley said. "Maybe yer shouldn't have killed him. Now they'll be trying even harder to find us."

Byram shrugged, massaging his heavy bicep.

Dudley smirked. "Best get a move on, old man. Us lads have another vault to visit."

CHAPTER SEVEN

Drake always got a feeling in his gut when things were about to kick-off big time; a kind of pre-emptive adrenalin burst that, if heavily diluted, one might feel when tipping over the top of the lift-hill of the world's tallest rollercoaster or sitting behind the wheel of the world's fastest and most dangerous dragster.

When Karin took the call and then turned *that* face upon them, the feeling hit him. "What the hell's wrong?"

Karin stared. "Unbelievable. About an hour ago there was a murder and unknown theft committed at the Smithsonian and they believe *Dudley* may be involved."

Drake couldn't make it compute. "What? *Our* Dudley? The mad Irish bastard who's in jail?"

"The mad Irish bastard who *escaped* jail, killed his drivers and guards in the process with the help of some old friends, and may now be back working for the Pythians."

Drake gripped the bridge of his nose between two fingers. "He escaped? And nobody thought to let us know?"

"We just brought him to justice," Hayden put in. "After that, he's all theirs. An escaped prisoner doesn't come under our purview and might not be brought to our attention at all."

Karin pursed her lips. "We're *that* agency that's so secret nobody knows to read us in."

Dahl disagreed. "We're not that bloody secret anymore. I think it's more admin based, no insult intended. We need some kind of a flagging system."

Drake shook it all off. "Just tell us what happened, Karin."

"The Smithsonian isn't exactly sure. Their secretary, the big boss, may have escorted three men into the vault earlier today. Units are en route to his house now. Using facial recognition the cops have identified one of the three men as Callan Dudley."

Drake sat down. Here they were awaiting word of Mai and something potentially bigger had dropped into their laps. If the Pythians were up to their not-so-old tricks . . .

"Make sure you reinforce and remind all the relevant authorities of Dudley's nastier connections," Hayden said. "I didn't expect the Pythians to bounce back so quickly after we killed three of their members. I guess I underestimated them. Or maybe it's something else. Now, let's start looking into Dudley's so-called friends and this Smithsonian heist." Her eyes stopped as they passed Drake's.

"I'm sorry we have to pull away from Mai at this time."

The Yorkshireman shrugged. "Aye, me too. But it'll help take my mind off what I'm going to do to her abductors."

Hayden nodded. Dahl sighed and rolled his shoulders, a man desperate to help out his friend but incapable of doing so.

"Need a way to ease some of that tension?" Alicia addressed the Swede. "We could always—"

Drake's phone rang, cutting her off. It was Hibiki. "Yes?"

Alicia finished lamely, "Hit the gym."

Hibiki's voice filled Drake's world. "I'm with an . . . informant now." The cop was panting. "Hold on, I'm just washing my hands . . ."

Dahl raised an eyebrow.

"Took an awful lot to learn this, my friend, but Mai is now the focus of the whole Yakuza organization. And they are the biggest criminal organization in the world."

Drake knew his face had gone white, emotions bubbling over, but he didn't care. "What can we do? Do you know their intentions?"

"Unfortunately, yes. The Yakuza, they rarely forgive. It's as much a trait of theirs as the rule 'once you're in you never get out'. It's hard to pin any Yakuza operation down not only because they're so connected and insulated but because they're into so many different criminal activities. It's a testament to their viciousness and cleverness that although they're universally known, they still haven't made many inroads into America or even Tokyo. I say this only to prepare you for what we have to do."

Drake felt Dahl's hand on his shoulder. "Which is?"

"Mai is being taken to Kobe, where they have their headquarters, probably by freighter. I'm not sure if you have identified the blood in the hotel room yet?"

"Not yet."

"Well, if it is Mai's don't worry. The bullet will have been to make her compliant, to help the snatch squad take her down. They will fix her up."

"How can you be so sure?"

"Because they plan to put her up on a vile pedestal for some kind of showcase trial. Before the entire Yakuza organization. And then they plan to kill her."

Drake felt a headache coming on. "A trial? Where?"

"They have a walled compound, Drake. A guarded

headquarters inside the city of Kobe. For real. The place is impregnable."

"And that's where they're taking Mai? Can we stop this freighter at the docks?"

"I have a few of the Kobe police looking into that. But . . ." Hibiki paused and sighed. "You have to understand the Yakuza and their *reach*. It is said they *own* the police. A few years ago one of their leaders was allowed to be honorary police chief for the day. There really are pictures, believe me. I can only seriously trust half a dozen people."

"But would *they* risk going up against the Yakuza?" Dahl asked. "In their home town?"

"Not a chance," Hibiki said. "In truth, Kobe is one of the safest cities in Japan. This is because no other criminal entities dare operate there and the Yakuza don't crap where they eat. But my police friends are strictly reconnaissance only. They will not challenge and they will not get physically involved."

"How many men do the Yaks have?" Alicia asked.

Hibiki laughed. "Normally? Only a thousand or so. But for such a showcase trial designed to inspire its members? To put fire in their bellies? You could double or treble that. And add a private video and audio network, I'm sure."

Drake suppressed the relatively alien rush of sudden panic. "So what can we do?"

"Seriously? If it were anyone else with lesser comrades-in-arms I'd say prepare for the funeral. I don't know what the answer is, my friend, but I do know this. You have to get yourselves over here. Over to Kobe as fast as possible."

Drake nodded. "Text me a location. We'll find you."

Dahl turned to Hayden, stony-faced. "We're going to have to split this team up."

CHAPTER EIGHT

Hayden watched as a major part of her team vacated the room, illogically intent on rescuing Mai Kitano from the world's biggest criminal organization in their own back yard. Of course she would not even try to stop them, and if it had been up to her, and Dudley hadn't just resurfaced, she would undoubtedly be climbing aboard the same plane with the same motives.

Once they were gone, however, the remainder of the team needed refocusing. Hayden encouraged Karin to concentrate on Dudley, his friends and Walcott, and what they may have stolen, then asked Kinimaka to keep tabs on the police visit to the Smithsonian's boss's house. Her own first task was to inform her boss—Robert Price the new US Secretary of Defense—as to Callan Dudley's new venture. The man sounded genuinely shocked and supportive, but Hayden was beginning to detect a peculiar detachedness there, as if Price didn't give too much of a hoot. Obviously, although he was in the same job as Jonathan Gates, the man's motives were a whole lot different. *Don't be surprised, most officials have different notions about how to perform their duties once they're in office. It's not unknown.*

At least Price was leaving them alone. But that only reminded her of Jonathan and how he had died. *A tragic, tragic waste. Same as my father.*

Karin spoke up. "Okay, well, the FBI have taken charge of the Smithsonian robbery. They're not taking any chances with Dudley. They've drafted in Walcott's underling, guy called Kyle, and one of the old relics who's worked there practically since he left pre-school. They think they've identified what was taken."

"Hayden leaned forward. "Which is?"

"The Peking Man."

"What's that?" Smyth barked. "Sounds old."

"You're right. Peking, now Beijing—the older English spelling was the Chinese postal map Romanization *Peking*—the city is three thousand years old. This city alone has *seven* World Heritage sites, including the Forbidden City, the Ming Tombs and the Great Wall, so it's not surprising that such an ancient, momentous find was made there."

"This Peking Man?"

"Yes. Discovered in the 1920s the bones are said to be three quarter of a million years old. The site also revealed teeth, bones, skulls and tools. Some of the fossils even ended up in Uppsala University." Karin smiled wistfully. "Neighboring unearthings of animal remains, and fire and tool usage were used to identify this find as the very first tool-worker, actually a great example of human evolution. He is chiefly a human ancestor and the earliest known ancestor of the Chinese people."

"So why the hell isn't he in China?" Smyth wondered. "Instead of being stored in a dusty vault underneath the Smithsonian?"

"Well, that's where it gets even more interesting. We know from the Odin quest that there are many out of place artifacts—OOPArt—in this world, artefacts that defy timestamping and challenge accepted historical chronology as being far too advanced for the accepted level of civilization of the time. These objects are usually collecting dust in some vault somewhere. Though not an OOPArt, the Peking Man has been subject to the same kind of concealment."

Hayden shared a look with Kinimaka. "I heard something about this. The bones were lost, right? And the Americans had something to do with it."

"Not *exactly,*" Karin stressed. "In 1941, while Beijing was under Japanese occupation, the fossils were squirreled away. Packed into two large crates they were loaded onto a US Marine vehicle heading toward northern China, near a Marine base at Camp Holcomb. This was of course before the outbreak of hostilities between Japan and the Allied Forces in the Second World War. From this camp they were to be shipped to the National History Museum in New York, possible for safe-keeping, or some other reason, no one really knows."

"And?" Smyth urged her.

Lauren put a hand on top of his. "Relax."

Karin continued, "They disappeared en route. Many, many attempts have been made to find the fossils, mostly frantic attempts by the Chinese, but nothing was ever found. Most theories suggest the fossils were aboard the Japanese ship, the *Awa Maru,* and that's where our mystery deepens."

"Shit." Smyth shook his head. "I'm gonna need espresso for this. Anyone else?"

Komodo gave him a thumbs up, also mentioning cookies. Lauren nodded. Smyth used Dolce Gusto pods to deliver the strong, steaming brews.

"In 1945 the *Awa Maru* was being used as a Red Cross relief ship, carrying essential supplies to American and Allied Prisoners of War in Japanese camps. An agreement—Relief for POWs—had been signed by all and was universally being adhered to. She was supposed to be given safe passage by everyone and all commanders had orders issued to that effect. Now, once she'd delivered her supplies the stories around the *Awa Maru* begin to get more captivating. It may be intrigue . . . but then again? In Singapore she took on several hundred marine officers, military and civilian personnel and diplomats. She also carried a treasure worth over five billion dollars, that's—"

Smyth choked. *"Five billion?"*

"Yup. Forty metric tons of gold. Platinum. Diamonds. There are even reports of the docks being cleared for several more precious cargos to be loaded in secret."

Hayden cleared her throat. "The Peking Man?"

"Like I said, nothing's written down in black and white. But the likelihood is there. It all fits. Her subsequent voyage coincided with the last sightings of the Peking Man fossils which were in Singapore at the time and, of course, priceless in their value. Many believe the bones were aboard that ship."

Smyth was intrigued, despite himself. "What happened to it?"

"On April the first, the *Awa Maru*, outfitted and sailing as a civilian and a hospital ship, under the protection of the Red Cross, was *mistakenly* identified as a destroyer by the US submarine—*Queenfish*. Intercepted in the Taiwan Strait and despite previously disclosing her route to the Allies, she was torpedoed by the *Queenfish* and sunk."

"Shit." Hayden and Kinimaka shook their heads, having heard something similar at different times before. The *Awa Maru* sinking was not something the American administration had been able to sweep under the mat.

"There was only one survivor." Karin grimaced. "Kantora Shimoda. And he later told authorities that no Red Cross supplies were aboard the *Awa Maru,* they having been previously unloaded."

"*What? Why?*"

Karin shrugged. "Clearly, it was a clandestine mission, the civilian transport front exactly that. A front. The *Awa Maru* was being used for another purpose."

"Okay, okay," Kinimaka said. "Say that's true. Why in hell was a US sub secretly in the Straits of Taiwan? And why fire on a ship supposedly transporting supplies to their own POWs?"

"Good questions," Karin said. "Both unanswerable for now. But the story isn't finished yet. In 1980 China launched one of the biggest salvage operations in history. Five years and one hundred million dollars were spent in their search for . . . what? It must have been something incredibly valuable, significant to them, or both."

"The treasure," Hayden said. "And the bones of the Peking Man."

"Sounds reasonable to me."

"What did they find?"

"Nothing. Not a single thing beyond a few personal artefacts. The ship was pretty much stripped clean."

Smyth looked shocked. Even Hayden was surprised. "They found *nothing?*"

The Lost Kingdom

Karin sat back. "Even the NSA were intrigued after that. They sifted through literally thousands of intercepted communications to discover what had happened to the bones and the treasure. Their conclusion was that it ended up in Thailand somewhere."

Smyth spread his hands. "Eh? The NSA said that?"

"My thoughts exactly."

Hayden placed her hands palm down on the table in front of her. "So," she checked off her fingers as she spoke, "why was the *USS Queenfish* hanging around the Taiwan Straits at that time? Why did they sink a known hospital ship? And what happened to all that cargo?"

"And what would Callan Dudley want with the Peking man?" Kinimaka added. "Which somehow ended up in the Smithsonian."

"If Dudley is working for the Pythians," Komodo said, a hand on Karin's shoulder. "The question is—what do *they* want with the fossils?"

"I just can't help thinking there's a reason the Americans were in *that* place at *that* time," Hayden continued, "As much as I love my country the motives of its power players sometimes lead me to despair."

Karin fielded a phone call. "They found Walcott," she said and proceeded to tell them the details of the man's kidnapping. "I'm just shocked both his family and he are still alive. The family were tied up and left in their house. Walcott was deposited on the Interstate. He did have one snippet of interesting information though—Dudley mentioned a *second* vault that he was about to visit."

"He means raid," Hayden said. "Shit, there's even more

to this than we know. Could it be another artefact? The treasure itself?"

"If there was any treasure," Komodo said. "I doubt that it's been sitting in a dusty vault for fifty years."

Hayden looked down as her cell rang. Seeing Robert Price's office she sighed and offered a few suggestions to the team. As she answered and waited to be put through to the new Secretary she couldn't help but remember General Stone's words: "In any war there are unintended casualties. Just ask your new Secretary of Defense".

What the hell had Stone known about Robert Price?

CHAPTER NINE

On the way to Kobe, Drake learned more about the dreaded Yakuza and recounted details of Mai's previous exploits at their expense. During her first, largely unsanctioned, operation she had engaged the local Yakuza gang, which had links to the head office in Kobe, taking them down to the last man. Head office, it now seemed, had previously blamed its own men for the defeat and damage rather than Mai Kitano, perhaps not comprehending the legend she had become. Old speculations had been reintroduced, however, when Mai humiliated the Yakuza for a second time during her whirlwind quest for her parents. Again Drake berated himself for not going with her, even though he knew he'd been embroiled in a life or death battle at the time.

"This Hikaru," he said. "According to Hibiki he's the guy who's been credited with capturing her. What do we know of him?"

Dahl answered that one. "Hikaru is the man Mai made the deal with at the Cosplay convention," he said. "Pretending she'd taken him out for the Tsugarai, he gave her time to set the trap. Assuming all went to type, the Yakuza will have punished Hikaru for his failure, despite his efforts in ridding them of a significant rival. It is all about honor and saving face, after all."

"Bollocks," Drake said. "So you're saying this is some kinda atonement? Making up for a fabricated loss?"

"It's much more than that now. Mai has been

romanticized as the Yakuza's nemesis by their bosses, mostly after her capture. A spectacle will be lapped up by their members."

"They're gonna get more than a fucking spectacle," Drake growled. "Believe me."

Alicia leaned across at that moment. "I just knew there was a reason I stayed," she purred. " 'Cause I ain't interested in one single hair on the Little Sprite's head. It's to hear you when you're angry, Drakey."

"Amazing. I thought you'd had your fill of that when we were teamed up together, working for the Ninth."

"Ninety-nine to oh-three?" She heaved a sigh. "I remember the years well."

"And you're full of shit. No way do you want to see Mai hurt."

"Balls." Alicia looked away, finding a sudden interest in the clouds floating over the wing.

The other two members of their team, Yorgi and Grace, smiled. Yorgi had been asked to come because of his world-class breaking-and-entering skills. Grace had been allowed to come because she practically screamed the house down when she heard about Mai's fate and promised to stay in the hotel room. Drake had more things to worry about now than Grace and her ill-fated past.

Later, when Mai's freed, I'll help. I . . . promise.

Not that he would ever again say such a thing aloud.

The hours passed and the airplane turned day into night and then into day again. As they were nearing their destination Dai Hibiki called.

"Just wanted to make you more aware of what you are

facing in Kobe. The Yakuza, though a transnational crime syndicate, are at war with each other. Several of the families do battle, but the one we face—the *Goda Kai*—are by far the largest."

"Typical." Alicia snorted. "Little Mai couldn't just piss of a tiny splinter group could she? Had to be the full Monty."

Now Drake smiled. "Same could be said for all of us. Look at this Ramses bloke. I'm guessing we're gonna have to set him straight on a few things at some point."

"One terror organization at a time," Dahl said.

Hibiki coughed to reclaim their attention. "They're very organized, strict, and deeply rooted in everything from crime to Japanese media. And despite their attempts at achieving respectability, including providing earthquake relief, much of their notoriety actually dates back to their origins. Called *Bakuto*, they were gamblers, an undesirable and disdainful image in older Japan. Gambling was illegal, and many houses cropped up in abandoned temples and shrines on the outskirts of towns and villages all over the country. Oddly, the name *Yakuza* itself refers to a losing hand in *Oicho-kabu*, a form of blackjack. *Ya-ku-za* or 8-9-3."

"We get they're a hard and nasty bunch," Dahl said.

"And much more," Hibiki insisted. "It is speculated that Japan's banking industry has ties to the Japanese underworld. Their property and realty market. Politics. And the young—a recent study showed that nine out of ten people under the age of forty believe that the Yakuza should exist. *That* is what you are up against."

Drake knew what Hibiki was trying to do. "Cheers,

mate," he said. "We'll make sure we're ready."

"Good. Now, on a separate note, I have information about this man Mai appears to be obsessed with at the moment. Hayami."

Drake sat up. "Anything would help."

"No, I don't think it would. Although Mai killed Hayami, a felony that could get her locked away I should point out, and disbanded the Tsugarai, the Yakuza felt that they still owed Hayami an honor kill. Who knows what he gave up in their organization, right? So, they visited his wife, son and daughter. Torture and promises of selling the women to the slave trade and local prostitution rings followed. Then death when they finally believed the family knew nothing more. Death was a blessing, you see, a gift, after what they had already done. But the girl, Emiko, she escaped. Now we have her in protective custody so she's a witness against them. The girl's an understandable mess, but we will look after her."

"Can she help Mai?" Drake asked, missing the point.

"Ah, she wouldn't even if she could. The Yakuza already told her who killed Hayami. Blamed Mai for everything that was happening. Emiko, she truly hates Mai Kitano."

Drake didn't know what to say. In one way Emiko had every reason to hate Mai, but in another, under different circumstances . . .

Finally, Dahl changed the subject. "We're an hour out, Hibiki. Have your men seen any sign of Mai at the docks?"

Hibiki sighed. "No. But over a hundred ships a day visit that dock. She will almost certainly be in Kobe by now, and many wagons roll out. We won't be able to prevent them from taking her to the compound, my friends. It is there, inside, that this battle will be won or lost. I have a detail on twenty-four-hour watch."

"What about at the compound?" Alicia asked. "Any increased activity?"

"Unfortunately, yes and no. Gang members have been arriving in Kobe all day, and many *Shateigashira,* local and regional bosses, accompanied by their own hierarchies. Their number increases by the hour . . . but none have actually arrived at the compound."

Drake clenched his fists. His stomach twisted at the thought of Mai being put on some kind of showcase trial before being killed in front of all these hard-headed maniacs. *I will not let her go out this way. Not Mai.*

"Then they'd better prepare for four more guests," he said. "And a battle that'll go down in history."

CHAPTER TEN

Mai stumbled as the two men lifted her to her feet. As instructed they were gentle, not wanting to rip open her stitches and further complicate her gunshot wound. The antibiotics were helping, as were the painkillers, and Mai could easily stand on her own. Hikaru, though, was taking no chances and, in addition to the two men helping her along, had directed a further four to watch her. Each man held a Taser and a sawn-off baseball bat in addition to the guns and knives in their belts.

Hikaru presented himself to Mai as the ship docked. "Your entourage." He indicated the assembled men. "I assume they're to your liking."

"If I didn't have this wound they'd already be dead."

"Agreed, Miss Kitano. That's precisely why you *have* that wound."

"Where are you taking me?"

"Not far. We have made good time. The members are still arriving. I believe your trial may not begin until tomorrow but that is good. It will give you time to prepare your defense." Hikaru burst into laughter, an arrogant and haughty expression fixed to his face. Mai spent a few seconds fantasizing about slicing it off with a blunt blade.

"I may be down, Hikaru. But I'm never out."

"We'll see if you're still feeling that way in a few days." Hikaru waved at her captors who urged her forward. Mai shrugged into the loose jeans and sweatshirt she'd been provided to cover her tank top and panties, showing absolutely no signs of pain or embarrassment as she dressed. Weakness was a drug to men like this. They thrived on it.

"Follow me." Hikaru led the way to the top deck, slowing to allow Mai extra time to navigate the stairs, then paused. Mai had her first view of the outside world in what seemed like days. Kobe was a port city, clustered around the coastline, tall buildings and motorways and bridges all lining up as if jostling for the right to sail away first. She stared across the water at a gray metropolis, at a place even she could get lost in, never to be found.

"Move."

Mai followed Hikaru's lead, and exited the ship's interior. What felt like a knife jabbed at the pit of her stomach—the wound stretching before it should—but she fought hard to keep the pain out of her expression, instead raising her face and gauging the horizon.

My future lies there, she thought. *Never forget it.*

Five men spread out behind her and now, as she looked over the side of the ship, Mai saw half a dozen more waiting on the docks below. The ship was already moored, a gangway fed out to the dockside. Two black cars sat among the men, doors thrown open.

"Kobe has been waiting for you," Hikaru told her with self-seeking pride. "But it is I who have delivered." He spread his arms. "I."

Mai gave him a hooded-eye frown. "Understand this, Hikaru." She moved closer. "Get your bucket list filled, boy, because I *will* kill you over the next few days."

Hikaru smiled quickly, not wanting to portray any fear, but the twitch at the corner of his mouth betrayed him. "Just get off the damn ship."

Mai walked down the jouncing gangway and onto solid earth. This was a quiet area, she noticed, probably cordoned off somewhere and belonging to the localized Yakuza yobs. Being Japanese, her own view of the Yakuza was a mixed one—yes their story was romanticized, they came from all walks of life but some *had* actually been abandoned or exiled by their parents, taken in by the clan. Mai could identity with that. Some were taken straight from Junior High. But most were common street thugs or members of other gangs. A Yakuza gang member cut all family ties, forever. They transferred their lives and their loyalties to their boss, and they referred to each other as family members. Their boss was often called "father". Mai could also identify with that; a youth abandoned or forced by siblings into a life of street crime would be crying out for a strong father figure and a protective family—the Yakuza would give him that.

It was their other activities that Mai could not condone. The criminal element. The power mongering that should not exist in any close family. She stared now at the grim-faced, emotionless men who awaited her, wondering who they could have been.

Guns were evident, held in every hand, even portable machine pistols. She entered the car they indicated and waited for it to drive away. No words were passed and Hikaru took the second car. Waves of pain washed through her body, making her want to lay her head against the window and close her eyes. But this wasn't the time. Fighting was all she knew how to do; for a long time now it had been the sole focus of her life.

Fight now.

Had she originally believed that a life with Drake might somehow take all the struggle away? Or was he a convenient harbor in the storm; a lifeline? One thing was certain—he had helped neutralize the pain. Perhaps he could do so again.

But first there was the Yakuza to contend with and, more importantly, the issue of the man she had killed and his surviving daughter, Emiko. What was the answer there? Yes, guilt swamped her but surely it would do no good to seek out the girl and confess.

I can't just let it go.

As the car started moving Mai found her thoughts turning deeper, more twisted, as she looked inward. The past could never be altered, but the future? It could be shaped, changed; amends could be made. But how?

Kobe passed her by, its main thoroughfares clogged with traffic and pedestrians. If anyone thought the two-car parade that headed away from the docks odd they didn't show it. Not a head was turned. Twice she noted policemen standing near traffic lights when the car slowed, but she was too savvy to seek their assistance. If they were Yakuza owned she would only make matters worse and if they were unsullied she would get them killed. Her mind flashed quickly then, becoming more responsive as drugs and painkillers wore off, and wondered how the SPEAR team would plan their approach. No doubts existed that they would attack the Yakuza. It was all a matter of when . . . and how.

Analyze the compound first, she thought. *And I should do the same.*

Kobe flashed by, the driver taking a well-known route. The men around her didn't engage eye contact; they sat alert and watchful as if always expecting an attack. And maybe they did. Mai knew that Kobe was one of the safest places in Japan so surely, with a kind of perverse logic, it would make the Yakuza stronghold less well guarded. Very soon she would be testing that theory.

Each street appeared similar to the last, but Mai kept the route in her head, memorizing street names where she could. The Yakuza headquarters was more than obvious to her when it appeared out of the gray, monotonous dirge—a smoked-glass-fronted high rise with wide spaces all around the first floor entrance and many black-suited men stood about. In Kobe the Yakuza didn't have to hide—everyone knew where they lived. Mai counted thirty floors before the building grew too close to continue and saw a smooth, peaked roof, clearly deliberate since the others around it were flat. Even Yorgi would have a hard time up there. More features lodged in her mind—the black windows that stood fully flushed with the brick walls, the lack of balconies and ledges, the positioning of the guards. Soon, the cars pulled up outside the building and everyone climbed out. Mai found herself entering the headquarters of her arch nemesis under a twelve-man shield.

Inside, the lobby was surprisingly small, no doubt designed that way. Glass formed partitions and walls everywhere. Mai could imagine the guns bristling on the other side of the two-way mirrors.

A sparse front desk, several women working the phones and computers—the first she had seen—and then a cramped trip in a highly polished elevator. Unsurprisingly it was down she went, into the bowels of the earth, even though the buttons only went in ascent from one to thirty five. Mai couldn't help but turn a wry smile upon her closest guard.

"Got that tip from the CIA? Or Hollywood?"

With no answer forthcoming she caught her reflection in the walls. Not good. She looked exhausted, white and ill. Hikaru, to her right, noticed and nodded.

"Don't worry. We'll fix you up for your trial." He mimicked injecting her with a needle. "Best cocktail you ever had."

Mai looked up at the roof, seeing at least the fiftieth CCTV camera so far. She badly needed to heal in order to take charge. They weren't going to give her that chance. And in this city she was isolated beyond belief. Yakuza here wore expensive suits, operated from offices like this and carried business cards. She found it odd that the trial would take place here and not at the walled compound in one of the wealthiest areas of Kobe, but perhaps with the arrival of so many significant Yakuza figures the office building could be better protected. It could obviously house more men.

Several floors down, she knew not how many, the elevator stopped and the doors glided open. A man in a doctor's robe sat waiting for her. He took one look at her form and rose quickly.

"More antibiotics," he said. "Before she gets locked away for the day. Otherwise you might have nobody to put on trial at all."

CHAPTER ELEVEN

Hayden stepped to the middle of the room.

"All right, guys, we have a number of questions that need answering. Why was a US submarine in the straits of Taiwan that day? Why did it sink a hospital ship? Why does the United States possess the Peking Man, lost for over fifty years? Why the hell does Callan Dudley want it? What's he after next and where is this second vault? We have a lot of odd pieces to this jigsaw, guys, and no way of fitting them together."

"And why did he leave that poor family alive?" Karin added. "Or rather, the other men he's working with."

"MI5 are checking," Hayden said. "As well as the Irish. We'll soon know all there is to know about Dudley and his degenerate friends."

"What will happen to Walcott?"

"Nothing. He was acting under duress. Perhaps now the government will pass some kind of bill that deals with this problem."

"Yes," Kinimaka said with his CIA hat on. "Don't forget there's the other side of the coin—a man *pretending* to be under duress and getting away with some priceless relic."

Komodo nodded in agreement. "Some of the twisted outlaws I've met would sell their family out that way just to make a few bucks."

Hayden waved her hands a little. "Okay, okay, let's focus. The sub and the ship are at the root of all this.

Obviously the ship's long gone but what about the sub? I need the name of the captain."

Karin checked the records. "A John Kirby. You know he'll be subject to something like the Espionage Act."

"Sure." Hayden nodded. "But I'm surprised he's still alive."

Karin sniffed. "Yeah, scratch that. John Kirby died in the eighties. His son would have been seventy nine this year but he also died. Now *his* son is forty five and still very much alive. Wow, I feel like I'm clutching at secondhand bendy straws here."

"Well, that's because we are." Hayden huffed. "If you have a better suggestion let's hear it, but we've very rarely been presented with a crime that doesn't actually make any sense. Our only lead has vanished. The Peking Man clearly plays a big part in all this so let's follow the damn fossil."

"Assuming it was on the *Awa Maru*," Kinimaka said. "Off Singapore dock, it should be at the bottom of the ocean."

"Shark infested," Komodo pointed out with a shudder.

"Or salvaged by the Chinese in the eighties." Karin nodded. "But it turns up *here*, in Washington. And at the Smithsonian of all places. Why?"

"I believe Hayden is way ahead of you," Smyth griped. "That's why she asked about the ship's captain."

"Maybe the US kept the fossil as leverage," Lauren suggested. "In my line of work—my *old* line of work—I came across this many times at high-class parties and establishments. They used facial recognition software to identify their shyer, more *influential* clients so they could leverage against them later."

Smyth looked wary. "Really?"

"Yeah, but don't worry. I doubt anyone would try to blackmail you."

"Oh, very funny. I've never—"

"Save it. I'm no judge."

Hayden acknowledged Lauren with a nod. "Leverage is possible, yes. Producing the fossil at the right time would give its owner immense power over the Chinese. Karin, where does John Kirby's son's son live?"

Several hours later, Hayden and Kinimaka parked their government-issue Escalade, with Smyth in the back, outside a house that sat on a pretty but quiet street in Virginia. The three SPEAR members had taken advantage of the steady drive and warm air-conditioning to unwind a little, sparing the conversation. For Smyth this wasn't a problem. For Kinimaka, concentrating on driving, it gave him chance to think about what he might say to his sister, Kono, when he finally greeted her. For Hayden however, it started out like a balm, soothing her anxieties and helping her relax recently bruised muscles, but after about sixty miles another concern intruded on her consciousness.

The air vent to her right on the passenger side was pointed straight at her.

So what?

Irritably she returned it to its normal position. Of course this might be her regular ride whenever she needed it but she imagined it wasn't assigned *only* to her. Was it? *I guess that's something I'm gonna have to look into.*

The glovebox still held her cheap sunglasses but there

was a fingerprint on one of the lenses. Her packet of chewing gum was more than half gone. None of these things were unexplainable but, together they caused a little twisting inside her gut.

Why?

No reason that she could fathom. It was as if . . . as if something wasn't quite right. Like the blackness in the corner moving when it shouldn't. The tree throwing too many shadows. The floor squeak that might have been totally innocent . . .

Might have been.

Hayden buried it deep as Kinimaka stopped the car. Together, the three walked side-by-side up a well-tended garden path and stopped outside a freshly painted door. Kinimaka knocked, his large knuckles producing a heart-stopping sound.

"Chill, dude." Smyth winced. "You're gonna break the door down."

Kinimaka grimaced. "Yeah, sorry."

Nevertheless, the door swung open. A good-looking man stood there, well-groomed, his tight white T-shirt bearing a designer slogan. "Help you?"

Hayden held up a badge. "Hope so. Are you James Kirby?"

"Yup." The fit-looking, middle-aged man peered hard at her credentials. "SPEAR? Really? I never heard of you."

"Probably a good idea to keep it that way," Smyth grumbled.

"We need to ask you a few questions, Mr. Kirby." Hayden flashed a smile. "Could we come inside?"

"Geez, I guess. I mean you *know* the FBI. You *know* the cops. But what are you supposed to say when SPEAR come knocking?"

"It's a fair point," Smyth said, stepping over the threshold. "The police don't even know we exist."

Hayden winced a little as she walked past Kirby. "He's just messin' with ya. You can always check our legitimacy later by calling the FBI."

"Later?" Kirby repeated. "Gee, thanks."

Hayden walked into a front room with a wide bay window. Kirby moved toward the deep sill and parked himself. Smyth sank into a chair, probably trying to appear less threatening. Kinimaka remained upright and large, as imposing a figure as Kirby had probably ever seen.

Hayden smiled once more. "Listen, Mr. Kirby, I'll be honest with you. Much of what I'm about to tell you will seem crazy. Bizarre—"

"I get it. You have your secrets, right? Truly I get it. My family has its fair share." Kirby laughed aloud.

Hayden paused, blinking. "It does? Well, that's interesting. What do you do for work, Mr. Kirby?"

"Don't you already know? You *are* part of the US government right?"

Smyth brayed from the corner. "My kinda guy. I like this one."

Hayden chuckled. "Of course. Builder by day, barman by night. Your wife lives with your son about two blocks south of here. Amicable break-up, amicable arrangements. You even play squash with her new boyfriend."

"What can I say?" Kirby spread his hands. "I'm a stand-up guy."

"Well, you shouldn't have a problem helping us out then. We have a few questions about your grandfather, John Kirby."

"Grandpa John? What's he done now? Talked the ear off a cherub?"

"Enjoyed a good tale did he?" Kinimaka asked.

"Every chance he got. Why is the government asking about my grandpa?"

Hayden bit her lip for a moment, thinking best how to phrase her next comment. "Well, we'd like to know how he was in the wrong place at the wrong time. Or was it the right place at the wrong time?"

"Say again?"

"Yup, you lost me too," Smyth said.

Hayden rubbed her forehead. "The *USS Queenfish*. Your grandfather was court martialed after he sank the *Awa Maru*, though later, incredibly, he continued his career and attained flag rank. I realize it's fifty years ago now, but did your grandfather or father ever mention those times?"

Kirby stared at them for a long minute, the confusion apparent in his eyes. After a while the military bearing and authoritativeness of his guests must have won through because he started speaking. "Are you kidding? It was all he ever talked about. Especially in his later years. Grandpa was what the English might call a crackpot; that's eccentric to you and I. Poor old man . . ." Kirby tailed off.

"Did he ever say why he was near Taiwan?" Hayden asked. "Or talk of an old fossil called the Peking Man?"

Kirby suddenly looked cagey. "Y'know, it's all just bullshit. No need to repeat all that crap now. Like I said, poor guy lost it after retiring, that's all."

"It might help us out with a related case," Kinimaka prodded. "That's all."

"Related?" Kirby looked doubtful. "How can anything be related to the Lost Kingdom?"

"Please." Hayden thought about the Pythians and Dudley and their past atrocities. The Pandora plague was only the beginning. Other campaigns were afoot. What if this was worse? "We need your help. Just knowing about this lost kingdom could save lives. Hundreds, thousands of lives."

"You're not telling me it's all true." Kirby started laughing despite the solemn faces around him. "How can it be? The lost continent of Mu? It never existed."

"That may be," Hayden agreed. "But some very, very bad men think otherwise. And they'll do absolutely anything to locate it."

CHAPTER TWELVE

Hayden saw disbelief mingled with suspicion make a dangerous mix in Kirby's eyes. In the end, though, the man's what-the-hell attitude won through and he found a neutral spot to stare at above their heads.

"Long time ago now. Even then my dad pitied him. Believe me, I was only eight, but I knew. Kids know. They pick up on everything, it's crazy." Kirby shook his head as if picturing his own son. "Grandpa John talked a lot about his sea voyages—he was a salty old dog. He spoke of his rescues, mostly, of which there were many. And how he commanded a 'wolf pack'. Typhoons and unknown waters. Islands that can rise or sink depending on the time of year." He shook his head. "But that was only the start of it. As he aged, he became less sure of his faculties and less able to keep his secrets, and Grandpa John started to give some away. Not that it mattered anymore. The war was long over. But that one voyage, that damn voyage to Taiwan, it became the *only* thing he ever talked about." Kirby took a deep breath.

Hayden sat down on the couch. "Go on."

"Don't say I didn't warn you. Grandpa John sailed to the straits of Taiwan on the orders of the US government at the time. He told the story as though he were given a map with directions, a map that led straight to the lost continent of Mu."

"Hang on," Smyth said. "I don't even know what this Mu is."

Hayden spoke fast, not wanting to dam Kirby's flow. "It's believed that early in our planet's history an extremely advanced technological civilization existed which was called Mu. It was destroyed by a natural disaster, probably flooding."

"Of course it's a myth," Kinimaka said. "Which makes Mr. Kirby's story here all the more interesting. You say the government gave your grandfather this map?"

"Yes . . . and no. It wasn't exactly a map. To explain I first have to shed light on something else. The Niven Tablets. Have you heard of them?"

Hayden swung the term around her mind, a trawler's net trying to snag a memory, but came up only with snippets.

"More history," she said. "Wasn't William Niven an explorer? Or an archaeologist? And he discovered something previously unheard of, right?"

"He was by profession a mineralogist, but in 1894 became involved with archaeological discoveries. Sorry if I'm droning on a bit, I've heard this a hundred times. He discovered prehistoric ruins in Guerrero for the American Museum of Natural History. He was a respected, connected man. In 1911 he discovered ancient ruins near Mexico City, the old home of the Aztecs, buried beneath layers of volcanic ash, rocks, pebbles and sand, he said the result of an obviously cataclysmic event. He found twenty thousand objects, so they say, most of which now reside in a private museum. Two thousand six hundred of these objects were known as the Niven Tablets."

"I never heard of them," Kinimaka admitted.

"They're very real," Kirby said. "Or they *were.*

Surrounded by controversy since their discovery, the Niven Tablets contain symbols, writing, that *has never been deciphered.* Associated with Scandinavian petroglyphs and widely interpreted, the translation remains positively unknown even today. Also called the Andesite Tablets, they all bore very similar markings and were said to have also been found in India and Egypt."

"Let me guess," Hayden said. "The tablets are said to be written in the lost language of Mu."

"Give that girl the prize." Kirby pointed at her. "But seriously, you guys want a drink? If I were you I'd be reaching for the friggin' whisky by now."

"I'm good," Hayden said, just as Kinimaka and Smyth both agreed to black coffees.

Kirby rose and walked out of the room. Hayden pulled a face at the two men. "Really?"

"It's been hours," Kinimaka complained. "I'm withering away."

Smyth snorted. Before he could comment Kirby was back with a plate of Oreos and a bowl full of Lays chips and separate dips. The Hawaiian's face lit up. Hayden waited patiently whilst both he and Smyth tucked in, trying to absorb everything so far. She wondered how the Niven Tablets and the *USS Queenfish* might intersect, but couldn't quite figure it out.

Yet.

Kirby returned with four coffees, and when she smelled the strong aroma Hayden was glad he'd ignored her.

"Thank you."

"No worries. Anyhow, it was postulated that the

markings on the tablets had their roots in the lost continent of Mu. After its ancient destruction various survivors are said to have found their way to Egypt and India and other places and recorded what had occurred, you see. Some say it's just another deluge theory. Others say a hoax, me included. But even I say: *Two thousand six hundred tablets, a hoax?* Really? I doubt that even the craziest fame-seeking conspiracy nut would craft that many, don't you?"

"If nobody could read the markings how did they decide it was the lost language of Mu?" Kinimaka said with a full mouth.

"Circumstance," Kirby admitted. "Tablets with the exact same markings had been found before in India, Egypt and Sinai by another man who told Niven what they were." Kirby coughed. "Whatever you say, whatever you think, the mystery of these tablets still remains unsolved today, international, and more than a little intriguing."

"All right." Hayden drained her coffee. "So where are they now? We've had what? Another hundred or so years to study them. Surely somebody has a theory."

Kirby smiled. "Unfortunately the tablets were lost. Niven sold them and they disappeared aboard a shipment from Mexico to the United States."

Hayden turned sharply, met the man's eyes. "The United States?" A link between the sub and the tablets was beginning to form.

"Yes, in the 1930s all two thousand six hundred tablets vanished whilst heading for the US. All that remained were the rubbings."

"I guess nobody thought that odd at the time." Smyth snorted.

Kirby spread his hands. "So it would seem. There were no enquiries made."

"Fuck," Kinimaka breathed. "What a fucking mystery."

"And it doesn't end there," Kirby went on. "The *USS Queenfish*, captained by Grandpa John, sailed for Taiwan in 1945, about ten years after the tablets disappeared. His 'map', he later babbled to us, was taken directly from the Niven Tablets."

Hayden somehow managed to stop her mouth from dropping open. "What? How?"

Kirby shrugged. "I don't know and would rather not speculate. But you asked what Grandpa John was doing in Taiwan. He was using the 'lost' Niven Tablets as a map to find the mythological continent of Mu, the first civilization of Man."

"So it's between Taiwan and China?" Kinimaka realized. "That ain't gonna go down well."

Hayden stored that insight away until later. "But why sink the *Awa Maru*? She was just passing by at the—" it dawned on her and she clammed up quickly.

Kirby nodded. "You're thinking *'Eureka!'* aren't you? I can see it in your eyes. Yes, Grandpa John says the ship spotted his submarine on their radar and questioned its presence. They reported it to whoever the hell was in charge. Grandpa received orders to fire upon it and, later, to salvage whatever may be aboard."

Hayden thought about it. "So the destroy order was given merely to mask the sub's real intentions? Searching for this lost kingdom, the sub was supposed to be a ghost. The US gave the sub up and called the sinking a mistake. Then, knowing through reports that a huge treasure was aboard the *Awa Maru*, and also the Peking Man fossil, they cut their losses and commandeered those also. Did they give up the search for Mu? And what happened to the Niven Tablets?"

"Grandpa John, he babbled a lot. An awful lot. I can't comment on the accuracy of what I have told you." Kirby tried not to look embarrassed. "I can't say even if any of it is true, though certain historical events like the disappearance of the tablets and Niven's claims and the sub's mysterious presence in Taiwan do back him up more than a little. Did the States steal the tablets? Did they decipher the writing? They could just as easily have worked off the thousands of rubbings that were made, though admittedly not as accurately. He mentioned the fossil and the gold bullion too but, to be honest with you, by that time we were all finished listening to his ramblings. Once he passed away my father drew a line under it all and never spoke of it again. Me? I got on with my own life."

"You remember it all very well," Hayden commented. "Maybe you wished it to be true? I just think—an eight-year-old kid listening to all that. Archaeology. Mystery. Lost kingdoms. Government conspiracy. Did you take it to heart a little?"

"Maybe a little," Kirby admitted. "But then I grew up, graduated, and real life became more important that a fantastical dream world. Hey, now I'd rather hit the gym than pick up a Kindle. Ya know?"

Hayden nodded at his physique. "I can see that."

Kirby grinned. "Membership includes a free guest if you're interested."

"Maybe some other time." Hayden rose, ignoring

Kinimaka's puppy-dog look. She was about to shake Kirby's hand when an unanswered question poked at the back of her mind.

"Sorry. Just one more thing. Did your grandpa ever say what happened to the Niven Tablets after he lost the captaincy of the sub?"

"It unloaded its secret and looted cargo onto a United States destroyer in the dead of night. Very clandestine stuff. Unbelievable really. Spies and conspiracies and super government agencies. It's only now that real people are beginning to believe that all this stuff really does go on."

Hayden said nothing.

Kirby continued, "Grandpa John may have been disgraced in the eyes of the world but he was still the true captain of that submarine. He took one for the team, so to speak. He had an interest in the tablets, since he'd followed their directions so far. The archaeologist who looked after them—I don't know his name—told Grandpa that they would be sent back to America and locked away until they were needed again. They had to let the dust settle, you see, and keep the tablets safe."

"It wouldn't do for another US sub to be spotted in the exact same area," Smyth hypothesized.

"Exactly. Well, they were sent to some vault somewhere and then forgotten about, I guess. Who knows? There are so many secrets these days, layers upon layers, like old skeleton bones crushed beneath the passage of so many years."

Hayden raised an eyebrow as he waxed lyrical. "Thanks for your help, Mr. Kirby. We'll be in touch if we need anything else."

On their way back to the car, Hayden stopped and turned to the other two. "You guys thinking what I'm thinking?"

Smyth cast his gaze down. "Not unless you're thinking about texting a thousand-dollar hooker called Lauren."

Kinimaka glared. "Or about jamming that guy's gym bag up his own—"

"Okay, okay," Hayden interrupted quickly. "So maybe we're not all reading from the same script. But Dudley's looking for a second vault, right? He's already grabbed one of China's great treasures—the Peking Man, which is linked to Mu and the tablets. Could it be that he's now after their greatest—the Lost Kingdom?"

"By using the tablets," Smyth barked. "But why? Kirby said there were rubbings that still exist."

"But not as accurate. Which the Pythians need. And maybe he just wants to destroy the tablets, who knows? Either way, guys, we have to find out where those tablets were stored and we have to go there. Right now. Dudley and his crew need to be stopped."

Smyth reached the car first. "Theory's sound," he said. "I'm all the way in."

Hayden reached for her phone as she climbed inside. Her first call was to Karin Blake, who would make high-level enquiries as to the whereabouts of the Niven Tablets. She was so engrossed in her work that she didn't feel the chill that hit her full in the face—the air vent aimed right at her.

Not for the first fifty miles anyway.

CHAPTER THIRTEEN

Former limestone mines are now used throughout the USA as secure vaults. The more you pay the more secure your valuables become. Bill Gates uses a refrigerated cave over two hundred feet below ground. Princess Diana's will rests in a vault below a reinforced mountain entrance. Other safeguarded riches include the original recordings of Frank Sinatra, law firm client files, the mysterious Mormon Vault. The servers of WikiLeaks are secured behind a forty-centimeter-thick door that's accessible through only one tunnel and capable of withstanding a hydrogen bomb. The JP Morgan vault, one of the largest in the world, the Vatican and of course the KFC vault, where the Colonel's original recipe is hidden.

An abandoned mine in Pennsylvania houses none of these treasures; rather it is less famous, dustier, and quieter. Instead of the usual all-embracing entry procedures which include two forms of ID, special clearance and blood-taking, a twenty-eight-ton, triple-timed lock and a quarter of a mile trip below the surface, this facility is touted as less illustrious than its big brothers, almost antiquated, and thus unworthy of much attention. There are no fees for storage; prospective clients are generally pointed elsewhere.

A gray-haired man wearing a tatty reflective jacket meets you at the gate and sends you on your way; he's never had to explain to anybody that he's ex-Special Forces.

*

Hayden, Kinimaka and Smyth arrived back in Washington DC in time to hear Karin trying to use Robert Price's influence and the SPEAR clearance level to learn the whereabouts of the Niven Tablets. Karin told Hayden she was sure nobody was trying to pull the wool over her eyes—it was more a problem of finding anyone who *remembered* them. No computer stored their file, no filing cabinet contained their folder. The best way to hide something you don't want found was to lose every record that it ever existed.

And create the backstory that they had gone "missing; somewhere between Mexico and the US".

Hayden heard most of what Karin told her. A small part of her mind still dwelled over the air-vent incident. Had she moved it before she left the car, even accidentally? Had Mano or Smyth moved it? She felt a little embarrassed to ask them.

Or am I losing my mind?

Maybe it was the gunshot wound. A virus. Damn, most likely she needed a vacation. To get away from all this. *As soon as we bag the Pythians.*

Barely believing her own promise, Hayden perked up as Karin swung around. "Nailed it. There's a curator works at the old Steel Mountain facility in Pennsylvania, near the city of Butler. Pretty much a forgotten records facility, he knows of more than a few dusty old treasures that were stored down there between 1940 and 1960. Records don't exist for these pieces and I guess once the older guys who know about them retire or lose interest then their existence will just pass to legend."

Hayden rose to her feet. "So what are we—"

"One more thing," Karin said. "The curator mentioned someone else making the same inquiry only a few days ago."

"Who?" Kinimaka asked. "Dudley?"

"No. This person came across as well-spoken, highly educated and powerful. And possessed a clearance level beyond ours."

Hayden narrowed her eyes. "What? But that's . . . did he get a name?"

"Names weren't passed, no. Just the clearance level protocol."

"Are we thinking—Pythian?" Komodo wondered.

Hayden nodded slowly. "Who else could it be? They're a downright sneaky bunch. Always a step ahead."

Karin tapped her keyboard. "They're only ahead because we don't know what they're planning next. It might be an idea to place someone permanently on the inside."

"A mole?" Hayden said. "A *Pythian* mole? Great idea, but we don't know where they are. We could ask Lauren. She said that Nicholas Bell didn't seem the sort. What do you think?"

Kinimaka and Komodo were already gearing up. Smyth shrugged into a vest beside them. "Shall we discuss all that later?" he said. "We have a robbery to stop."

Less than two hours later the team exited their plane and were approaching the storage facility by car. The skies were dark, the roads picked out by full beam. The mood inside the car was grim as the soldiers prepared for a fight.

"Nothing heard from the facility for over an hour," Hayden reported. "Damn. Dudley could have gotten in and out by now."

"My guess is—he won't," Komodo said unhappily. "That man loves his chaos and now he's brought his friends along." The soldier shrugged. "I'm surprised the Pythians are still using someone they can barely control."

"We hit them hard in Niagara," Smyth said. "Bastards are still in recovery."

Hayden grunted in approval. "You're probably right. Which means if we hit them just as hard this time we might take 'em down."

The facility appeared up ahead, the mountain rearing up behind it. Soft, sparse floodlights made inconsequential pools around the gated entrance, giving the impression of a low-level building. Kinimaka stopped the car right outside.

"Everybody out. Heads up."

The night closed in. Hayden raised her gun and approached the entrance. Karin's voice filled their comms. "Still no contact. It's now ninety minutes."

Smyth crouched at the gate. Beyond, splitting a patch of yellow light, a sprawled leg could be seen sticking out. "Contact confirmed," he said. "Something's definitely wrong here. Call the cavalry."

Karin affirmed and then Smyth pushed at the gate. It opened easily. "We still have to secure those tablets," he said.

"I don't see any trucks around," Kinimaka said as he ran through the gate. "How do they intend to move them?"

"Trucks will be inside the facility, I guess." Hayden

moved to the front of the four-man team. "Or they could be taking pictures. Finding the tablets and photographing them could be what's taking so long."

The team folded their bodies into the shadows and approached the large entrance to the mountain storage unit. Pausing for a moment they cast about, searching for any signs of life. Through previous contacts Hayden knew Dudley wasn't exactly the kind for covert and careful infiltrations but she wasn't about to start taking chances. The entrance was comprised of two doors, one enormous and perfectly able to admit a Mac truck; the other about the size of a large man.

"We need an override code," she told Karin. "For the facility. Right now."

Two minutes passed and then they were on the move again. Kinimaka entered the code. The door clicked open. Hayden was first through, squinting slightly and slowing as the light hit her. Komodo produced a prepared map of the unit and pointed off to the right.

"Past the booth, turn right and we're into a tunnel network. The tablets are on the fourth level if the old timer's faculties haven't deserted him."

Hayden proceeded with caution. The booth was empty, as were the tunnels. Their next problem was the length of the tunnels, hundreds of feet with no niches or exits or junctions; if they were spotted by Dudley and his men they would be sitting ducks.

"Bank of elevators," Komodo said. "About two hundred and fifty feet ahead."

"Let's make it fast." Hayden broke cover, senses on full

alert as she sprinted hard down the smooth, white-painted tunnel. Strip lights mounted to the ceiling lit the way, though her route was arrow straight, angling slightly downward. Kinimaka ran at her back, with Smyth and Komodo behind him.

They reached the elevator bank. Hayden scouted for a set of stairs. "Four down?" she confirmed. "Let's go."

The ordinary staircase switched back twice for every level, so it was seven sets later when she slowed. The door to the fourth level stood just below, closed and unmanned.

"It's been over one hundred minutes," Karin breathed in their heads. "Be careful." She added a tender word for Komodo which the rest did their best to ignore.

Hayden approached the door, cracked it open. She took a moment to catch her breath. Beyond, the room opened out into a huge, arched vault, a veritable Aladdin's cave of unknown and unspeakable treasures. High shelving filled the center of the place but much more space was taken up by haphazard, endless piles of boxes and crates and other paraphernalia.

"It's a livin', breathin' pirate's cave," Komodo said, peering over her, grinning. "Used to love all the ole pirate stories, I did."

"Hey! Where's that Drake guy? Or Myles? Me brother said yer might be all coming."

Hayden processed the situation at the speed of light. The Irishman's voice came from behind, which meant he'd been hidden somewhere in the lower stairwell, and was undoubtedly armed. She dived through the door, rolling; Komodo followed. Kinimaka and Smyth also managed to squeeze through just as the Irishman started firing. Bullets whacked the door and fizzed through the narrowing opening.

"Come on!"

Hayden ducked behind the nearest crate, a high and wide timbered casket large enough to house a small car. Smyth covered the rear whilst the others tried to get their bearings. Komodo referred to the map.

"Um, I don't think we need that anymore."

Kinimaka pointed around the left-hand side of the crate. Six men crouched around the bottom shelf of one of the racks, two of them aiming weapons his way.

"They're photographing the tablets," Hayden said. "I'd put my sanity on it." Not the most astute bet she'd ever made. "See any civilians, Mano?"

"No. Just six guys carrying weapons. What do you want to do?"

"Dudley?"

"Yeah. I see him."

"Take 'em down!"

Hayden burst out of hiding, firing ahead. Kinimaka ranged to her right, Komodo to her left. All three of them stayed low and veered their run toward another potential shelter. Straw and polystyrene and even dirt coated the floor. High above, strip-lights swung around the rafters. Dudley's men returned fire, the four who were taking photos cursing loudly and scrambling to the side. Hayden saw one of the tablets fall from its leaning position and crack in half. About the size of two laptops laid on end they were dark gray in color, with the addition of a dull red pigment. Symbols and markings covered their surface. Hayden saw several piles of them just as Dudley's men started to destroy them.

"Oh no you don't!"

She fired first, peppering the men and sending them reeling. No blood flowed so she guessed they wore vests, but two fell to the floor, groaning. Dudley's evil smiling face turned toward her.

"And who the hell are you, missy?"

Hayden let her gun do the talking. Dudley and his men scrambled away, ducking around the end of an aisle. One of them clutched at a leg and this time she saw a trail of blood on the floor.

At her back, Komodo and Kinimaka kept moving. Nobody wanted a stalemate here, too much was at stake. *Too many unanswered questions.* She kept up a steady fire on the Irishmen's hiding place as they sought to get closer.

Behind them, Smyth kept the other Irishman at bay. Dudley's *brother.* Evidently, they needed to research the whole crew when they returned to the HQ, when and if they captured any of them.

"Where is everyone normal?" Komodo said. "Guards and curators. The question of hostages exists, guys. I just hope these mad Irish bastards didn't kill everyone on their way down here."

Kinimaka fired off a shot. "Low key facility," he said. "Nothing ever happens here. Purposely. I bet their staff numbers in the low teens."

Hayden was still evaluating Komodo's other statement— "mad Irish bastards". The soldier was spot on. They needed to push their advantage because these guys weren't going to stay pinned down for long whether they had a viable escape route or not. A sudden cry made her look back. Smyth was racing toward them, head down and legs pumping, a metallic object rattling around in his wake.

"Grena—" he managed.

Then the place erupted. Deadly shards made them all hit the ground; the concussive sound blasted their eardrums and their senses at the same time. Hayden recovered fast, Smyth and Komodo doubly so, but then all their assailants burst out of cover.

Behind Smyth, the single Irishman capered and shot his gun off in all directions, performing an actual Irish jig, but only for a moment. When his comrades appeared he fired at an angle, effectively trying to stop Hayden and the others from hitting them.

"They're the worst kind of enemy," Komodo groaned. "Trained fucking madmen." He rolled behind the large crate, joining the others as a bullet whizzed off the framework, narrowly missing his bulk. In that instant Kinimaka's cell rang.

Hayden stared at him, suddenly lost in the past.

Kinimaka frowned and dug the unwieldy object out. "My fault," he said. "Should have switched it off. Ah, shit."

Komodo glanced over. "Who is it?"

"Kono. Sister who's probably madder at me than all these Irishmen put together. Oh, well." He turned it off. "Hayden? You okay?"

The ex-CIA agent struggled to speak. Her mind had been transported back many months, to a time when she fought alongside young Ben Blake. Ben often received and took phone calls in the midst of a battle, usually from his mom or dad.

All gone now.

Hayden swallowed drily, hearing the click in her throat. It wouldn't do to lose focus at this point. She ignored the guys and rolled to the other side of the crate, still struggling. But then Dudley's manic voice cut through her melancholy.

"Yer really think yer can stop us? The 27-Club are back, bitch, and yer country is our amusement park."

Hayden peered around just in time to see a rocket launcher settle over the madman's shoulder. From across the huge vault his brother broke down into fits of laughter, literally falling to his knees. Dudley's men darted around him, unable to conceal their glee, their lust for blood and lunacy.

"Goodbye," Dudley intoned.

Hayden called a warning, and shot out from behind the crate, firing blindly to stop the Irishmen taking potshots. She needn't have worried. They were too busy tracking the missile to watch the damage it caused. When the RPG struck the huge crate the four SPEAR members were sprinting away; when it hit they were suddenly flying away—airborne, meters off the ground, lit by an expanding fireball and twisting amidst debris and planks of timber and metal fastenings. Hayden felt the whoosh of air and the unstoppable force, helpless, crawling through thin air and then coming down hard, slapping into the ground with her shoulder and then her skull; her hip and then her shins. Sliding across the floor for a moment and then she lay still, ears throbbing, ringing, body screaming to be left alone.

But what was Dudley going to do next? A sane man would use the opportunity to escape. This guy . . .

Hayden fought every nerve ending, every warning signal, every impulse from her brain, and forced her body to turn over.

There he was, sniggering, still talking, standing right over her. And over his shoulder, now pointed down, he still held the rocket launcher.

"Always wanted to do this to a feckin' cop."

CHAPTER FOURTEEN

Horror made Hayden's eyes widen, her face turn white. Staring up at the rocket launcher she momentarily froze.

Surely he realizes he would die too?

Maybe, maybe not. Truth was he didn't care. To this man it was all a deadly game, a boy's day out, and each successive high intoxicated him to try the next. Her vision, her world, was filled with metallic death and a wide drooling grin.

"C'est la vie, bitch," he drawled.

His finger tightened on the trigger. Hayden couldn't look away. The missile shook slightly. And then the rocket struck.

But it was a rocket of hard flesh and bone, an enormous man-made rocket called Mano Kinimaka, and he smashed into Dudley hard enough to snap him in two. The rocket launcher tumbled away and then hit the ground and fired— its unstoppable missile speeding toward the rear of the vault. Kinimaka tripped over his own blurry feet, falling and rolling. Dudley coasted helplessly into the air at least six feet, then came down on his back, stunned. Komodo was on his knees, lifting a rifle.

Dudley's boys laughed hard as they closed in behind him.

One leapt at Komodo, taking advantage of the soldier's befuddlement, and added to it, striking him in the face. Another started kicking at Kinimaka, dancing out of the

Hawaiian's reach and then darting back in. Two more lifted Dudley, unable to stop from cracking unintelligible jokes. That left two surplus and Dudley's brother, who now sat near the shelving, finishing off with the camera.

"Best get goin', lads," he said. "Backup'll be here soon."

Most of the men complained, enjoying their fun.

"Ach, I don't mean this minute," the brother drawled. "Kill the feckers first."

A shout of pleasure went up. Hayden rolled away from her attackers, seeing the world spin at least three times. Nausea rose within as a sharp kick connected with her spine. Damn, they were at such a disadvantage here. It was then that she thought of Ben again, and her father's sacrifices, and so many others—all that they had lost—and a feeling of pure anger rose within her.

What the hell am I doing here? Curling up into a fucking ball?

At least she was still alive to live out her hopes and dreams. Ignoring the discomfort, the vertigo and the heavy pounding, she kicked back, using the momentum to jump to her knees. The world turned violently, but she thrust it away, focusing on the men before her. One came at her with a knee, which she deftly palmed aside. Now she spied her Glock to the left. A second attacked with a rush and she fell under him, risking a roll and paying dearly for it. Again the world turned, her head screamed and she threw up. But her attacker sprawled in her wake, smashing his head to the floor.

Hayden reached out for the Glock.

To her left Komodo wrestled with another Irishman,

looking stronger with each passing second. The initial concussion was wearing off, the soldiers were trained to fight through it. Smyth, flat out and groaning until now, suddenly sat up and there was a machine pistol in his hands.

An Irishman kicked it away, then collapsed as Smyth punched his thigh. Hayden grabbed the Glock and aimed it at her nearest attacker.

"Hey now, lassie, hey now. It's all just a bit of fun."

He backed away. His compatriot jumped up, grinning. "Time we got the feck outta here."

They rushed her. Hayden squeezed a shot off, winging one, but got a knee to the face for her trouble. Blood flowed. She fell backwards again, groaning, but used the fall to twist her body around so that she now faced their fleeing backs.

"Stop!"

She could stop them, wound them, but her team needed her more than her mission. Without pause she whirled once more. Smyth had thrown off his attacker; the man was already in flight. Komodo threw his to the floor. Kinimaka had caught a boot intent on breaking his ribs and was now twisting an ankle.

"Let 'em go," a voice rang out, Dudley's brother. "And we'll let yer live. Can't do fairer than that."

Hayden evaluated their position. Three machine pistols were pointed at them—one by a dazed Dudley. Kinimaka, Smyth and Komodo were starting to get the best of the other four attackers, though there were no guarantees in this fight. Quickly she raised her Glock, nodding at the same time.

"Go," she said. "Get the hell outta here. We'll see you soon."

Her team was bruised and battered, like her. This deal was as good as it was going to get.

Dudley stretched his clearly aching body. "We'll be counting on it, bitch. Counting down the days. And next time, yer'd best bring some real men."

"Then go." Hayden, with her body starting to relax and the adrenalin seeping away, was trying hard not to see double. "Before I change my mind."

Dudley's brother was walking away from the pile of tablets, machine gun trained upon them. "Whadya say, brother?"

"Make a bleedin' mess, Malachi. Yer know yer want to."

Dudley's brother grinned, but Hayden suddenly rose to her feet. "No! Stop. You destroy one of those tablets and the deal's off!"

Her three colleagues rose to stand at her side, weapons reacquired. Dudley blinked as he regarded them.

"Mexican standoff, eh? Well, we did get the rubbings too, and it'll sure help yer's find us again, right?"

Hayden squinted. "Yeah, whatever you said. If it helps you run away then just go."

The Irishmen backed off, covering the Americans the entire time. No more words were passed and by the time they were alone, Hayden was crouched down in front of the tablets.

"Go make sure they leave without killing anyone else," she told Smyth and Komodo. "And send the backup down here when it finally arrives. We need to secure these tablets and find out what they say."

Kinimaka laid a hand on her shoulder. "You okay?"

"Barely, Mano. Barely. I guess that's another life gone. One of these days I'm gonna find I ran out."

"Don't say that. And besides, we run out together. You got me?"

Hayden found herself smiling. "I got you."

Kinimaka crouched down at her side, an arm now draped over her shoulder. His left knee struck a precarious tablet, sending it crashing to the floor. Luckily, though cracking from side to side, the object stayed in place.

"Shit."

"I guess some things just never change."

CHAPTER FIFTEEN

Since the SPEAR team found and brought the tombs of the gods to the attention of the world, unearthing a language expert had never been a problem for them. Several were still employed on translating the writings found and photographed in the tombs, chief among them Torsten Dahl's good friend, Olle Akerman. The Swedish language expert had proven to be fluent in old Akkadian, Sumerian, Babylonian and even the Nu Shu of ancient China, so Hayden wondered how he might fare with the lost language of the lost kingdom of Mu.

With the nightmare logistical problem of guarding two thousand six hundred tablets, organizing an approaching force of two hundred men, the SPEAR team's widespread distribution, and Olle Akerman being in Sweden at that time, Hayden parked her butt in a tiny office and thought about what to do.

Tylenol was the first order of the day, followed by an entire bottle of water. Hayden sat in the dark, trying to steady her head. The facility's employees had been found, three locked in a room with bruises to most parts of their bodies, two security guards murdered with shocking brute force, and six other workers in the far-flung reaches of the vault who had no idea what was going on. The most promising development was that Steel Mountain's boss had been located and told them that the Niven Tablets had actually been photographed years ago, the prints archived.

He was currently searching them out.

Hayden checked her watch. Forty five minutes had passed since Dudley escaped. That meant that the Pythians—she assumed—now owned the Peking Man and also a potential map to the lost kingdom of Mu. Their endgame and purpose, however, still remained a mystery. Was Mu a link to Atlantis? Was it, by itself, worth as much to China alone? Did it even exist? The Americans had been searching for Mu fifty years ago. Why did they stop—simply because a ship had been sunk? At the time, Hayden imagined, tensions must have been so very high between the countries involved that prudence would have come into immediate effect. Thousands of people died aboard the *Awa Maru*, and it wasn't until twenty years later that even the Chinese decided to try salvaging the vessel.

Her first decision was made. Olle Akerman had come through before and would undoubtedly be delighted to hear about an undecipherable language. Hayden placed the call.

"Hello? Ja? Who is this?" Olle answered immediately, his voice loud as if he stood right next to her.

"Olle, it's Hayden Jaye. I hope you remember me."

"Ja, ja. Of course, how could I forget? I follow the world for your exploits. I wish I was following you right now. Ha ha."

Same old Akerman. Hayden remembered how he used to tease Dahl about his wife. She launched into a full explanation for her call, missing nothing out. Akerman listened intently, not interrupting.

"What do you think, Olle?"

"Of course I have heard of the Niven Tablets. They are

famous, considered a hoax. But a very good hoax. So many tablets, so elaborately constructed. Why go to so much trouble? Why not stop at a thousand tablets or even five hundred? Recent years and events have taught us that old artefacts once considered anomalies, inexplicable, or clever pranks, may actually be genuine. Indeed, as science advances so do the unexplainable mysteries it gives rise to. I thought everyone had forgotten the tablets."

Hayden shrugged in the dark. "I believe they had."

"But not these—what do you say—*Pythians?* They remembered, eh? Even knew where to find them. Ja? So where are the tablets now?"

Hayden didn't answer for a moment, thinking that Akerman had uncovered a rather sore point there. How *had* the Pythians known where both the Peking Man and the Niven Tablets were stored?

"They're with me. Here. At Steel Mountain. The warden is digging out a set of old prints."

Akerman fell silent before coming to a decision. "Ja. Well, this is what I think you should do. This Mu, it is no different to Atlantis. A myth or an ancient, dead civilization. All gone. But clearly, if you are hunting Atlantis—or Mu— you need an expert's view. I have a friend in Washington— one David Daccus—who will be able to help. I believe he wrote a paper on both Mu and the tablets and is also a language expert, though not in my class of course. In *any* discipline."

Hayden caught his drift. "Olle, you're sixty three."

"Give me the chance, my dear, and I'll show you how a lifetime's experience improves one's . . . virility."

Hayden couldn't help but laugh, whilst also feeling a little horrified. "Give me his number, Olle. And go take a cold shower."

The Swede found Daccus' contact details and signed off. Hayden placed her next call and put Daccus on alert as she awaited the arrival of the prints. Kinimaka reported that they'd located an industrial scanner in the vault's main office along with several other modern accoutrements. Hayden paused a moment longer, savoring the peace and the dark and the quiet. But the world always moved on. It moved millisecond by millisecond, minute by minute, hour by hour. But it always moved on.

And danger befalls those who didn't move with it.

Once the many prints had been fed through the scanner, compressed into a file, and sent to David Daccus; once the vault had been secured; Hayden thought about returning to Washington. It was late—or more accurately very *early*; and her team was worn out. Back at base Karin was manning the communications, giving Hayden's team the entire flight home to relax. Once they arrived, Hayden had no trouble directing everyone straight to the Pentagon. There would be no returning to their apartments or houses just yet.

Hayden guessed about three hours had passed. She wondered how Daccus was faring with the tablets, how Drake was proceeding in Japan. She wondered why she viewed her little attached office differently, as if searching for small things amiss. Of course, they were inside the damn Pentagon. What could be amiss?

Just a niggling. A voice in my head. The first sign of madness?

How did the Pythians locate the fossil and the tablets so easily?

The absence of an answer worried her. She swallowed more pain killers and joined the team for an early morning round of black coffees. Karin sat nursing Komodo's injured knee. Kinimaka sat alone, cradling his ribs as Smyth rolled the kinks from his own shoulders.

"Took a few whacks?" Hayden sat opposite the big Hawaiian.

"More than a few. Think I said *aloha* to my spleen."

"Those Irish boys take no prisoners."

"They'll die the same way."

Hayden pretended not to have heard that last remark. Instead, she swung her body around, keeping her head as still as possible, to regard Karin.

"Any news from Daccus?"

"No. But I also have the warden from Steel Mountain going through every inch of his records. We have to believe the Americans at one time translated these symbols. Otherwise why would they be in Taiwan?"

"Ya think the translation might be in the archives?"

"Why not? It sure makes sense."

Kinimaka now turned around. "I never heard of the lost continent of Mu," he said. "What exactly is it?"

Karin nodded. "Me too. So, I did a little extra research whilst you guys were away. Older than the ancient Greeks, the Babylonians, Persians and Egyptians, the civilization of Mu was far more advanced than any of them. It existed fifty thousand years ago and had inhabitants that migrated to the places I mentioned, taking their expertise and legends with them. The tablets themselves confirm the creation of the earth and then humans, who originated in Mu."

"So it's the birthplace of humanity," Kinimaka said. "*If* it ever existed. A place quite important then."

Karin laughed. "To say the least. It was also said to be the location of the Drug of Immortality. Don't smile, Mano. As we already know most modern day academics don't go seeking controversy such as lost continents and inexplicable relics for fear of losing credibility among their peers and ultimately their whole careers. But searching through the histories of both China and Taiwan I have read innumerable accounts of sea voyages to discover this lost kingdom. The *Ling Wai Tai Ta* text tells of a great bank of sand and rocks in the Great Eastern Ocean and states that 'a great castle of red walls lies somewhere submerged beneath the sea'. Then, in 1981 a diver found the battlements of what appeared to be castle walls in the Straits. This is *right below* where the *USS Queenfish* found its notoriety. Coincidence?"

"A strong one," Hayden admitted.

"Anyway, amazingly this story of castle walls received absolutely no attention in the west, despite a British Channel 4 TV series. The structure he found consists of two colossal walls, running hundreds of meters in length; these ruins lie in a place that would have been above sea level during the last glacial period about ten thousand years ago. Now, both Taiwan and China have ancient flood myths, so which country would claim Mu?"

Hayden swirled her coffee, staring into the black liquid. "They both would."

At that moment her phone rang. She stared at the screen,

still lost in thought, and saw the name of the warden at Steel Mountain flashing up. "Hayden Jaye here."

"Hi, it's Carl Preston, the warden. I haven't discovered anything pertaining to the translation of the tablets yet but I wanted to apprise you of something nasty that we *have* found."

Hayden put her cup down. "What is it?"

"If you remember rubbings were made of the tablets. Old rubbings made by William Niven himself and his colleagues. Though some were later found and released to the world at large, most ended up here, one way or another, inside these archives."

"Out of sight out of mind," Hayden said. "I get it."

"Yes, well, all the rubbings are missing. And *not* taken by these Irishmen of yours. Camera footage shows a blackout about a week ago. We believe that is when they went missing."

"Any suspects?"

"Yes, a prominent member of our security team who suddenly quit a few days ago. He's missing too."

Hayden hung her head. "All right. Send me his details. We'll start an inquiry at this end." She ended the call and looked around. "Any ideas?"

"Could still be the Pythians," Karin said with a shrewd look. "First they went simple—tried the rubbings. When they didn't pan out they took the tablets themselves. Didn't someone say the rubbings weren't accurate?"

"The guard was working for the Pythians?" Kinimaka repeated. "Possibly then he was paid off. Relocated."

"Or buried," Komodo growled.

"Don't forget the Peking Man fossil," Smyth added. "How is that involved in all this?"

Hayden shook her head. "Shit, my brain hurts. Getting blown up has done nothing for my cognitive process. I'm actually thinking Drake's got it easy right now, over there in Japan. All he has to do is break Mai out of a compound, right?"

Kinimaka nodded gloomily. "Right."

"So let's find Mu," Karin said. "Obviously it's critical. Let's find the Lost Kingdom."

CHAPTER SIXTEEN

Drake paced the carpet as he waited for Dai Hibiki to join them. Alicia, Dahl and Yorgi sat in various states of repose, clearing their minds. Grace nibbled on snacks she'd taken from the mini-bar. They expected this operation to take the form of a swift, clandestine, well-executed strike of the dagger—in and out before the Yakuza knew it, leaving them reeling and none-the-wiser. The team needed to be prepared.

The knock at the hotel door made them all take offensive positions. Drake put his eye to the peep-hole and waved them down. "Only Hibiki."

The Japanese cop entered the room, a resigned expression vying with the weariness already engraved into his face. Without smile or greetings he walked to the center of the room. "Mai wasn't taken to the Yakuza compound. She was taken straight to their headquarters in Kobe. That explains why we've been seeing all these arrivals and no guests physically arriving on site. This HQ," he shook his head, "it is virtually impregnable."

"If we have to we'll use sheer firepower to break her out," Drake vowed. "Headquarters or not."

Hibiki sighed. "I truly wish it were that simple. I've been wracking my brains for a suitable plan ever since I heard. Their HQ is huge, ultra-modern, almost a skyscraper. The very first and least of your problems would be locating her. After that, well, how do you infiltrate a heavily guarded, ultra-secure, modern building? There is no parking garage. No windows or roof that you can access without setting off a hundred sensors. No grounds. No pliable security guards or staff. The place is run purely by hardline Yakuza. It is . . . a fortress."

"Calm down, Dai-Dai." Alicia rose quickly, a sickened look on her face. "What the hell's wrong with you? I never took you for a bitchin' pussy. Got your thong on back to front?"

Drake stared at him. "Bitch has a point."

"Damn right she does." Dahl rose too.

Alicia glared at them both. "Hey."

Hibiki stared from one set of hard eyes to the other. "I'm open to any suggestions, my friends."

Alicia started counting on her fingers.

Drake screwed his face up. "What are you doing, love? Counting Yakuza?"

"Nah, just counting how many guys there are still alive in this world who can get away with calling me a bitch. I'm at two, maybe three."

Drake gauged the space around him. "Am I one of them?"

"You're still standing aren't you?"

Hibiki caught their attention. "Look. You can't just blast in and out of there. It has to be done a certain way."

"Your way?" Alicia asked. "Pussy style?"

"Let me give you an example." Hibiki frowned. "The way you guys charged that arms bazaar. Remember? Using the Light Brigade method. Though successful, what has that wrought upon you?"

Drake pursed his lips. "You mean this Ramses bloke? He's a myth. I can't see there being any kind of real terrorist royalty."

"Well, believe me when I say that there *is,* and that the threat is very *real.* But that's not our problem. Your brazen attack has caused you complicated issues down the line. You simply can't defeat *all* the Yakuza. So what do you do?"

"Do have a plan?" Alicia looked confused.

"Denial is everything." Hibiki said. "You can't have an organization like the Yakuza hunting you for the rest of your life, ergo they can't know for sure that it was you. For starters, your careers would be over. No security force in the world would touch you. So, you can't kill them all. The cops are infiltrated. The building is impregnable. What do you do?"

"Hang on whilst I pour a bloody rum." Drake made a show of heading for the mini bar. " 'Cause this round of question time is giving me a headache."

"Okay, okay. There's this. I think Yorgi, with his bespoke skills, could probably break in. Alone. But he could never get Mai out. And he couldn't locate her on his own so he'd be forced to take somebody with him. Which wouldn't work because the Yakuza are already watching all of you. That leaves us with many problems, the first of which is to actually locate Mai. I know only one way to achieve this."

"Spill." Dahl looked threatening.

"Send in a girl."

Everyone blinked. Drake and Dahl looked at Alicia as the Englishwoman looked straight at Yorgi.

"What?"

"Of course, every structure has a weakness, even a seemingly indestructible brick wall. The Yakuza are primarily young males. They admit girls to their compound, and their HQ, every day."

"But aren't they . . . Japanese girls?" Dahl asked.

Alicia glanced at Yorgi. "Damn, looks like you're off the hook."

Hibiki nodded. "Yes, primarily. Of course, this is a HQ and they admit prisoners too, most of whom leave in body bags without being seen." He blinked. "Somehow. Now, in Yakuza-run Kobe a foreign woman would stand out like a forest fire. Only a Japanese woman would be able to infiltrate unnoticed."

Drake saw now where this was all headed. "No way, pal. I mean, shit, how would you explain it to Mai? She'd fucking *kill* you."

"Like I said before—if you have any other suggestions . . .?"

"Impossible." Dahl turned away. "After all she has been through? I won't allow it."

Alicia stared at Hibiki with shocked eyes. "Are you mad?"

The cop took a step back. "Well, I expected an objection but not quite so much."

Drake waved a hand at Grace. "She's a seventeen-year-old kid and only here because we couldn't lock her up back in bloody DC. She stays in the room, Hibiki."

Grace looked slightly affronted. "Hey, I handled myself okay for . . . a lot of years. I think."

"Ah, now I see. No, I wasn't referring to Grace. The

Japanese woman I propose we send into the Yakuza stronghold is Chika, Mai's sister."

For a second Drake froze as he tried to compute. Though not as radical as sending in Grace, Hibiki's suggestion still drifted as close to the edge as anyone would surely like to sail.

"Mai's *sister?*" Alicia repeated. "Dude, you have a death wish." It was a statement of fact.

"If we can't get her out of there soon she's dead." Hibiki's voice was edged with deep stress. "And there's no other way to find out where they're keeping her in such a large building. The girls will at least have some free run."

Alicia eyed him closely. "You do know what you're asking of your girlfriend then?"

"Fuck." Hibiki walked to the nearest chair and threw himself in it. "Of course I know. It's . . . it's the only way. And even then it's practically suicide."

"You're a cop," Yorgi said. "Do you not know girl you can use?"

"Not a girl I would trust with Mai's life," Hibiki moaned. "The only person I'd truly trust to get in and save Mai is Mai herself."

"All right, well I have to ask," Dahl said. "What was Chika's reaction?"

Hibiki squirmed a little. "I haven't asked her yet."

Alicia groaned and turned to Yorgi. "And we're back to you and those delicate cheekbones. Think you could fit in a size ten?"

The Russian glared, but Hibiki spoke up strongly. "No. No, this will work. I'm sure of it. I have a way, I think, of getting us all in. We would assume all the risk, and the rescue. Chika would only mark her position."

"Wait, you said it was impregnable," Dahl pointed out.

"It is," Hibiki said. "Nobody has ever broken in, nobody has ever broken out. No team could enter that building without being seen. But there's another way. A cleverer way."

"What way?" Drake was intrigued, despite everything.

"Well, it was the American White House that gave me the idea . . ."

CHAPTER SEVENTEEN

Chika Kitano was a survivor, a fighter. Though young, she still remembered the day the bad men took her sister, the agony etched in her parents' faces and eyes, the way they aged ten years overnight. Though far wiser now, she still felt a touch of hatred for them. Growing up hadn't been easy for her—she had waged a constant war against hunger, poverty and perverted old men. She had resisted education until she finally realized it was her way out—not the only way but the best way.

Finally, settling into her life as well as a hand fits into a glove, reunited with her sister and not knowing nor caring where her parents were, the older Chika Kitano had landed a great job. Then Dmitry Kovalenko struck, the Blood King kidnapping her and forcing Mai to hand over some dusty old relic for her return, which even then was achieved only by Mai's abilities. Another month, another job, and her résumé was starting to look like a scribble pad. Though Kovalenko's men had treated her fine she still harbored the fears the episode had given rise to. But fear could be overcome and Chika had not forgotten her roots, nor the trials she overcame there.

Always, a fighter.

Then Dai Hibiki entered her life and, though some part of her craved the security such a man offered, she initially pushed him away, fearing she would lose her own fighter's instinct by depending on another. But, through tentative months, she came to understand that together the two of them strengthened each other. Their relationship shored up their inner drive and together made them incredibly durable.

Chika thought there might be nothing on earth that could defeat the two of them.

But when Dai Hibiki came through the door the look on his face instantly told her that there was.

Torn again, shredded, she listened to his story; to the consequences of Mai's old actions, her new activities in murdering Hayami, humiliating Hikaru, the Yakuza and even helping to prevent the Pythians from unleashing the Pandora plague. Though a fighter, Chika found herself almost defeated. *Mai? Oh, Mai . . .*

Unable to speak, battling her inner fears, doubts and old memories, she knew that there was only one way to get through this. To be as one. Both her and Hibiki. Together.

"SPEAR are in Kobe," Hibiki was saying. "But the Yakuza have taken Mai to their HQ, not the compound. And the HQ," he shook his head. "It's pretty much impregnable."

Chika felt a bolt of fire. "What are you saying?"

"That this is going to take all of us, working together, and that the risk . . . is high. Higher than high, it's off the scale."

"Of course it is." Chika said. "This is the Yakuza in their own city."

Hibiki spun on the spot and walked over to a window. Beyond the lawn and the road outside, the city of Tokyo sprawled, a forty minute plane ride from Kobe. Chika walked up to him and placed a hand on his shoulder.

"What is it? Is this story the only reason you pulled me out of work?"

Chika had recently landed a job with a video games designer, one of the biggest in the world. Working her way up to chief publicist would be tough, but it was her ultimate goal. Somehow, she loved the idea of being the spearhead for a new game, the public image, the influence and drip-feed behind a new release and the person who stoked and watched the hype intensify.

"No," Hibiki said softly. "You're going to have to take some time off."

Chika sat down as Dai explained his plan, that she gain access to the Yakuza headquarters alone by posing as a . . . *as a what?*

"Are you saying you want me to be a Geisha?"

Hibiki wouldn't look at her. "Something like that."

Chika tried to adjust. "Because . . . because it's the only way in?"

"No. Because it's Mai and she will be safely locked away somewhere. We can't make our move until we know where she's being held."

"But how would I . . . where would I . . . what—"

Hibiki still didn't turn around. "The girls stay for the night. There are so many of them, you should be able to wander a little. They change the girls every day. And you have an excuse if you are seen. We believe Mai's trial is tomorrow, so . . ."

Chika fended off a dagger of ice that threatened to split her heart. *"Tonight?* You're telling me I have to go in tonight?"

"Nobody wants this—"

"Oh. Do you think?" Chika shouted at her boyfriend and then felt instantly sickened. Not because of what she was being asked to do but because she hadn't agreed immediately. *This is Mai. My sister. She's already gone through Hell a dozen times for me.*

Hibiki's head fell. "I'm sorry I'm asking, Chika."

She turned his face around so that their eyes finally met. "Do you know what you're asking? I mean, forget about Mai for just one second, but . . . do you know?"

Hibiki tried to turn away but she held on. "Of course," he hissed. "Of course I fucking know what could happen in there."

"I have to ask, since you're a policeman, is it because you don't want the force involved that you haven't found someone else?"

"Not only that," Hibiki said. "Yes, the force all the way from Tokyo to Kobe and way beyond are probably compromised in some way, but even with the best intentions word of our operation could get back to the Yakuza bosses. And it's also because I don't trust them with Mai's life. I don't trust them to put everything on the line for her. I don't trust them to push and push and search every square meter." He licked his lips. "That's it."

Chika's own mouth was dry. She poured them both a glass of fresh mango. "SPEAR don't have a contact?"

"They have Lauren Fox, but she's too far away and an American. It's you or we go in blind, Chika, and we *are* going in. But you don't have to do this. Nobody is forcing you."

Chika set her glass down hard. "Mai is as much my responsibility as I am hers. And we're more important to each other than even you could imagine. You really think there's a choice? That I *want* a choice?"

"I—"

"Just get me on the damn plane. We'll talk tactics on the way."

Chika turned away before Hibiki saw the fear in her eyes, the twitch in her grim smile. She turned away before she started to cry. She turned away to let the fighter live once more.

CHAPTER EIGHTEEN

Before darkness fell over Kobe, Chika Kitano made herself ready to join a fresh group of girls being admitted to the Yakuza building. Exiting out of a line of limos they would look like party girls, intoxicated by the night, but nobody was really fooled. The cops turned a blind eye and the girls were gone come the dawn. The Yakuza's security remained intact because they used their own sources; nothing was left to chance.

Hibiki's face changed from passive to surprised, to scared and then terrified as Chika changed from city business woman to Geisha girl in a little over thirty minutes. Then, a little more conservatively, the six-inch heels were changed in favor of three, the hemline lengthened, the lipstick applied a bit less gaudily.

Alicia gave the finished girl a critical once over. "Y'know, I've done this a million times. The question is—do you want your suitor to be the weasely little ferret-boy with the nasty glint in his eye or someone with a bit more sophistication? Deck's loaded either way."

Dahl reached for an apple. "A *million* times? Whoa."

"Not the sex act," Alicia quickly amended. "I meant getting through security and into the building."

"Of course." The Swede kept a straight face. "Sex act, maybe only half a million, right?"

"Fuck you. Hey, I just heard a click. Was that your wife snapping her fingers? Better get running, Torsty."

Chika felt a freezing sensation in the pit of her stomach that deepened with every passing second. "If we could focus on the building and the blueprints again maybe that would help take my mind off things."

Alicia smoothed out the plans across a table. "Entrance. Elevator shafts. Recreational area." She tapped the drawings as she worked. "Twelve potential upper levels. The building does have lower levels but they're not detailed. My guess is, because that's where they take the girls and other, um, guests."

Drake stepped into view at that moment. "And Mai, we hope. It's unlikely that they'll be holding her inside the business levels of the building."

"Can you be sure?"

Drake shrugged. "Not really, love. She could be anywhere."

"And you'll be coming?"

"Right when you tell us to."

"You're sure you can get inside?" Chika tried to shut down her fears but hearing Drake reassure her was already helping.

"Yorgi can, Spidey style. And Hibiki's plan for our entry is sound."

Chika smoothed out her skirt and stood in front of a floor-length mirror. "Oh wow, I look so . . . different."

Alicia held out a little blue pill. "If you get chance, slip this into the bastard's sake. It'll dissolve fast and put him out like a light. For the entire night."

Chika reached for it with relief. "Thank you. I think I can make that work."

The Lost Kingdom

Hibiki stared at Alicia. "Have you done *that* before too?"

"Why Dai, don't you remember?"

The cop managed a smile. "Not the time, Alicia. So not the time."

"Hey, nobody ever said I was the insightful type."

Drake handed her a small handbag. "No tracker. No weapon. They'll search you pretty thoroughly. Just remember who you're doing this for and it'll be a doddle."

"I'm not likely to forget," Chika said a little haughtily. "Is it time?"

Hibiki nodded. "I have an arrangement with one of the traffickers who supplies the Yakuza. We busted them a few months ago. I can get you in through him."

"Arrangement?"

"He gets twenty four hours head start. That's all."

"Dai," Chika breathed. "That's jail time if you're caught."

"Well, even if we get Mai out of there she isn't exactly out of the woods. We're all putting it on the line here, Chika. Everyone in this room."

Chika made a huge effort to hold back the tears, knowing it would ruin her garish makeup. "Thank you."

Drake touched her arm. "Be safe."

Hibiki turned toward the door. "Let's go."

On joining the group of girls bound for the Yakuza stronghold, Chika sensed immediately that her job was going to be much harder than even Dai had imagined. The problem was the girls themselves, of course. Chika should have guessed. It wasn't that they were abusive or violent in any way; it was the suspicion. These girls ran in relatively small circles—somewhere along the line one always recognized another—but when nobody in the large group of thirty women acknowledged Chika some of the more attentive ones noticed.

Whisperings began.

And she didn't move like they moved, didn't speak like they spoke. Conspicuous to say the least, she kept herself in a corner as men directed them to their limos. She spoke to no one. All she had to do was gain access, pair off, and drug her suitor. Her mind ran over the blueprints Alicia had made her memorize. That was all good, except they didn't map out any lower levels. Time was short. Life might be even shorter. Chika kept her mind on the blueprints and Mai, and kept her silence.

The limos drove smoothly through the heart of Kobe, threading traffic and sticking to the main roads. Four in all, they kept together, obeying stop lights and staying courteous to other drivers. Inside, the girls helped themselves to drinks from the onboard bars—mini and chilled, jiving to the loud music and swapping stories. Chika followed their lead, taking a tumbler and pouring two measures of whisky. The warm liquid helped shore up her dwindling self-confidence.

Fight.

She checked the time—9 p.m. According to the chatter the girls were provided after the 'businessmen' had concluded their daily affairs—mostly local guys but also some visiting dealmakers and gang members. The visitors would have their pick and then the locals would choose from the rest. Chika gathered that this was almost regarded as a 'night off' for the working girls; it was certainly better than roaming the streets and sleeping in what amounted to nothing more than a filthy hostel.

A woman leaned forward from her place opposite Chika, her PVC skirt squeaking across the limo's leather padding. "Wrong with you, baby? Looks like this your first time." She squealed with laughter, almost spilling her drink.

Chika lifted her tumbler to her lips, gaining an extra moment to think. "First time back," she said. "Been a few weeks."

"Beat up?" the woman speculated. "Someone gave you *otoko no ko?*" She reached out to pat Chika's belly. Chika flinched. The woman's eyes narrowed until they were slits.

"You not like being touched, eh? Maybe you in wrong car? Wrong place?"

Laughter filled the confines of the vehicle. Chika turned away from it, watching the passing lights and darkened structures. People on the sidewalk stared at them, some enviously, not knowing that *they* were the lucky ones.

The woman touched Chika's knee, tapping hard. "I am called Asa. I watch you. I watch you close."

Chika embraced an urge to do battle. "So watch, bitch. Maybe you'll learn something."

Asa backed off, but turned to the other girls. "Something wrong there, mark me. She ain't one of us. You know it. I say we turn her in to the boss."

Chika thought about striking out. Isn't that what a street girl would do? Defend her honor or something? Care a bit less?

Be stronger.

"Leave her the fuck alone, Asa." A voice spoke up from the far side of the four-person seat. "She got her own business, that fine. Nothing to do with a troublemaker like you. Keep it to yourself, bitch."

Chika turned a grateful look upon her savior but received only a cold glare in return. They wanted none of her, and Chika didn't blame them. The limos pulled up outside a modern high-rise with walls as flush and white as paper, its windows gleaming. Men came forward from a covered entrance to open their doors.

"Move," they said gruffly. "Out. Now."

Chika exited and drifted apart from Asa and the others, thinking it best to enter with a different group. With only minutes to practice she watched them walk, listened to them talk, and prepared as best she could. Mai's life depended on her acquiring a certain competence. Gaining entry would surely be the hardest part of her night.

The doors were held open as the girls walked into a small lobby, divided and bordered by smoked glass screens. Chika kept her gaze straight, her head slightly lowered. She fell in behind a girl who looked just like her. Should it worry her that her boyfriend and Alicia Myles had, at least outwardly, turned her into a street girl in less than forty minutes? They shuffled toward an elevator bank, each girl having to pass through a metal detector and then enter separate rooms. Armed guards surveyed them without emotion. Chika held strong to her mission, clenching her fists. Around her the girls chatted. Through the lobby-height windows the streets outside appeared normal. Chika wondered if Dai and the

SPEAR team were out there, planning their entry.

The line moved forward, and she passed through the metal detector. Her visit to the closed-off room would be next.

Drake readied himself. If Chika was going to come through it would be within the next few hours and the team wanted to be ultra-prepared. Hibiki's plan to get them inside the Yakuza HQ was good, but relied on several unknown factors.

The first of which was Karin Blake's skill.

Back in DC, the young genius was tapping away at a computer, analyzing records and infiltrating security systems. Her own omnisciently designed shadow program was sniffing its way around the digital highway of Kobe, searching every rooftop, underground garage and blind corner. Drake left her to it, gearing up with Dahl, Alicia and Hibiki. Grace watched it all in silence, ignoring even her cellphone and favorite social media sites. Yorgi knelt in a corner, casting a careful eye over the equipment he had brought with him from the States.

Drake drifted over, pistol in hand. "Ey up, pal. What ya got there?"

Yorgi sat back on his haunches. "PDMS sheets. Pretty new invention, not at all associated with buildering and forced entry but still quite useful and effective." He showed Drake a palm size sheet of plastic. "Sheet is covered in fibers just like hairs on a Gecko's feet. The hairs produce what is called . . . intermolecular van der Waals forces, which let them stick to surfaces. Walls. I can attach them to my pads," he pointed out the handheld device, "And climb any wall, vertically."

Drake touched one of the sheets. "Had any problems with letting go?"

Yorgi grinned. "Not yet, my friend. This is first time I'm using them."

Alicia, overhearing, also drifted over. "Yogi, I never even thanked you for helping us out in Paris last week. You pull this off I might even let you . . ." she nodded suggestively.

Yorgi smiled. "And follow in Beauregard's footsteps? Not likely."

"Not adequate enough for me?"

"Not *crazy* enough for you."

Drake fought a strange urge to question Alicia as to the Frenchman's intentions by shouting out to Dahl. "Any news?"

The Swede was chatting to Hibiki. "I'd say so. For you at least."

"Eh? Whaddya mean?"

Hibiki waved a hand. "After dropping off Chika I spent a little time discreetly quizzing the local police. They know you are here, Matt, with a team. And they are watching for you."

"Bollocks."

"Only your face was recognized by the spotters. Perhaps they lost you or had very little time. But we can't risk you coming along on this mission. We can't risk Mai's safety, and we need somebody to safeguard Grace and man the comms." He gestured at Drake.

"Well bollocks again. No way am I sitting on my arse whilst Mai's in trouble. Besides, you need me."

Dahl loaded his weapon as he spoke. "We need Alicia. We need Hibiki. They need a strong, skilful, capable bodyguard. So, see, we don't need you at all, Yorkie."

"Seriously," Hibiki broke in before Drake could react. "They will spot you the moment you exit this hotel. Then they will follow us. You're out of it, Matt. Sidelined."

Drake took a breath but couldn't think of anything to say. The wind had been well and truly taken out of his sails. *This is Mai,* he thought. *Surely there's a way.* The problem was, Hibiki's rationale made total sense.

Karin's voice spilled from the laptop's speakers. "Guys. Guys? I think I've found it. Hope you're ready."

"To take on a few thousand Yakuza in their own headquarters in their own city on their own terms?" Dahl's grin would have illuminated a sea cave. "Looking forward to it."

CHAPTER NINETEEN

Chika exited the secure room feeling relieved. Not knowing what to expect she had imagined all sorts of horrors, but the uninterested man inside had asked questions about her boss—questions that Hibiki had prepped her for—given her a cursory frisking and then emptied out her small handbag. It contained only lipstick, a compact mirror makeup case, condoms and a cellphone, all of which were expected.

"Follow house rules at all times," the man said as if reciting a script.

"Yes, sir."

The elevator arrived and Chika got her first clue as to where she might be taken. A man holding a compact machine-pistol urged her group inside and pressed the button for basement level two. She noticed there were three lower levels in total. All around her the girls chatted and the men ignored them. The elevator dinged and the doors whooshed open. Chika found herself facing a narrow corridor with doors to each side and an outsize open-plan room at the far end. She noticed a stairwell access door to her left. It was into the far room that they were herded. Throw cushions, leather suites, loungers and pouffes sat everywhere. To one side stood a number of curtained-off booths; to another a full-size bar with waitress service. More ominously a raised, black-lacquered stage formed the room's showpiece, complete with dancing pole. A clock on the wall read 9:35.

"Make yourselves at home, ladies," a voice rang out. "Our guests shall be along shortly."

Chika headed for the bar. As she ordered a drink several tattooed men appeared dragging a youth between them. The youth, though dressed well, sported several cuts and bruises to his face and the way he favored his right side made Chika guess at a number of broken ribs. The youth was dragged unceremoniously through the large room, his captors not acknowledging the presence of all the girls.

"Take him to lock up," one of the men said, and then he too headed for the bar. As he ordered, Chika saw that his knuckles were bloody. She looked away.

"Young men," he breathed knowingly. "All the same. All think they know what is best. If he lives he will learn."

Chika sipped her whisky, and kept an eye on the youth's progress. The elevator doors closed after the press of a button and a green indicator light told her that the elevator was heading down.

So the lock up was on level three. A positive starting point at least.

She wondered if the girls were allowed to initiate conversation. Several questions sprang to mind that would help pinpoint Mai. Then she caught Asa staring straight at her.

She walked over. "I still watching you," she said, waving at a barman. "I see where you are looking."

"Leave me alone," Chika hissed. "I'm only here for the guests."

"Now ladies," the man with bloody knuckles said, smiling. "Be nice. You are all here to help us unwind, yes?"

He studied Chika. "The classy," his gaze whipped to Asa, "and the crude. Make your guests happy, yes?"

He pointed at the door. Several men filed through; business types, all bearing the hassles of the day on their faces. The bar came to life and the music started. Chika flowed to the center of the room, ignoring Asa's murderous gaze. Dread for Mai kept her inner strength at an elevated level, her outward demeanor intact. This was not her; the person she played was not even in her arsenal.

Fight on. Remember how you felt when Mai returned. When your parents returned safe. When Mai saved you . . .

"Hai," A man bowed very slightly before her. "You are mine for tonight. I will take that," he relieved her of her glass. "And you will fetch me another. Quickly now."

Chika hid her distaste well, rose and walked toward the bar. It struck her then that, even after the nail-biting ordeal she had already been through, this night was only just beginning.

Drake listened attentively as Karin helped turn Dai Hibiki's outrageous plan into something that might achieve fruition. Though gutted at the outcome of events, his behind-the-scenes role in running the op was imperative and he needed Karin's knowledge. Grace, on the other hand, had now started to officially ignore him, given that he'd seemed so traumatized at having to stay and guard her.

Too busy to worry, he concentrated on Karin's words.

"I have to admit, when Hibiki first stated he got this plan from something he heard about the White House I was more than a little sceptic. This *is* the Yakuza we're talking about, a Japanese mob network, not the Secret Service. But it may have paid off. When Hibiki told me about all the prisoners that the Yakuza interrogate inside their HQ, all the bodies they create, all the hospital visits that must ensue, all the high-level deals that simply can't involve someone just walking through the front doors of either the HQ or even the compound, then it makes absolute sense that they have built a small tunnel network underneath Kobe."

Hibiki coughed. "Not quite a network, but—"

"We don't know that," Karin admitted. "But we do know this. I spent an hour trawling through deeds of ownerships. Most were easy, some a little vague, but only one led me through several dummy corporations from places as far apart as Zurich and Australia, Nigeria and New York. Only one presented half a dozen dead ends, fake corporations and even faked personnel, including directors. Finally, I tracked the company's ownership to a Yakuza-run gambling conglomerate with outlets all over Japan. It owns the three-story building across the road and to the side of theirs. It's actually the closest of the lot."

"So they use that building to admit their various *guests*. People, for one reason or another they don't want seen even in Kobe, and take them through a man-made tunnel into the true headquarters." Dahl cleared his throat. "A clever set up."

"They have been involved in this business for so long," Hibiki said. "It would surprise me if they didn't have every detail perfected by now."

"Let's hope they don't," Dahl said. "For all our sakes."

Alicia addressed Karin. "Any communications into the place?"

"You mean anything special? Not that I can find."

"Can you tap their network?" Hibiki asked.

"I can do anything. Why?"

"We'll stand a better chance of access if they know we're coming," he said, then laughed. "Amazingly. Alicia, I realize this is a stupid question, but would you like to be tied up?"

The Englishwoman licked her lips. "Depends. By who?"

Hibiki rose and pointed to himself. "By Yakuza!" And nodded at Dahl. "And by foreign devil enforcer looking for reward. "Don't worry, we won't hurt you."

Alicia raised an eyebrow. "Then you're no fun at all. Ya gotta take it to the limit, Dai-Dai, or you'll never know just how much you can take. Or what you might like. Ya get me?"

Drake made a pretense at laughter but his eyes spoke otherwise. Alicia read them in an instant, reminding him how well they knew each other.

"Moving forward," she reiterated. "Never stopping, never looking back. That's me, right? The Girl Dynamic." Somehow Drake knew she meant it as a title. "Look back, pause for a second, and I'm dead, right?"

"It doesn't have to be that way and you know it."

"Ah, and when I crash and burn who's gonna be there to catch me? Who's gonna manage the fallout? You?"

"If you want me to."

Alicia stared as if she didn't believe him. It was Dahl who interrupted their moment.

"C'mon, Girl Dynamic. We have a lot to do."

*

Chika swapped whisky for water as the night grew deeper. The lights were dimmed, the music amplified, the women grew louder and the men became drunker. Chika tolerated her beau's hand on her thigh and getting up every fifteen minutes to refresh his drink. The fetching and carrying became a welcome relief as did his frequent trips to the restroom, though she suspected he was doing more than what came natural in there judging by the powder that began to collect around his nostrils. At this rate she wouldn't even need to use Alicia's blue pill.

Still, the night dragged on, the hands of the clock turning far slower than they should. Well aware that there was nothing she could do until the party died down, Chika sought to hasten its windup by drawing her admirer's attention to the rooms nearby, now with doors standing open. Those around her caught on and some of the men decided to make their parties more private.

"Little minx." Her friend sought to whisper, but actually shouted in her ear. "Want to get me alone do you?"

Chika thought there was nothing she'd like better than to get him alone, and winked. "Ready when you are."

"One more drink," he said. "And . . . and a quick trip." He headed off, shambling toward the restrooms under the guards' watchful eyes. Chika readied herself. When he came back she plied him with another quick drink and then half dragged him away from the party. Thinking ahead, she chose one of the open rooms nearest the elevators and stumbled inside, turning to lock the door behind them.

Oh, oh, first problem. There's no lock.

That meant anyone could check on them at any time

during the night. But it was also a factor she couldn't control, so she ignored it. The second thing she did was to scan the room for any obvious cameras, and found nothing. The third was to grab her man in a bear hug and swing him over toward the dresser.

"Are we dancing now?" he grunted. "You didn't want to dance back there? On the stage?"

"Now, I'm in the mood," she whispered, swinging him around.

"Oh."

Together they hit the dresser, knocking over both the lamp and empty vase that sat there, breaking both. Now, at least if there were any cameras inside, they had innocently moved position. The only other place a camera might be secreted was inside one of the recessed ceiling down lighters, but again she could not affect that so ignored it.

Now, for the poseur.

He was standing on the bed, stomach sucked in, in the throes of taking off his shirt. Chika made a pretense of admiring his pecs and then turned to the in-room bar. "Drink?"

"Later. C'mere."

Chika eyed him in the mirror. He was standing with his thumbs hooked into his pants, grinning like an evil clown on Halloween night. Carefully, she ignored his request and bent over to grab a bottle of water and a miniature whisky. As predicted, the man just watched. Chika poured his drink, added a splash of water just how he liked it and then moved to block the tumbler.

Now all she had to do was add the pill.

Damn.

Problem was, the tiny blue capsule was tucked into the waistband of her underwear. There were no toilets in this room, so no way of slipping inside. Chika took a deep breath and turned around; the smile plastered across her face slipping even as she met the man's eyes. Luckily, he was both drunk and slightly stoned and finding it hard to focus. As he slipped his trousers down, Chika slid her own hands down the front of her skirt.

Where the hell . . . ?

Feeling more than a little foolish she withdrew her hands, still smiling like a crazy woman, and trying to keep the pill hidden between her fingers. The man jumped down from the bed, trying to affect a dance routine but failing badly. He stumbled, caught himself by grabbing her belt, and then rose quickly, suddenly inches from her.

"Let's have a kiss, lovely."

Chika froze, her entire body stiffening. If she wanted anything she wanted to smash him on the tip of the nose. "No kissing," she said. "We're here to fuck not to fall in love."

His eyes went wide, his face slackened. Chika turned away, using the distraction to slip the pill into the waiting whisky. *Now, just one minute. One more minute and . . .*

The door opened. A guard popped his head around.

"All well in here?"

Chika nodded quickly; her friend barely noticed the intrusion. So maybe there had been a camera on the dresser. The guards knew it had fallen over and were checking. Chika slipped her arms around the man and winked at the guard.

"We're fine."

He withdrew with a shake of the head. Chika reached behind, bringing the drink around and pressing it to his lips.

"Kiss that whilst I undress, lover boy." As she twisted away, regaining a little space, she realized she had no idea how long the drug would take to work. And when it did, lover boy really should be on top of the bed. She would find it exceedingly difficult to drag his dead weight up there. Quickly, she climbed onto the bed and watched him drink up.

"Come here."

Apprehension raced through her system. *What am I going to do if this doesn't work pretty damn quick?* The man climbed up beside her, eyes rolling, but was it the drink or the drugs? Was it the pill? She tried not to flinch as his hand fell on her exposed leg. She covered it with her own, pressing hard. His other hand came around and gripped her shoulder, pulling her in.

"One kiss," he slurred. "Just one . . . little . . . kiss."

His head went down, body slumping across her knees. Chika felt a world of relief open up inside of her. *Oh thank you, thank you!* With some effort she managed to drag his comatose body up the bed so that his head rested on a pillow and then covered him over. Then she rearranged two spare pillows as best she could, making the lump under the covers appear to be two shapes rather than one.

Next, her handbag. The cellphone. She dialed a number, whispering, "Hello? It's me."

Dai Hibiki sounded relieved. "Hey, it's good to hear from you. How . . . how did it go?"

Chika felt a little devilment rise. "Do you want the details?"

"*No!*"

Alicia, hooked into the same line, grunted, "I do."

Chika let her boyfriend off the hook. "Pill worked before anything went down." She shuddered. "Not that I could have gone through with it." She tried to ignore the impossible choice that might have arisen, the one that included saving her sister's life.

"They're heading for the other building." Drake's voice was low and tinny, fed through two sets of comms and finally through Hibiki's cell. "Where are you?"

"About to start my check," she said. "Providing the party's ended. I'll be in touch."

Without further comment she finished the call, slipped the phone back into her bag and checked the door. Happily, the handle turned freely. Butterflies flickered through her stomach, though if they saw her she still had a way out even now. She cracked the door an inch, saw only empty corridor. Another inch.

Rooms across the hall were closed, every one. Before, they had all been standing open. That was good. She pulled the door further and poked her head around the frame. The corridor all the way to the party area was clear, though figures moved slowly through the room, most likely cleaners. Chika waited two more minutes. Nothing stirred.

With the restroom next door, Chika played her last card and headed for the door. Beyond it, as she knew, stood the door to the staircase and the elevators. Still, she was alone. If there were cameras at this point she was lost, but none were in evidence. Maybe they limited their surveillance to the main areas. In her head, reasoning to keep herself brave and sane, it made sense.

Chika passed beyond the restrooms and entered the stairwell. Silent and chilled at this time of night it was an alien environment, fraught with danger. Uncarpeted, the risers echoed at her first footstep. The far wall was a vertical line of one-way glass, affording her a view into the outside world, more a hateful taunt now than a comfort. She steeled herself and padded down the first switchback, pausing on the landing to listen.

No sound. The Yakuza building could be a morgue.

Slightly lifted, she pressed on, descending the second switchback and arriving at the lowest level. The door that faced her was as bland as they come; nothing screamed *Yakuza Prison and Torture Level!* but at the inner sanctum of their highly guarded stronghold would they really need bells and whistles? The only people foolish enough to be down here were the careless and the already dead.

Mai had been careless, she thought. Yes, even her seemingly indestructible sister had failings. What did that say for Chika?

Ignoring the self-deprecation she opened the door, expecting alarms but hearing nothing. Moving on she listened hard. The space beyond the door was the mirror image of the one above, except that the row of doors that lined the corridor all looked reinforced and possessed a Judas window at about head height. This was where Chika scored a small victory. The Judas window might give the guards the facility to check on their captives at any time but it also gave her the chance to effectively search for Mai.

She moved into the center of the corridor, ignoring any fears now as she came closer to her goal. There was no turning back, no easy way out. Even the mighty SPEAR team were depending on her. The first tiny window looked onto an empty cell as did its twin across the hall. The third showed her a small, thin man curled up on a bare bunk, knees tucked up to his chest. She recognized him as the youth from earlier, but closed the window quickly when she saw him start to stir. At this point she paused, thinking it prudent to check the shadows at the far end of the corridor. On her level this was a recreational area; down here she didn't like to speculate, but the inky darkness at least told her that it wasn't in use.

The next two windows looked onto barely clothed men in varying forms of health, neither of them good. But it was the sixth window that made her catch her breath and stare with widening eyes.

Oh help us . . .

Mai was chained inside, kneeling on the floor and facing the window, arms outstretched to the wall and loops at her back. Her black hair fell over her skull, hanging down so that it almost scraped the floor below. The muscles in her arms were taut, strained. Her knees were red raw. For a dreadful moment Chika saw no movement at all, but then made out a slight rise and fall near her spine.

Mai was down but she was not out.

Chika bit her lips hard, drawing blood. Every sinew, every instinct in her body wanted to cry out, wanted to at least make some kind of contact. But the mission was clear—no time to waste. Dai and Drake and the rest needed Mai's exact position as soon as possible. They could already be on site.

Chika withdrew fast, fumbled about in her bag and made the call.

Drake answered. "I'm running ops. Did you find Mai?"

Chika gave him the location.

"Bloody good work. Mai would be proud."

Chika fought the tears back and the urge to tell Drake how Mai looked, that he had to hurry. They knew the situation and it would only slow things down. Her job done, her situation still precarious, she backed away and made for the stairwell.

Now, it was out of her hands.

Back up the stairwell and across to her room she trod lightly and carefully, feeling a deep sense of relief and now hoping that Lover Boy remained in his comatose state. Hopefully the girls would be made to leave before their suitors awoke. A reasonable assumption given some of their identities.

Inside the room all was quiet. Chika let out a sigh of absolute relief. Maybe she could now begin to breathe properly again.

Until Asa's nasty little voice made her heart leap. "Knew you were trouble, bitch. Where you been?"

The guard she had summoned stepped out from behind the door. "See this big fucking gun?" he said, waving it from left to right. "Answer her. Or it will make a real mess of that pretty little body."

CHAPTER TWENTY

Alicia struggled in the grip of her two captors. They had made the bonds on her wrists tight, but not enough to stop her blood flow. They held her upper arms firmly, bruisingly hard, but she knew she could take it. Dahl fought to make her move forward from the right, Hibiki from the left. When she didn't move fast enough the Swede threw her up against a brick wall, pressing in close.

"Quit it. I don't want to hurt you."

Alicia, her face squashed by the brick, mumbled. "Oh, Torsty, what's the first thing you think about when you have a girl up against a wall?"

"Stop with that swaying. We're here."

As Dahl pulled her away from the wall they saw the small squat building ahead, barely lit, its lobby shrouded in shadow and its upper floors completely black. No guards were in evidence, no human presence of any sort.

Dahl propelled Alicia toward it. "I hope you know what you're doing, Hibiki."

"My girlfriend and my friend are inside. So do I."

Though Karin had identified the Yakuza-owned building wherein Hibiki speculated the Yakuza preferred to admit their more 'precious guests', she had not been able to identify any entry protocols. That problem was left for Hibiki to deal with. Using the only cops he could trust in Kobe and one of their informants, he had been able to put together a good idea of the etiquette and procedure.

But first he'd had to use the hours since Chika left to pass for a member of the Yakuza.

Tattoos had been painted around his neck and on the backs of his hands. Behind his ears. Anywhere that the skin was exposed. The ink would resist water but wouldn't exactly stand up to a good scrub. Despite his reservations, Hibiki was happy with the quality of the tats in the time they'd had available.

Alicia had taken a picture on her cellphone. "For later," she said. "For blackmail."

Now, they approached the barely illuminated frontage, a set of glass doors. Hibiki put his hand on the vertical, brushed metal handle and paused, looked up to the top right where a tiny, inconspicuous camera watched.

He stared, dragging Alicia into view, and waited. After a long time the door clicked and Hibiki pulled it open.

"Keep your mouths shut," he whispered. "I'll do all the talking."

Alicia wriggled in their grip. "Now you know *that's* gonna be a problem. Never been one to—"

Dahl pushed her so that she stumbled inside. Hibiki pulled. All three of them surveyed the quiet lobby as they walked across a polished floor toward an unmanned desk. If anyone was present they were certainly doing a good job of concealing themselves. Hibiki stopped at the desk, staring above it at a blank TV screen.

Alicia knew what he was doing and took another moment to study the place. The area was about as mundane as an accountant's weekly schedule. The likelihood was that many of the people who worked here didn't realize what went on in the lower levels. Maybe during the day they even used a different entrance; this place did have a lower parking garage after all. Hanging her head, she switched her attention back to the front, now beginning to feel bored and about to say so.

The TV screen flickered to life, a hard Asian face staring out at them without an ounce of emotion. "What is it?" he asked in Japanese.

"Prisoner." Hibiki clearly knew better than to elaborate by referencing the HQ. Such things were obvious.

"Where you from?"

"Tokyo."

The barest flicker of uncertainty. "Your boss?"

"Rei," he said, using information provided by his informant. Still, his heartbeat all but doubled.

Alicia listened, understanding nothing but knowing Hibiki was swinging it rather close to the edge. She struggled. Dahl, possessing the same instincts, clubbed her over the head.

"Be still now. There's a good girl."

The activity distracted the impassive face. "And the Englishman?"

Hibiki shrugged. "He's . . . he used to work with her. It's complicated."

"Go down. We'll see you."

Another click and a door to their left swung wide open, a door they hadn't even noticed was there. Set into the wall at the back of an alcove it was seamless and handle-less. Hibiki knew that the Yakuza weren't at risk even now; this was but one layer of security—the real test would be conducted in private where imposters could more easily be made to disappear.

Alicia allowed herself to be dragged through the door, down a set of stairs, past more CCTV cameras than she could count and onto a brand new level. Here, directly before them was another unmanned desk and a bank of elevators. The right side was already standing open. Hibiki ignored it and the desk and pressed the button on the left, another protocol successfully passed and now the guards must have gained at least an element of trust. They traveled down for thirty seconds and then the doors opened. Hibiki pushed her out first into a white glare.

"Stop."

Down here it was different, more akin to the environment she preferred. The bright lights came from directly ahead and the shadows of men holding guns stood right before her. One of them stepped forward and lifted her chin.

"Who is she?"

"An informant's girlfriend." Hibiki chuckled.

"Your plan is to use her to turn him back to us?"

"That is for the boss to decide." Hibiki shrugged. "I'm just a soldier. The informant has betrayed his family, our trust." He gripped Alicia's throat and then sighed, letting go. "Either way, she must not be harmed until he determines."

"Bad timing," a man said. "The trial means you won't be able to leave soon."

The Yakuza guard lifted his rifle and waved them past. Alicia blinked the glare from her eyes as the bright light dimmed. The area around her was basic, all plastic desks and hanging bulbs. Open packets of food lay on the tables, some upturned, and a deck of playing cards. Coins stood in piles everywhere. Men sat around, hard-faced and smoking or toying with their handguns. A hundred comments came to mind but she bit her tongue, struggling to keep them down.

Damn, now there's a first. Maybe it is *time to start making that change.*

But not today. Never today. Her vision finally fully returned, she spied a heavy door behind the men and a keypad set against the wall. They were close. But still the Yakuza weren't pacified.

"And the big one? He is your responsibility."

Hibiki nodded. Alicia saw these men weren't guards in the truest sense of the words—they were minders at best. Of course nobody would actively seek to gain entrance to a Yakuza stronghold; nobody in their right minds, and probably never had. If a person did, and even passed this level of security they only gained entry to a building full of even more of the same. She put her head down, hiding her face, because she just couldn't figure out how to imitate that broken, terrified look of the frightened captive. Better to stare at the floor.

Together, they approached the heavy door. One of the guards entered a six-digit code and pushed it open. Beyond Alicia saw a roughly hewn tunnel, shored up by heavy spars set into the walls and illuminated by a row of strip lights. It was rudimentary, but effective and perfect for the Yakuza's needs. No more words were passed as the door closed behind them. Hibiki started forward, saying nothing. Dahl coughed and Alicia looked up at him.

"Keep your mouth shut," he said, his meaning twofold, both as a token threat for unseen eyes and as a warning to her—their enemies could yet be playing them, allowing them to venture further into their territory.

The tunnel ran straight, cold and damp in parts, but sturdy enough. Nothing trickled or drifted down from above. Cameras were attached to every second spar. Alicia imagined the busy road above; the cars that passed over every day having no idea as to the activity going in beneath. How many other cities in the world had this kind of set up? London? Washington? New York? *Those,* she thought, *and hundreds more.*

It didn't take long to traverse the tunnel. The far side was composed of a glass cubicle, which the three of them entered and waited inside. Completely enclosed they assumed that again they were being vetted. Hibiki stood patiently until a door opened automatically and allowed them access to another room; the mirror of the one on the opposite side. Yakuza guards stared at them as they passed through and entered another elevator.

Hibiki caught both their eyes. His meaning was clear.

We've done it.

Alicia allowed herself an inner smile. Dahl's grip on her arm relaxed. The elevator doors whooshed open.

And a scene of dangerous bedlam met their eyes.

Guards were rushing around, guns up. Outside the elevator a man stopped as he ran past, took a look at Hibiki and his captive.

"Better keep a low profile for a few hours," he said. "Check in over there and wait." He pointed to yet another unmanned desk. "The guy should be back soon."

Hibiki's face was surprised, and the expression was not faked. "Considering where I am," he said, "I'm wondering what the hell is going on?"

Shouts were flung through the air all around them. Men who looked like boys helped double the guard near the front entrance to the building. Suited individuals with a sense of authority shouted order, themselves looking flustered.

Hibiki coughed. "Please. What is happening here?"

"We've been infiltrated." The man shook his head in disbelief. "A woman. She came in here with the girls. The entire building is in lockdown, all the guards up and armed. Damn, if this hasn't happened before."

Alicia watched as Hibiki struggled to contain himself. "What girl? Why?"

"They think it is the sister of one of our *special guests*. You know, the one scheduled for trial tomorrow? Well, they think it's her and that she has help. But don't worry, they caught her."

"They caught her?" Hibiki's words all but trembled.

"Of course. And now they have both of them." The man laughed. "Should be a real showcase tomorrow."

Alicia closed her eyes, feeling actual gloom for the first time since they locked handcuffs on her, and then reopened them to take in the chaotic scene. Hundreds if not thousands of guards—all getting organized and ready for battle. Dozens of bosses. More weapons than she could count. Untold security precautions.

And now they were smack bang in the very middle of it.

"Fuck," she said aloud.

The Japanese man stared at her. "I don't know what you're worried about. Nobody's going to be interested in you for at least two days."

Hibiki grunted. "I only came to drop the bitch off."

"Then you're out of luck. Nobody's getting in or out of here, my friend. Nobody. Not even Special Forces could get through those doors now."

Alicia unobtrusively caught Dahl's eye, both of them having the exact same thought.

No. But I bet Matt Drake could.

When he took Chika's call Drake felt elation. Against the odds but with stealth and the unexpected on her side, Mai's sister had completed her task. Hibiki's operation had also passed with relatively little hiccup—that was until the trio gained access to the Yakuza HQ. It was then that Drake, listening through the comms, learned Chika's fate and saw the new dilemma.

Shit, we have a team inside that can't operate. One sister about to go on a showcase trial and the other about to join her. How did all that happen?

He sat back in the chair, pushing it away from the table and rubbing his eyes. They were on a knife edge. Could he bridge the blade one way or another? His watch read: 3.13 a.m. So there was time. Time to come up with a new plan. But it would have to be concise—Hibiki needed to be a part of it and Drake's involvement thus far had been passive— they had not communicated for fear of alerting Yakuza security measures. Deciding on a plan and relating it had to be a one-time deal.

The only other person in the room brought him a mug of black coffee. "Thanks, love," he said a little gruffly. "This isn't turning out quite bloody right."

Grace plonked herself down next to him. "You will do it," she said. "And if I can help . . ."

"We're in a world of shit."

"Hey, stop sugar coating everything will ya?"

Drake turned to her. This was a seventeen-year-old runaway with no good experience to draw upon, her old past a jumble of newly emerging hateful memories. Raised later by the Tsugarai and in particular her brutal master—Gozu— the same man who had trained Mai, her life until this moment had been a tapestry of evil. As she told it she was now determined to let the past go, to embrace her future potential. To rise from the depths of Purgatory.

"It's not all like this," he said lightly. "Sometimes we even have a laugh."

"Next time maybe."

Drake focused his attention fully on her. *Next time?* "We're *soldiers,* Grace. Trained ones. You shouldn't even be here. If Mai knew she'd blow her top."

Grace blinked. "Eh?"

"Y'know. Like a volcano. Nobody ever said you would be part of the team, Grace."

The young girl clenched her jaw, eyes filling so that Drake suddenly felt like a major bastard. He reached out but she flinched away.

"Don't touch me."

"I'm sorry. I didn't mean anything. I know . . . I know . . ." He was about to say *I know what you're going through.* But how could he? He was being insensitive, bloody condescending to be honest. But it was the damn job, the situation, cluttering his thoughts.

"They're still searching for your parents," he said. "You're still young enough to have anything you want. Any job. We're all here to help. You have a new start at life."

"Could I be like Karin?" Grace suddenly asked, eyes now filled with excitement. "A geek? I'd like to be a geek. I'd wear glasses and everything."

"You don't need to try so hard to fit in." Drake smiled. "You're already one of us."

Her smile now included him. "Family?"

"Family."

Drake fought an instinct to hug her, turning instead to the window before she could see the surge of empathy in his eyes. "And you can start by helping me plan how to save 'em. How to save 'em all."

"There is one thing," Grace pointed out. "What has happened to Yorgi?"

CHAPTER TWENTY ONE

Mai came fully awake as the guards invaded her cell. Her stomach wound flared as she tried to stand. Two men pulled her upright, the cramped muscles in her arms screaming in protest. Guards fanned out in front of her, each one toting a mini machine gun. When she was fully vertical and alert the mass of guards parted as if split by a cleaver, leaving enough space for one black-suited man.

He stopped a hair's breadth away, disdainful and disrespectful of her skills. "Today the Yakuza see you for what you really are," he spat out. "Tomorrow we get to see you die. No more insolence, no more freedom, no more dreams for you, Kitano *bitch*."

Her inner fury lived in her gaze, which locked onto his like a heat-seeking missile. To speak would be wasteful, expending energy which she knew might yet be needed, and attract only cruelty which she also knew these men would never have the courage to risk if they were alone with her. Cowardly, spineless, they would dare challenge her only now, and only to plump themselves up in front of their men.

So, simply, she remained mute.

The Yakuza boss barked an order, sneering in her face. His men urged her forward, pushing her out of the clean cell and into a corridor. More guards lined the walls, all with raised automatic weapons. Mai had never seen so much security, not even surrounding President Coburn in the hours after his escape from the Blood King. Were they expecting an assault? Surely all these safety measures couldn't be for her.

The Yakuza boss read her mind. "So many bosses have come to watch you die," he said with an air of sentimentality. "It has been a long time since we all came together. For that, at least, we have you to thank. The atmosphere up there is electric, euphoric, a thing I thought I'd never again see in our stronghold. Today," he nodded, "will go down forever in Yakuza history as a day to be remembered."

Mai didn't doubt it. Her legend was strong among the police and governmental authorities. Her demise would deflate morale at the very least and leave some important individuals crushed. The optimistic part of her mind knew that Drake and the rest of the SPEAR team would have tracked her by now, starting with the symbol she drew in her own blood, but even that failed to ascertain her actual *rescue*. Not without bringing the damn building down. But then, if they knew civilian casualties would be non-existent, even that wasn't beyond them.

Mai walked the line, traveled up several floors in an elevator, exited and then walked another line. By now, the corridors were wider, the men more smartly dressed. She knew they must be close to their destination. She passed empty room after room, seven floors up judging by buildings she could view out the far windows. Her only thoughts were of Drake and Grace and the man she had murdered, Hayami, and his poor daughter, adrift in the world.

I no longer feel like the strong woman I once was.

Her dilemma in a nutshell. Incident and consequence had sapped her inner strength and calm. Now, since no avenue of escape automatically existed she didn't waste time trying to concoct one. At last her entourage slowed and finally stopped before a huge double door, but rather than fling them dramatically open she was shown a side door and made to make her way along a darkened corridor and into a spacious room.

"Wait here," somebody said.

She looked around. Whiteboards propped on easels stood everywhere, as well as a lectern and other conference paraphernalia. Of course, there was only one room big enough to house all these mobsters—the building's premier conference room. So she was about to head out on stage for the first time in her life.

Smyth would be proud, she thought. Maggie in the limelight. Maggie standing proud. Maggie undefeated. And Drake? Where was the Yorkshireman now? The darkness around her crawled with Yakuza. And as she put her mind to it, as she concentrated on her peril instead of her problems, she heard the murmurings of a gathered crowd.

"They're waiting for you." The boss's mouth was so close his dry lips brushed against her ear. "Time to face your accusers, Kitano. Time to face those you wronged."

She struggled to remain mute, to keep from crying out: *No you're not! I wronged Hayami! I wronged his family! Emiko! That's who I wronged, not some inked-up, arms trafficking, lethal organization that destroys hundreds of lives every single day! Never that!*

The rear of the stage protruded into the room and was

reached by a set of small steps. For now she was shielded from the conference area by a wide accordion-shaped partition. As she waited a great cheer split the air.

"You're up."

A door opened and she was guided through, then left alone. A great hubbub swelled all around her, straight at her, filling her head. An overwhelming force, it swept all else aside, leaving her stunned. But she stood tall against it; a sturdy oak in the eye of a hurricane, a survivor refusing to bend in the face of all her aggressors.

The men sat before her, arrayed around the room in their hundreds if not thousands. She stood on the stage, watching their hostile gestures, their violent fake lunges. Not one of them would stand against her alone. Not one in several thousand. Yet here . . . here they were kings and gods and unstoppable tyrants. Their words—*only words,* she reminded herself—threatened every manner of degradation and shame and vicious death.

"Approach the stage." She spoke aloud into the storm, her words whipped forcefully away and unheard so that only those who could read lips knew what she said. "Come now. Just approach."

None did. It took many minutes for the abuse to die down and nobody immediately brought the trial to order. There were no judges here today, only prosecutors. If any germ of hope existed in the far corners of her mind it knew that the longer this trial went on, the more chance she had of being saved.

Let them rant.

At length, the men relented and were served drinks. As

this process continued Mai finally heard the voice of someone she knew.

All too well.

Hikaru rose from his, no doubt honorary, place in the front row. "You are accused of dishonoring the Yakuza family, Mai Kitano. What do you say?"

Mai ignored the little weasel, preferring instead to examine the faces beside him. These would be the most powerful then. She wondered if she might seize one of them.

"What do you say?" Hikaru repeated, voice rising.

"I say it takes at least three people to have a trial," she said. "The accuser, the accused and the judge. I see no judges here today. Only killers. I say this is no trial at all."

"Oh damn, you got us." Hikaru hooted to the sound of laughter, jeers and some disapproving looks from the older men beside him. "This is what you Europeans call a holiday. Some time off for jobs well done."

"I am Japanese," Mai pointed out.

"But show no respect for your countrymen. We are Yakuza; we live and die here as our ancestors did. We are family with a family ideal. Many of our members are outcasts, betrayed by their so-called parents. And yet you have now disrespected us twice."

You are a bunch of deluded killers, Mai wanted to say but her composure won the day. Maybe she could turn this into a long-running debate. "I was doing my job."

But Hikaru and his betters saw her reply only as a further sign of contempt. Hikaru snorted, "The police work for *us*. Not us for them. But not you. Never you. Not until now, at least."

Mai caught a change in his tone, a cunning that hadn't been there before. Instantly she was on her guard. Perhaps she had underestimated this homicidal mixture of deviants.

Hikaru waved in a general manner. Mai saw movement over by a far door. A loaded moment passed and then the world fell out from under her. Even she, trained and tough as she was, felt her knees buckle.

Chika came into the room, restrained and bloodied, a gun pointed at her head.

The world would never be the same.

Hikaru began to laugh.

CHAPTER TWENTY TWO

Hayden Jaye stared into the heart of chaos, wondering how to make sense of all the evidence scattered around her. Never in her life had she known so many clues to exist that led nowhere. First—the Lost Kingdom. It was out there somewhere, probably submerged between China and Taiwan, though the jury was still out on that one—their language translator, David Daccus, still engrossed in his thankless task of deciphering the symbols and characters nobody had ever managed to decode in all of human history—those found on the Niven Tablets.

Or had they?

The *USS Queenfish* was looking more and more like it might have been an exploration vessel, and had been ordered to sink the *Awa Maru* to conceal its real intentions in the South China Sea. Such an appalling tragedy. Either way, it had helped spirit away a fortune in glittering treasure and an ancient, priceless one—the Peking Man. And now Dudley, his crazy crew and the Pythians possessed the old Chinese treasure and a potential map to an even older and more controversial one.

The lost kingdom of Mu. It would be a find beyond belief, she reasoned, but also an enormous bone of contention between China and Taiwan. As if they didn't have enough already.

Their curator back at the Steel Mountain facility was busy checking for an old translation of the Niven Tablets, but had come up with nothing so far. The physical tablets had been saved by Hayden and her team, but Dudley still escaped with the photographs. Hopefully it would take the Pythians time to put so many pictures together, but her gut and Karin's knowledge of cutting edge technology, told her otherwise.

"Seconds," the Blake woman told her. "Once they get the photos loaded onto the right machine it will render them in seconds."

As time marched on she decided to take a break and call Matt Drake. It would be early morning for him on the night Chika was due to infiltrate the Yakuza. She paused with her finger hovering over the button. Should she risk the call? The team could be in the middle of something finicky.

What the hell . . . Mai once made a call that saved Smyth's life!

Fortunately, the call was answered immediately. "Yep?"

"Matt? Can you talk?"

"Aye, could do with the break actually. Things have gone right to shit here."

Tell me about it, Hayden thought. She sighed aloud. "What's happening over there?"

Drake ran her through the high- and lowlights. Hayden listened then poured herself a black coffee. "Quite a dilemma. Remember, Dahl and the others are still likely to get the job done. Mai may be down, but never count her out. My issue would be with Chika and Yorgi and the length of this so-called trial. Can you get another night out of it?"

Drake said he didn't know. Hayden caught the edgy tone and decided to change the subject a little. "Bringing you up to speed," she said. "The Pythians have the fossil. Dudley's still on the loose with help from his old gang. We believe the lost kingdom may be real and that the Pythians are trying to find and use it in some way."

"Any idea where it is?"

"Oh, yeah, plenty. But this damn language has to be translated—which takes time—or we have to find an old translation. Nothing has turned up so far."

"An old translation? You're saying the US already did it and kept it all a secret?"

"I know. Big shock there, right?"

"But why? Surely it's a great archaeological find that the whole world can get behind?"

"We're not sure. It may have something to do with a sunken ship. Or diplomacy. Or nothing more sinister than passing time." Hayden shrugged even though he couldn't see her.

"I guess China wasn't a world power back then," Drake said intuitively.

"Sure. We've thought of that too and the current consequences. Either way, this can't end well." Hayden put the coffee down as her stomach started to growl, reminding her that she hadn't eaten in about twelve hours. Looking around the office, at the team all working on adrenalin and enthusiasm she suddenly realized that everyone might need to take a break and refuel. She shouted out as much, insisting that everyone take a couple of hours off.

To Drake she continued, "We know for sure the Lost Kingdom lies somewhere under the South or East China Sea, probably near China and Taiwan. The boundaries are disputed as you know. With that in mind I'm already organizing a first-class diving team in the area as well as several other specialists in their field. I was hoping you guys might be able to supervise."

Drake was quiet for a moment, but then his reply was exactly what she wanted to hear. "I guess I'll go rescue 'em all and then head to Taiwan then. No worries. Catch you later."

If only everything were so simple.

Hayden signed off and motioned to Kinimaka. "Let's get out of here for a while."

"Home?" Their rental was only fifteen minutes away.

"Why not? You can knock me together some of that sausage, eggs and rice you love so much."

"Sweet bread?"

"Damn right."

The couple said their goodbyes and headed out of the office. Hayden heard Karin and Komodo ordering from the on-site restaurant. She couldn't force them to relax, just hoped they would have the sense to realize that sometimes taking a breather was better than powering through. Kinimaka drove their large 4x4 through the early afternoon traffic, a big man in a big car, taking care not to sideswipe anything. As ever her antennae was up, but nothing appeared out of the ordinary.

Once home, Mano headed into the kitchen whilst Hayden took off her jacket and flung herself down onto the sofa. Staring straight ahead, vegetating, she found herself studying the few ornaments and single picture they had placed on the white mantelpiece. All was well, she was sure, but where had this new pastime come from?

Tyler Webb. During the Pandora event the Pythian leader had promised to come into their homes; even boasted about having pictures and video of them, but had never shown an ounce of proof.

Why?

Now she heard the noise from the rear of the house and it wasn't Mano. It wasn't her imagination. The rear French doors had just slid open or closed—the catch made a peculiar sound whenever they did so. Drawing her weapon she advanced through the front room and turned a dog-leg to reach the rear. Nothing looked out of place. The doors were closed.

But—

Something didn't feel right. Was there a faint cologne in the air? A fading imprint in the carpet? Her eyes fixed on something and she called Mano through.

"You see that?"

"What?"

"The picture on top of the bookcase. It's facing the wrong way."

"Okaaay. Do you want me to set it straight?"

"Mano. I think somebody's stalking us."

The Hawaiian's face passed through a multitude of emotions, mostly hilarity to surprise and then to seriousness. "Because the frame's the wrong way around? It fell down yesterday. I probably replaced it backwards."

"You did?" Hayden felt a moment's relief. But her gut still told her something was wrong. "How did it fall down? Did you knock it over or did you *find* it on the floor?"

Kinimaka reached out to hold her, but she twisted away. *This shouldn't be happening to me. I'm an ex-CIA agent and leader of the best special operations team on the planet.* Was this how it began? How people felt every day when they knew something was different but couldn't quite put their finger on it?

Was this how it all started?

First the niggling nervousness and then the denial. Next the deep fear, the burning sensation in the stomach and again the denial. Then the paranoia; evaluating every little thing until every little thing began to drive you crazy. Truth be told, you could find suspicion in just about everything, every day of your life.

The man with the phone—was he texting or taking her picture? The guy three shops over—was he following her? The slightly cracked open wardrobe. The shadow that crossed her window. The crackle that may or may not be the boards settling.

Kinimaka walked over and righted the photo. Hayden watched, then took out her cellphone and began to take pictures of the room. She ran through the house as her boyfriend finished making their meal, cataloguing everything. No mental notes this time, no room for error.

Downstairs, Mano was waiting. "All good?"

She forced a smile and picked up the proffered fork. "All good."

"Find anyone?"

"Funny. Look, don't you remember Tyler Webb saying he had pictures of us?"

"Oh yeah." Kinimaka laughed. "But the guy's a total

whack job freakazoid. Now just try that sweet bread." He smacked his lips loudly.

"Mano," Hayden said softly. "What if he was telling the truth? What if he's been watching us for weeks? What if he's *been in our house? With a camera?*"

Kinimaka put down his fork. "This isn't like you, Hay. You're stronger than this. Tougher. Some maniac with a god complex trying to unsettle you is all it is. Any case," he started shoveling eggs into his mouth again. "All he'll get is me falling over two or three times and you stepping out of the shower." He waggled his hand. "Meh."

Hayden kicked him under the table. "Hey! There's a lot of guys would like to see me step out of the shower. And into it for that matter."

"Do we have time to test the theory?"

Hayden didn't even check her watch. "Stupid question. C'mon."

As they left the table, their meal almost eaten, Hayden fought down the unsettling feeling that the sound of the rushing water would leave her deafened, that the smoked glass screen and even Mano himself would leave her practically sightless, and that she had never once taken her gun into the shower.

Why did she feel the need to now?

CHAPTER TWENTY THREE

Tyler Webb was a happy man. Not only had Dudley now secured two major bargaining chips; not only were the Chinese about to be made to sit up and beg; not only had his small, expensive team of translators pinpointed the location of the Lost Kingdom so accurately he already had men heading to the site—he had now sent Dudley and his highly capable crew to the site too.

And that wasn't the best part. Not by a long shot.

His train of thought broke as two monitors set before him flickered to life. Clifford Bay-Dale and Nicholas Bell stared out at him.

"We are the Pythians," he said. "What news have you?"

Bay-Dale, architect of the lost kingdom project, spoke up. "We are the Pythians. As you know we have located the ancient site. It's too early to provide any absolute proof yet, but we are working on it. Incontestable proof would take many months, perhaps years, but we can provide a formidable corroboration when the find is combined with evidence provided by the Niven Tablets, the American expedition of 1945 and the Peking Man. Startling corroboration. The Chinese will be forced to give us all that we want once our ultimate terms are laid out on the table."

"Superb," Webb said. "And Nicholas?"

"Zoe Sheers, our new primary member, is up to speed. I will have her ready to speak at the next meeting. Do we have news on your Lucas Monroe?"

"As you say—up to speed. And Clifford? Last we spoke you hadn't found the time to vet a new member." He allowed the sentence to hang.

Bay-Dale surprised him. "I made time, Tyler. If we make time then we make things happen. I do have a candidate, a man called Julian Marsh, ready to go. Such an excellent choice I'm surprised I didn't think of him before. Anyway, as you both say, next time we convene . . ."

"Good. Good." Webb shut his misgivings away. He didn't enjoy giving the others even a modicum of control, but the way the Pythians were branching out meant he had no choice. "Now, Clifford, what about the haters? What about those who would seek to derail our new discovery?"

"The press," Bay-Dale admitted. "I have made a shortlist of some of the rags that take themselves too seriously. Men in power who would seek to profit." He coughed delicately. "The ridiculous academics who are so short-sighted they barely see what's beyond their own snooty noses—"

Now Bell coughed, only raucously. Webb knew why. Such words coming from a man like Bay-Dale—a controller of energy prices—sounded ludicrous.

"Prices rising again are they this year?" Bell clearly couldn't help himself. "Price of oil up is it? Another tsunami maybe? Extra investment? How many houses do you have now anyway?"

Bay-Dale ignored him utterly and completely. "We have eyes on as many haters as possible. And we have leverage. I believe a significant amount of haters can be swayed to our side. Enough to make all the difference."

Webb claimed both their attention by declaring operations open on the hugely important next level of their project. "So onward. The Chinese are teed up, waiting for our call. Shall I make it now?"

His question was designed to magnify excitement within Bay-Dale and Bell and it certainly worked. Bell sat up straight, eyes widening with pleasure and even Bay-Dale appeared surprised.

"You have them interested already?"

"I have my go-between standing by. He's more a . . . procurer . . . of wishes. He makes things happen. He will get our demands to the government of the People's Republic and in particular up to the State Council and all the way to the top—the Paramount Leader. We will be taken very seriously, gentlemen."

"Fire across his email," Bell said in a predictably crass manner. "I have more than one wish list I'd like *procuring*."

"He has no email." Webb sighed. "No address. No paper or digital trail. He does not exist apart from to those whom he invites to be his clients. Now, be quiet whilst I contact him."

The process was laborious, necessarily so, as the call rerouted through half a dozen countries and servers. Despite all that, when the line started ringing it was answered immediately.

"Yes."

"This is Mr. Webb. Following on from our last conversation we now hold both the Peking Man fossil and the location of the lost kingdom of Mu, either of which will cause a stir in the Chinese government the like of which you have never known. Not one but two legacies are at stake. Now, as we all know the Chinese like to play hardball in their negotiations and are masters of the double-cross. Please tell them there will *be* no negotiation beyond the provision of authenticity. And any double-cross will end in unprecedented disaster. Our demands will be met within forty-eight hours or the fossil will be destroyed live on YouTube. What will happen to Mu will be far worse."

"Worse?"

"The whole area between China and Taiwan is being secured by a primed daisy-chain bomb."

"And your demands?"

"The code boxes we spoke of, your so-called Z-boxes. The Chinese may not have developed a quantum computer just yet, I know, but those little boxes are almost as good for code-cracking. You say the People's Liberation Army and their Cybersecurity Division have developed three? I want three."

Webb signed off to quiet laughter.

Later, alone, he spoke to Callan Dudley, the Irishman on his way to China.

"I have new information for you, Mr. Dudley."

"Oh, aye? And what might that be?"

"You're headed to Asia, yes? Well, I have news that the SPEAR team, including the woman who beat you, are currently somewhere in Japan. If you come through for me, I will do my very best to facilitate some kind of . . . meeting."

"Yer very best? Hey boys, the people who locked me up

be in this part of the world too. Looks like we might get a showdown."

Webb heard drunken cheering in the background. "I'll be in touch."

Webb sat back in silence, allowing his thoughts to drift. Today had been another major step forward for the Pythian movement. The wheels were turning. China would relent and then Taiwan would protest. The code boxes would be delivered. The US would shudder. New primary Pythians were on the way. From this lofty tower the world below was nothing but a game board to be played, manipulated and controlled. With that idea in mind he pressed a button to call the private elevator and allowed himself to be whisked fifteen floors down to an equally private lobby. There, a chauffeur awaited, the car already burbling. Webb stepped straight into the back seat, stretching out across the luxury leather.

"The hospital," he said quietly.

His driver knew which one. His driver knew all the local addresses of the entire SPEAR team after multiple visits from Webb and other furtive operatives. As they negotiated traffic, Webb changed clothes and added spectacles and a comb-over to his appearance. The good thing about a city's CCTV cameras was that they were all passive outside of extremely sensitive areas, which meant Webb could move freely without too much worry about facial recognition software. Only if authorities suspected he was in the vicinity would proactive measures be taken.

You can't police all of the city all of the time.

Webb entered the hospital along with everyone else,

wincing at the too-warm entry area and ignoring the information desks. Lines of people waited at the coffee shop to his right and at the convenience store to his left, as if there weren't two deserted duplicates directly across the road. His eyes turned up briefly to check the signage, ensuring he was headed in the right direction. Inside, deep down, he was so fully alive his heart was racing, his temples practically pulsing. The prowl was on. The danger was exquisite, the outcome potentially delicious. A nurse smiled at him. The corridor bent at a right angle, passing a restaurant and an employees' shop. A bank of elevators took him to the first floor and now Webb forced himself to slow down through fear of overexcitement. Her private room stood one hundred yards away. He strode on, a confident visitor to all appearances, but when he reached the small window he slowed. It was covered by a closed blind but he knew who lay on the other side.

The door handle turned. He didn't bother to hide his face. The syringe lay cupped in his pocketed right hand, not that he wanted to use it.

And look at that.

He grinned outwardly. She lay sleeping, face turned away, monitors beeping nicely. The room was cozy, perfect for the recovering plague victim. Webb knew this woman was an expensive escort, but had no clear idea how she fitted in with the SPEAR team's international efforts. No doubt she was a procurer of information, but he didn't like to hang presumptuous hats on a person until he'd properly stalked them and learned their every inner secret—dirty, precious, miserable, heart-rending, the more priceless the better.

He opened her personal drawer, rummaging through the items of clothing there. The top drawer was locked but there was the key—right next to her water glass. How quaint. He sipped from the glass, flicking his tongue around the entire rim. He pawed through her locked drawer, finding a purse and a cellphone, which he quickly cloned. Many people kept information on their cellphones that couldn't be accessed elsewhere, even by him—house alarm codes, obscure passwords, pin codes, highly personal details . . . for instance, the way to contact her escort service. All the time Lauren Fox lay sleeping at his side, breathing softly.

He slipped in beside her, ever so careful, ever so quiet. The syringe was now exposed, but he really didn't want to use it. It was so much better when they were fully conscious. The sheets covered them both. A little snore escaped her luscious lips. Her hair smelled of almonds. He savored it for one more moment before climbing out, ecstatic.

Even in his rapturous state Webb didn't want to tempt fate too much. It was time to leave a memento and get back to the real world. *Why do these moments have to end so quickly?* For that was all they were—moments. Yes, he could enter their lives, their homes, prowl around whilst they were out, but the truly perfect encounter was right here and now. In his mind it had a name—the *Live Prowl*. It was real time, full risk, and gave him the most intense thrill.

Webb drew a stylized 'P' on Lauren's wall, right beside her peacefully sleeping face. This was the first of many, and would be necessarily large, obvious and crass. The ones to follow in the days and months to come would be far more intimate and thus more shocking.

Job done, Webb exited the room, but before he did so he placed his lips so close to Lauren's own he could almost taste them; her breath mingled with his own. It was enough.

For now.

More was to come and soon. Excited, he decided he wasn't yet done for the night.

Tyler Webb left the hospital and told his driver to head for home.

"*Theirs,*" he said. "Not mine."

CHAPTER TWENTY FOUR

Alicia waited impatiently for Hibiki to move aside. Since Dahl and the Japanese cop dragged her into an elevator last night their situation had been getting more and more complicated. It wasn't bloody easy being a prisoner. To escape the Yakuza crowd they had quickly moved away, melting into the din and chaos of it all. Hibiki had pressed the button to ascend and their fate was set. The higher floors were work areas, deserted, with plenty of places to hide and wait. Hibiki soon remembered the information he'd gleaned regarding Mai's showcase trial and how they were even going to beam it over the TV. He decided the reality was they would broadcast it over an internal secure network for those unable to attend. By early morning he had identified that network and by the time Mai's trial began he was watching the live feed.

Alicia placed two fingers against his temple and pushed. "Shift over."

Dahl guarded the entrance to their obscure little office on the fourth floor. It was still early morning but the trio were gambling that the entire building's workforce had been given the day off—the Yakuza wouldn't want anything interfering with the legendary Mai Kitano's final day of judgement.

Alicia studied the video feed. The quality was low, the camera angle limited, but she could easily see there was no chance of a frontal assault.

"Has to be a diversion," she said. "But what and when? Best if we knew what Drake was planning." She licked her lips. "What would Captain Jack do?"

Hibiki, acquainted with her love of all things Depp, turned around. "Captain Jack Sparrow? Well, he wouldn't go full frontal that's for sure."

Alicia started. "Shit, now there's an image."

"Diversion," Dahl rumbled form the doorway. "Any idea how long Mai has?"

"All day." Hibiki sat back, thinking. "But after that? The hope is that they make this last for two days and we can figure something for tonight."

"Didn't work too well for Chika," Alicia pointed out. Mai's sister lay crumpled on the stage, barely able to support her weight. Hibiki closed his eyes at Alicia's words.

"Hey, man," she saw his anguish, "don't worry. We'll get 'em out of there."

"Be quiet," Dahl hissed, ducking low. The covert sound of a door opening reached Alicia's ears and the soft padding of footfalls. Dahl sank even further and then slithered into the outer room, sliding among desks. Alicia left him to it. The Swede *was* one of those men she trusted to take care of business in the right and proper way.

On screen Hikaru was ranting. Mai stood before the gathering, covered on all sides by men with weapons, but still managing to appear menacing. Alicia saw the bandage strapped to her stomach—such a wound would diminish the Sprite's abilities for several weeks to come. A scuffle brought her attention around and she turned just in time to see Dahl hauling a small figure through the door.

"Yogi." She laughed. "Where the hell have you been? Delivering pizza?"

The Russian thief shrugged away from Dahl's grip. "It's Yorgi. I googled *Yogi* few days ago and it is *not* flattering. Please . . . it is Yorgi."

"All right, Yogi. So what's your story?"

Dahl put himself back on watch. Hibiki stared at the screen, eyes unreadable. Yorgi sighed, a sound of grudging tolerance, and took a seat by her side.

"Building was tough, walls ungiving. Took me longer than I thought to break in, da? Then I heard the anarchy. I hid, thinking to let it pass. Searched every floor . . ." he shrugged. "Here I am."

"No cameras up there?"

"Not in office space or staircase, no."

Alicia waved his attention toward the screen. "So, we're fucked. Any ideas?"

Yorgi looked pleased to be included. He needn't have been. Alicia regarded him as part of the team now, especially after his exploits in Paris. The thief was a thinker, a planner, and settled in to watch. He wouldn't suggest anything until he was sure it would work.

The hours passed. The foursome drank the last of their water, ate the last of their supplies. Nobody had thought to plan for an extended stay. Lunchtime came and went. A perfunctory Yakuza patrol scoured their floor, but made no real effort to check every office. All entries into the building would be secured and had been since last night. The guards had no reason to assume anyone else was already inside.

Dahl eventually drifted back, casting eyes across the TV

monitor. "Barring a foolish assault from Drake," he said. "Which, of course we can't rule out, it has to be tonight after they're all resting. Let the trial play out today. We go in hard after midnight. We contact Drake then, and hopefully he'll be ready with some kind of diversion. In addition we have Yorgi, not a fighter but we can use you to create a further distraction. Any questions?"

Alicia stood up to stretch. The problem was Dahl's idea, flawed and as uninspiring as a day at boarding school, matched her own. They couldn't use the comms to liaise with the world outside yet because the Yakuza would probably spot the signal and realize somebody else was inside. They couldn't use the office phones for the same reason and, this being a planned military-style strike, nobody had packed a cellphone. Hibiki continued to watch Mai's trial, identifying members of the audience with distaste and, on occasion, with astonishment.

"Yowza, we've been searching for that old man for years! Old boss, mean son of the Devil. I know an aristocrat who would pay ten million dollars for him."

"Yowza?" Alicia repeated sarcastically then, as Hibiki finished, "Which man?"

The hours stretched like resistant elastic as the sun waxed and then waned in the skies, throwing its rays through the heatproof glass, dappling the wooden floors and the plaster ceilings. As the shadows began to stretch Hibiki called their attention to the monitor.

"Something's happening."

This was the moment of truth. All hopes were pinned on the Yakuza drawing out Mai's show trial for one more night, but if they started showing signs of an early execution the soldiers were still prepared for a blitz attack.

Hibiki turned the sound up a little.

"And so we have it," Hikaru was saying. "The gravest sins of Mai Kitano are those she committed against the Yakuza brotherhood. Our family has suffered all these years even though we did not know. In the police, the government, the military, the boardroom there were whisperings of our humiliation. Now . . . we should make a bloody example," he paused and sneered. *"Two* bloody examples."

An old man rose from the front row, trembling as he leaned heavily against two knobby walking sticks. "Do you have anything to say, Mai Kitano?"

Hibiki leaned forward. Dahl looked ready to burst into action. Mai, who had barely moved a muscle all day, now stretched her legs and arms. Weapons were steadied on all sides but she ignored them, holding the old man's eyes.

"They say a warrior deserves a good death. I am and always have been a warrior. My sister is a civilian and has nothing to do with this. Let her go and give me a good death. That is all I ask."

The old man looked a little surprised, perhaps expecting argument, rebuttal, or at least an appeal. Hibiki shook his head without realizing and even Alicia couldn't quite put her finger on what the ex-ninja was playing at. *Does she want to die? Is she trying to save Chika?* She recalled the recent glitch that had inserted itself between Mai and Drake. Was this her confession and absolution all in one?

"Chika Kitano," Hikaru spoke up, "inserted herself into

this building, into our midst, to rescue her sister. It is fitting that she receive the same kind of justice."

The old man looked over at Mai, giving her the chance to speak.

"She only came here to save me. Which one of you wouldn't do the same to save your brother, your family?"

"Should she even get an opinion?" asked a younger man in the front row, rubbing a balding head.

Shouts rose, some for and some against. The old man tapped a stick gently on the floor. "We are not murderers. We are not heartless killers. Some would paint us so, but they are wrong. Mai Kitano—you were never going to walk away from this, of course you weren't. The Yakuza would hunt you to the ends of the earth, non-stop, and with no lessening in resolve. It is a matter of honor."

Hibiki turned his head to look back at Alicia. "See what I mean. That's why it's imperative they don't know the SPEAR team and I were ever here. I actually think the extra day's wait has done us some good. The tunnel guards won't even remember we were there tomorrow. The problem is . . ." he tailed off.

Alicia didn't need it explaining. "Mai and Chika. We save their asses and they're gonna be Yak targets forever."

The old man had finished his spiel and looked to Chika. Mai's sister stood off to the left, her hands tied, face crusted with dried blood. "I think," the man said, "that they will die together. For *her* sins. Think on that, Mai Kitano, as you spend this night, your last, alone." He spat on the floor. "Take them both away."

Mai then clearly saw no drawback in taking action.

Alicia watched her lunge for the old man, splitting the air between them like a finely shot arrow. Her elbow came down on his nose, sending him reeling into the front row, her body then revolved three times, bringing her to Hikaru's side. Alicia couldn't hear what the Japanese woman said, but the man's face went whiter than Alpine snow and his body flinched away. The guards rushed her, unable to use weapons because of the half-panicking human mass all around, but they were no strangers to unarmed combat. The Yakuza would have picked their best warriors to watch her. And Mai was wounded. Still, she caught Hikaru by the windpipe, two vice-like fingers squeezing together, and backhanded the first guard to arrive. He went down, gushing blood from his nose. Attendees scrambled away to either side, and those at her back tried to jump over their seats to get away. The second attacker skipped around her strike and kicked at her midriff. Mai breathed in, curving her body away from the attack, then coming down on the outstretched leg hard enough to break the ankle.

Hibiki put his head in his hands. "She has no chance. And we can't move. This is completely the wrong time."

Alicia knew how he felt. Her hands and feet moved unconsciously in time to Mai's, almost like a car passenger sometimes imitates the driver; her breath caught in her throat. Dahl came over and cheered. Mai's grip on Hikaru was absolute, unbreakable. The man who had captured and shot her—his eyes were rolling back in his head, his legs gone to jelly, body held up only by Mai's incredible strength and agility. Another Yakuza guard accosted her and received an elbow to the mouth for his trouble. He doubled over, blood and teeth spraying. Mai's lead foot smashed him in the same place again for good measure, achieving a high-pitched scream.

"Stop! Stop!" The old man had recovered remarkably quickly, and was now waving one stick at her. "You will stop or we will kill you now!"

"You just chose to kill my sister and I," Mai returned calmly, the knuckles of her fingers that gripped Hikaru's throat now turned white. "Do you expect a warrior to take it lying down?"

"No, but you will desist immediately or we kill her now." He pointed his stick at Chika. Instantly the guards stopped surrounding Mai, turned and focused their weapons on her sister. The only thing at Chika's back was a thick red curtain. Mai pushed Hikaru away, the man only slightly more alive than dead.

She held her hands above her head, wincing at the pain in her stomach. Alicia winced along with her. The old man shuffled to her side, ignoring the blood that flowed down his face.

"Tomorrow, at dawn," he said. "We will see how tough you are, Mai Kitano."

"And will my death be honorable?"

"Do you want to fall upon a sword? Battle a group of men, one at a time? Pistols perhaps? I will decide overnight what your fate will be." He wiped blood from his nose and flicked it onto the floor. "But whichever way it goes it will be hard. For both of you." His stick finally stopped waving.

Alicia rose and walked over to Dahl, stretching her limbs. "A few more hours and then we contact Drakey?"

"Yes. He would expect an attack after midnight. This . . ." he hesitated. "Is not going to be our easiest offensive."

Alicia laughed at his tact. "You're telling me. Dude, this could well be the hardest thing we've ever done."

"And the stupidest?"

"Nah, not where family's involved. It's never stupid."

"I always thought you hated Mai."

Alicia looked away. "The thing about me, Dahl, is that you never know what I feel. You never will. That's how I like to play it. Mai can be a bitch. So can I. And so can you. Does that make us any less valuable to the team?"

"Of course not."

"Then get yer lube ready, Torsty, 'cause where we're going—it's gonna be tight."

CHAPTER TWENTY FIVE

After midnight the team made their final preparations, knowing nothing could be gained from waiting any longer. Indeed, if there was any kind of celebration this night its racket would help mask their rescue attempt. Dahl led them all to the elevators and then switched the comms signal back on.

"Drake? You there?"

"Dahl? Pal, are you a voice for sore ears. What's going on in there?"

"Mai and Chika both okay. It's all about the speed now, Drake. Are you ready?"

"I have a way of escaping Kobe. Probably."

"It doesn't involve fast cars does it?" Alicia snatched a line. " 'Cause I wasn't even in the last bloody race and I'm already bored hearing about it."

Dahl ignored her as he opened the stairwell door. "Can you help break us out the front, in about twenty?"

"Not a problem. I have a plan B, C and D ready to go."

"Good. Then keep a comms silence until you hear from me."

"On my way."

Alicia followed Dahl into the stairwell, Hibiki at her back. All three of them slipped on masks that Yorgi had provided. Yorgi had already been sent on his mission and was now descending in the elevator, looking to start a small fire on each floor. The office behind them was filling with smoke, courtesy of chemicals and cloths found in a cleaning cupboard and a lighter found in a desk drawer. Alicia heard the door swing shut above them just as the sprinkler system went off. As one, they rushed down the stairs, heading for the lobby where they would have to switch stairwells to access the lower levels. Hibiki and Dahl carried their weapons, but Alicia was empty-handed.

For now.

She moved fast behind Dahl as the Swede pushed through the final door, exiting out into a corridor that led to the lobby. Thirty feet ahead the entrance area gleamed in semi-darkness and beyond that the windows and glass doors sparkled with random lights.

"Hope they're not all downstairs," she whispered.

Dahl stopped beside a new elevator bank, recalling the blueprints, and pushed at the adjacent stairwell door. As half-expected, it was locked, even today with no day staff around. Dahl aimed his gun.

"Stand back. This is where the fun starts."

He shot out the keypad and the vision panel but still the door only rattled in its frame. "Damn."

"What did you think, genius? Breaking its keypad would destroy the lock?" Alicia watched the lobby as a shout went up.

Dahl swore loudly, put his shoulder down and charged the door. Thankfully it exploded off its framework, shattered timber flying everywhere and clattered down the stairs.

"Could you make a bit more noise next time?" Alicia patted his arm.

"Next time?" Dahl grunted. "I'll throw *you* through it."

Down three more levels they went, hitting the lowest at a run, then slowing as they reached a carpeted corridor with heavy doors to both sides, evidently leading to the cells where Chika found Mai earlier. No doubt she now occupied one herself. Alicia saw Hibiki hesitate, taking a deep breath before continuing. The cop had more on the line down here than any of them.

"Keep moving," she said helpfully. "Can't save 'em standing with your dick in your hand."

Dahl pressed on, checking the first whilst Alicia lifted the metal flap of the second. Empty. It was then that, further down the corridor, she heard excited murmurings and expressions of disbelief. Somebody up there had gotten wind of something.

Knowing their luck was about to run out, Alicia checked the second and third doors on her side of the corridor. Men occupied two of the rooms—shirtless, pantless, bloodied and bruised. They were wretched figures, heads hung in defeat, not even bothering to acknowledge the sound. Behind her Dahl grunted that he'd found Mai. At that moment Alicia opened the viewing panel of the last door and set eyes on Chika.

"Bloody hell."

Mai's sister was chained to the wall, arms above her head, legs together. Her head hung and her black hair was draped across it. New discolorations and bloody weals covered the exposed flesh across her collarbone, arms and below the knees. She moved aside for Hibiki and turned to Dahl.

"Keys."

"On it."

The Swede marched toward the sound of voices, steadying his gun. He paused to one side of an open doorframe, giving Alicia chance to make ready.

"Now."

Together they peered around, prepared for anything. What they saw was a small surveillance room—rows of TV monitors and chairs, some desks, and a bunch of men crowded around just two screens. A low table and wall off to the right-hand side was practically festooned with pain-dispensing instruments from blades and electrical-prods to hammers and whips, all heaped together along with their guns. Alicia noted the blood still dripping from one of the leather handles and embraced her sudden rage. Most of the men were jabbering away and gesticulating wildly, trying to get some point across, others were sat staring and letting their cohorts rant, but every one of them had their backs to the door.

Alicia saw instantly the object of their interest—a bank of cameras had been tasked to chase the outbreak of fires above and now, finally, one of them had spotted Yorgi.

A man reached out for a walkie, his eyes flicking backwards.

"*Hey!*"

Alicia grabbed a gun and fired, hitting his arm and then his chest, knowing he would never hurt anyone again. Dahl put three double-taps into a trio of heads and that left just one. Alicia saw a blade flash and dodged as the weapon skimmed by her face. Then she leveled her gun.

The Lost Kingdom

"Give me the keys and I'll make it quick."

It was the only language this Yakuza guard would understand. There would be no bargaining with them. His eyes flicked to a metal cabinet. Alicia never knew whether it was a voluntary gesture because a moment later he was dead, cheek blown away by Dai Hibiki.

"Torturing bastards." Tears stood out in his eyes. Alicia rushed over to the cabinet and yanked it open.

"We must hurry," Dahl said. "They have hundreds of guards inside this building and they can bring every last one down upon us."

Alicia grasped a single key and also a bunch attached to a large iron ring, figuring the first was a master for the doors and the second for the chains. She turned and ran back to Chika's door, unlocking it and throwing Dahl the single key. Hibiki was at her heels. Now, Chika's head whipped up, the abject fear in her eyes followed swiftly by confusion. Alicia whipped the mask up and then down at super speed.

"Al . . . Alicia? *Dai!*"

Hibiki ran to her and leaned in, helping to take the weight off her chained wrists. Alicia reached up and tried several keys before finding one that turned. The chains rattled down as Chika's hands came free and she stumbled into Hibiki.

"Hold on," he whispered. "Just hold on. We got you."

Alicia raced across the hall, throwing the key ring at Dahl. Mai was already alert and asking about Chika. "She's good," Alicia said. "On her way now."

Dahl helped Mai out of the chains then stepped back.

"Are you able to fight?"

"I'll kill them all if I have to."

"Good, because we're going to have to go through every one of them if we want to get out of here."

Alicia nodded toward Mai's stomach. "How bad is it?"

"Just a bullet wound. I can work around it."

Chika stumbled into the cell, saw Mai and ran over. The two sisters embraced whilst Mai eyeballed Hibiki over her shaking sister's shoulder.

"We have a lot to talk about, Dai Hibiki."

The cop winced, practically shuddering. "Yeah, let's get out of this hellhole first though, before you start chopping things off."

Alicia led them back into the corridor and at a fast sprint to the stairwell. "Wait." Dahl spoke up, the beginning of a grin twisting both sides of his lips. "How about taking the elevator? It's faster and it'll give them one hell of a surprise."

Alicia drew in a sharp breath. "Risky."

"It will put us nearer the exit."

Alicia quickly broke comms silence. "Outside? You ready? Do you have the Russian?"

Drake replied. "I'm outside. He's here and we're raring to go."

"We're coming right now," she said. "And it's gonna be fucking noisy."

"Noisier the better. Just do it."

"Buckle up, soldier boy," Dahl said. " 'Cause the Yakuza are about to be taught a hard lesson and they're gonna be plenty pissed."

"Bring it, nancy boy. I'm here to help."

Dahl pressed the button for the elevator, took a breath, prepped his weapon and then looked around.

"Ready?"

CHAPTER TWENTY SIX

Alicia was armed in every way possible as the elevator doors opened out onto a jam-packed lobby. Pistols, knives, spare ammo, electrical prod, even one of the dead torturers' bloody hammers. Her compatriots were similarly armed, fired up, and ready to wade through blood to make their escape.

Fucking good job, Alicia thought as the path to freedom greeted her.

Yakuza were everywhere, from those groups milling about and looking bored to those taking charge to others who rushed around carrying out tasks. The opening doors sent many pairs of eyes flicking in their direction.

Dahl was a mountain of dependable violence. The instant their presence was noted he opened fire and waded into the mob, shooting with one hand, crushing with the other, using his feet to further hinder those who fell. The crowd would have closed around him but it was Mai who came next and she had a score to settle. With lithe movements she used knives to slice and carve her way in Dahl's wake and ribbons of blood painted a trail through the air behind her. As if that wasn't enough, she was followed by Alicia, and the Englishwoman was more than angry. Enraged by the terrible, but matter-of-fact room below she wanted to crush bones. The first Yakuza ended up with a flattened nose and shattered teeth, the second a bullet wound in the stomach. The third ran on to her knife but she didn't end it there, dragging the blade sideways. They came from all sides, a screaming throng, and they hit hard, but never had they encountered foes like this.

Blood slicked the floor and painted nearby surfaces. Hibiki and Chika stepped into the open, both armed with handguns, and picked off aggressors who stood between them and the glass exit door. Alicia emptied her magazine into two more Yakuza, then spun with her knife, a sinuous target, cutting flesh as she inserted a fresh mag almost with one hand. Dahl met resistance ahead, the sheer mass of their enemies slowing him down. Still, he fought just as hard, never still, a twisting, turning wedge of pure muscle, violence and sheer elegance that defied belief. Weapons clattered to the floor; screaming men fell sideways. Mai and Alicia collected the enemy weapons when they had to, their sudden movements only adding to their evasiveness. When a Yakuza grabbed one of the women around the neck or the waist, the other taught him the error of his ways. At first, Alicia saw no difference in how Mai fought, the bullet wound not hindering her, but as the battle went on and they took more and more knocks, the Japanese Ninja began to slow down.

Anyone else would be on their knees by now, but not Mai. In addition to a lifetime of experience and training she now had vengeance in her heart, and hatred, and fear for the safety of her sister. As she glided by Alicia saw her wound had torn. Blood seeped. Mai fought even harder.

Drake could barely believe his eyes. Never had he seen anything like it a—a lobby so crowded, a battle so violent, men and women so determined and motivated. He sat astride a red Ducati, deep in shadow, with three more fast bikes behind him, currently being watched by Yorgi and Grace. The streets of Kobe that he planned to use were narrow and twisting and easy to get lost in—the bikes were perfect.

And Alicia mentioned that thing about car chases . . .

This should piss her off nicely then. But now, as he stared, a man used to adventure, war and death, but still awed and shocked at the nightmare vision before him. A simple question jabbed at him—how were they going to get out of there alive?

Alicia rammed in her third mag. One knife had been torn from her grip by a passing ribcage and now she employed a second. A fist slammed against the bridge of her nose but she barely felt the blow; adrenalin invigorated her every muscle and sinew, and acted as a pain killer.

Dahl smashed fists, elbows and knees into assailants before her but the crowd was just too thick, bodies fell and had nowhere to go. And whilst their demise caused their brothers intense problems it also hampered the SPEAR team.

Mai strove in a different direction, cutting a path to the right of the doors. Alicia sidestepped in her wake, jabbing her elbow into three noses with three steps, using her other hand to deliver three knife strikes.

The blade twisted from her hands.

She covered the momentary loss with the gun, aiming for hearts, necks and heads, wondering who these men imagined they might be beneath these black blank masks.

But then they were gangsters. They probably didn't think that way. Alicia withdrew the electrical prod and pressed the button, making it fizz against several adversaries and seeing them twist away in anguish. The prod was going to be a good weapon whilst it lasted then, enabling her to incapacitate enemies faster than she could with a gun and its limited supply of ammo. She jabbed to left and right, faster and faster, and the path opened up.

Hibiki and Chika watched their backs, the latter battered and bruised but determined to survive. What she lacked in skill she made up for in resolve. Hibiki protected her as best he could, whilst also watching out for himself. He had been given the most weapons, lacking the highly tuned skill of the SPEAR individuals, and he put them to good use, but even he was running low on ammo.

The great glass doors loomed in their sights.

Dahl growled and launched into a huge final effort. Alicia prodded and kicked, and loosed bullets. Mai, crying out in pain, twisted her body several different ways to rain blows upon her enemies, sometimes in the air, sometimes falling to the floor, using one man to gain momentum enough to fell the next, twisting their limbs together so that each hindered the other, forcing their bodies into unnatural angles. Every move was instantly measured to produce maximum harm and maximum interference. Alicia, at her side, paused between electrical charges.

"Little Sprite, you're a fuckin' death machine."

Mai's quick glare reminded her of the Japanese woman's inner turmoil and made her wince. *Shit, Myles, aren't you the tactful one?*

Since when did she even care though? Alicia was here

for the good of the team, showing support for the men and women whom she regarded as family—*not* just for one person.

And if she was that person sure wasn't Mai Kitano.

Brawling Yakuza then took every ounce of her concentration as they barreled in from all sides. The electric prod disabled three before it too was torn from her fingers, making her cry out in frustration. She took a blow to the ribs. Some fool fired his weapon in the surrounding melee, taking out his own comrade, but the bullet passed straight through flesh and bone and came dangerously close to Alicia. A baseball bat, such a clumsy and surprising weapon but not out of place at this moment in time, slashed down toward her. She moved fast, hitting men to her left, and the bat glanced off her shoulder. Still, the pain was intense. Unable to help herself she flung her last knife, taking the bat-wielder out of play.

Weaponless, she turned to hand-to-hand combat.

Dahl had been in that situation a while now. The big Swede blocked and slammed and barged. The noise of screaming, yelled orders and battle cries that curdled the air around him was like nothing Alicia had ever heard. Faces kept appearing all around her, warped by hatred and cruel intentions, striving to join the battle. Their eagerness blunted much of their effectiveness. Desperation set in among the Yakuza as the few insurgents and the legendary Mai Kitano herself, moved closer and closer to the exit.

Thus, came a desperate measure—machine guns.

Alicia heard the screams, saw the parting of the throng to her left, saw Yakuza throwing their own brothers in all directions to help clear a path. Dahl nipped into the space and the rest followed, the exit doors suddenly looming above them. Many Yakuza were slow in responding to their superiors, so caught up in battle rage, but the shouts continued and the machine-gun toting men began to find a way through. Mai threw her last knife, its blade thunking into one's forehead, but still four remained.

Alicia had saved bullets for the glass door, as she hoped had the others. But could they reach them in time? Men still assaulted her from the right, but she could only afford them half her attention as the machine guns were raised.

The Yakuza are risking hitting their own men.

It's not gonna stop them.

Concentration carved their features into hard relief as they lined the insurgents up in their sights.

Alicia saw Dahl start to run at them. It was a desperate measure. No way were they all going to come out of this one alive.

CHAPTER TWENTY SEVEN

Alicia lived the next few minutes in an agony of slow motion, positive she was about to see her own death and worse, the deaths of her friends, at the hands of these gangsters. Dahl grew optimistically close to the gunmen; Mai cleared the final stragglers away from the door; Hibiki and Chika were as close as they'd ever been; Alicia threw a facially tattooed man over her shoulders and into his brethren.

Keep fighting. Just . . . keep . . . fighting.

But they were out of time. Yakuza bosses were standing up on the lobby's reception desk, aghast at the bloody mayhem but still calling for deaths. Mai Kitano's last stand would be long remembered. The tales would be even more legendary once they surfaced, and surface they would.

"Kill them! Do it! Do it!" a man cried.

Yakuza all around Alicia scrambled aside or fell away. Dahl was a finger-length away from the first gun barrel when its owner was ready to fire. Then came the horrible instant of pure disappointment.

We failed . . .

The first crash was loud enough to disrupt everything—all eyes and focus switched to the front entrance. Something huge hit the glass very hard and even Alicia felt alarm. Her first wild reaction was to remember the old *Godzilla* movie and how the beast had trashed Tokyo. Hairs rose along her spine. But then reality checked in and she saw somebody had driven a small truck into one of the stanchions that supported the front of the building.

Jarring it.

Next came a hail of gunfire, aimed wild and high into the windows, and the crunching impact of another vehicle, this time into the reinforced glass frontage. Alicia saw cracks appear in the windows, spider-webbing across their entire surface. The bullets did the rest, sending the overlarge shattered panes crashing down like rolling torrents of lethal water. Alicia saw an opportunity and gripped it by the scruff of the neck—grabbing Hibiki and Chika, lowering her head, and charging through the piles of fragmented glass. Her feet slipped and skidded out from under her but she kept her balance. The heaps shifted and slewed but she jumped from one to the next, feeling a little like a fell-runner. If Chika stumbled, Hibiki steadied her and Alicia steadied him. More gunfire slammed into the building, loud and deadly, aimed high but the Yakuza couldn't be certain about that. They fell away, shocked and distraught at being assaulted on their own turf, most still in a state of disbelief, some beyond their limits and just trying to stay alive.

Of course they had never come up against anything like the SPEAR team before. Even half of it.

Dahl wrenched a machine gun free and sprayed the men in his vicinity. Mai grabbed his shoulder and urged him out of there. Still some bullets whizzed past him. Still a man attacked from his side waving a machete. Dahl let the huge blade slice a millimeter past his right ear, ramming the wielder's face with the full force of his shoulder. Blood sprayed his back. Machete Man went down, twitching.

Alicia felt the outside air wafting around her face, cooling her skin. Yorgi struggled to rise off to her left, having jarred his ankle as he jumped out of the second vehicle that had struck the front of the Yakuza building. Drake stood in the middle of the road, waving his arms.

"Come the fuck on! My bloody grandma would've gotten outta there faster'n you and she's been dead twenty years!"

"Piss . . . off," Alicia panted and hauled Hibiki and Chika along. Yorgi managed to gain his feet and limped up.

"We good?"

"Yes, Yogi, we're good."

Dahl ran up, hunched over, Mai at his side. "We're sitting ducks," he growled. "Where the hell's Drake?"

"Fuckin' *lucky* ducks, I'd say!" Drake shouted, urging them toward him. "Hurry. That was plan C. Ain't no plan D."

"I hope you have an escape plan." Dahl glanced back into the devastated lobby, toward the surging, enraged crowd of mobsters who now looked even angrier than before. "They're not just going to let us stroll out of here."

Drake snapped his fingers. "Bollocks. Never thought of that." He led them at a sprint into a nearby alley, pointing out the waiting bikes.

Mai set eyes on Grace for the first time. Her sudden exultation was then tempered by disbelief. "You brought her *here?* Are you insane?"

"Long, long bloody story," Drake grunted. "Hurry!"

Alicia checked out the scene at their backs. The Yakuza lobby was a seething mass of bodies, most yelling and strapping on weapons, some already running toward the apparently innocent building across the road that also included a parking garage.

"They're starting to get their heads straight," she said. "Some are already going for their vehicles."

"Then let's move." Drake turned his bike on and readjusted his mask. "Follow me."

The team jumped astride the other bikes without any more words. Alicia would have liked to thank the Yorkshireman, as might Dahl in his unique way; Mai might have liked to hug Grace and Chika and possibly slap Hibiki; Grace herself looked as if she wanted to embrace everyone at once—but fate had already rolled the dice and not in their favor.

Yakuza swarmed into the streets, weapons bristling like endless stalks of corn, as Drake spun his Ducati around on its back wheel and then fired it like a rocket deeper into the alley. Alicia clung to his waist. Behind them came a black Honda CBR and a slower Yamaha, one driven by Mai with Grace behind her and the other by Hibiki with Chika at his back. Dahl fired up the last in line, another Honda with Yorgi riding pillion. Alicia dug her fingers in as Drake shot along the dark, blind alley, scattering garbage and accumulated debris to both sides.

"Crap, you don't have to grab hold of my actual ribs, y'know."

Her mouth was alongside his ear. "What would you like me to grab hold of?"

"Balls!" Drake cried as they blasted out of the alley, crossed a road and missed a passing car by mere inches.

"If you insist." Alicia reached lower.

"Stop that! I should know better, but it's good to see you all. I didn't think you were gonna make it."

Affirmations filtered through the comms. Drake flung the bike down as they exited the next alley, traveling along a narrow road garlanded with colorful signage for a hundred meters before flinging them up yet another unlit backstreet.

Alicia had gotten her breath back, the incredible deadly lobby battle already a memory. "Hope you know where you're going, Drakey."

He tapped the side of his head. "All up 'ere, love. No PDA required."

She shook her head. "Not sure I like the sound of that."

"Well, you can always jump the hell off."

He slowed at the end of the backstreet, making sure the following three bikes were keeping up and then listening for followers. Already, a cacophony of engines was beginning to rise in the distance.

"They will never give up," Mai said prophetically. "Never."

Alicia felt sorry for the Sprite and her sister, the only two identities that the Yakuza knew without question. "Our problem for now," she said. "Is that they only need one person to spot us. Then the entire group will follow."

"Don't stop movin'," Dahl said.

"All right S-Club." Drake opened the throttle and aimed for the white lines on the center of the road. Alicia heard the Swede's comment over the comms.

"What's that supposed to mean? Is that more northern slang?"

"An old pop group," Yorgi, his partner, said. "From the nineties, I think."

Alicia allowed her mind to relax as they pushed between rows of shops, restaurants and apartments, threading the city of Kobe and heading southeast. With no imminent threats she began to consider what would happen once they escaped Japan.

Put Mai and Chika in hiding? Will their presence with the SPEAR team increase its risk? Would the Yakuza ever stop hunting for them?

Shit, so many questions it hurt her brain. Instead, she switched to easier contemplations. Like what would *she* do next—rejoining Team Gold for a while and resuming treasure hunting with Crouch and co sounded like a fun diversion, but it couldn't last forever. Still, it filled her immediate future and that was enough. Maybe it would make SPEAR see what they were missing. Maybe it would even make Drake—

A shout from Dahl interrupted her reverie. "Whoa, Drake, what's *that?*"

"The Akashi Kaikyō suspension bridge," Drake replied evenly. "The longest in the world."

"And we're what? Heading for it?"

"Unless you have quick access to a couple of speedboats or a sub then yes. We're heading for it."

Alicia surveyed the white suspension bridge that spanned the Akashi Strait, its hundreds of taut white cables glaringly illuminated by the night lights, its two crisscrossed support towers rising almost a thousand feet like white behemoths out of the rolling waters below. The comparatively thin plane of concrete stretched impossibly long across the bay, an emaciated but beautiful escape route.

Drake squeezed even more power out of the Ducati, lowering his head behind the front screen. Alicia was forced to stretch out atop him, still gripping his midriff tightly with both hands. The Kenritsu Maiko Park passed in a blur to their left and then they were on the final approach to the bridge, the toll road. Drake saw the lowered barriers and the line of manned ticket booths and couldn't afford to take any chances. Slipping out his small automatic he blasted the barrier apart, chunks of plastic-coated timber bursting to left and right. Mai's black Honda squirmed alongside and then Dahl's roared close to his back tire. Hibiki raced to the other side, quite at home atop the motorcycle. Alicia knew from Drake's movements that he was less than happy atop the crotch rocket, as was Torsten Dahl—the big Swede looking a little ungainly—but the bikes spoke for themselves as the best means of escape. Twisting slightly, she looked back now that the road was elevated a little, checking for signs of pursuit. At first she saw nothing back there but mostly darkened buildings outlined by brightly lit streets and even more colorful landmark skyscrapers—her spirits started to soar—but then the true size of their pursuit became progressively apparent.

"Oh, shit," she said. "Oh wow, that can't be good."

Drake spurred the bike on. "Helicopters?"

"Nah, don't be daft. They have a plane."

"A fucking *plane?* Are you kidding?"

Alicia clamped her fingers together.

"Ow, I guess that's a 'no' then. What *kind* of a plane?"

"Shit, how the hell do I know? It's stripy and it has wings."

"Actually it is seaplane." Yorgi was twisting around behind Dahl. "Two pontoons where wheels should be."

The four bikes came to a halt at the start of the bridge. Pursuing vehicles were probably five minutes distant, which gave them some leeway, but the plane was a bad sign. Drake passed his automatic to Alicia.

"I know you guys probably don't have a whole lot of ammo left, but hand it to your passengers and let 'em try to take that plane down."

A car passed them going the opposite way, its passenger gawping, but it was the only one at this solitary hour. The entire span of the bridge lay before them. Drake blipped the Ducati's throttle.

"Ready to race?"

Without waiting for an answer he burst forward, front wheel temporarily leaving the ground. By now the sound of the approaching plane could be heard as the four bikes attacked the Akashi Kaikyō Bridge. Alicia cursed out loud, finding it hard to get her head around a situation where she couldn't physically stop an enemy from pursuing her. The white plane came over the bridge, able to fly over its length until the first row of suspension cables started climbing toward the top of the first pylon, sinking as low as it dared.

Alicia steadied an elbow on Drake's spine, much to his annoyance, and let loose a salvo from the back of the bike. Yorgi did the same from his position. The seaplane shot sideways as if it had been electrocuted, zipping out of easy range. A single bullet breached its hull, its ragged entry standing out like a single forlorn wrinkle on the hide of an elephant.

The bikes ate up the bridge, passing cameras and callboxes, running alongside the barrier that separated the three-lane highway from its sister. The plane buzzed them again, but not as low as before, its occupants no doubt irate, and then pulled up as the first pylon approached. Alicia glanced both ways across the vast strait, seeing a huge expanse of heaving blackness, scattered with pitiful lights. Far out to the west lightning struck the seas, a vertical flashing white bolt, crackling along its length, then vanished into the night, the afterimage strong across her retinas.

"Damn that plane," Alicia said. "It's just going to follow us. What's the escape strategy, Drake?"

"I have speedboats waiting in a quiet marina on Awaji Island." He nodded at the body of land they were speeding toward. "Not far."

"Does that plan factor in the presence of a seaplane?" Dahl asked.

"No, mate, it doesn't."

"Well, maybe next time—"

"Stop bickering you two!" Grace suddenly blurted out. "We need a new plan!"

Alicia grinned in the dark. The new girl was showing more and more promise as she overcame her affliction. Perhaps the Sprite hadn't been wrong after all to draw her into the fold.

"Actually," Drake sniffed. "I do have a backup to plan C."

"Isn't that just plan D?" she wondered.

"No, just grab my sack." Before she could comment he added, "And be careful. It's loaded."

Alicia couldn't help but wonder about the

Yorkshireman's wording as she felt her way around his rucksack. "Hello, something's pleased to see me. What the hell's this? A rocket . . . where's the rest of it?"

"Yorgi has the launcher in his pack. Couldn't fit it all in mine."

"Where did you *get* it?"

"From the friggin' Yakuza. Where else? I had to take half a dozen of the little bastards out to crash that truck y'know."

"Oh, diddums. Slow down."

Drake was already slowing and pulling alongside Dahl. The Swede fixed him with a suspicious stare. "Yeah?"

Drake shook his head, knowing the Swede would be keeping up through the comms system, then swerved his bike so that his left knee was almost touching Dahl's right. Both bikes steadied. Above, the first pylon shot past, white and enormous against the vault of the night, standing starkly beautiful in its unending battle against the seas of Mother Earth. Alicia reached over and took the launcher from the fumbling fingers of a nervous Yorgi, berating him over the comms.

"So you can climb up the outside of a building without fear, but put a few hundred CCs between your legs and you're suddenly all aquiver? I thought you were better than that, Yogi."

The Russian remained silent, clearly unsure what to say. Drake gunned the Ducati so that it spurted ahead. "Time to gain us some ground." He pulled away quickly from the other bikes, staying low, the gray concrete and white lines flashing beneath their tires, the engine screaming. Alicia stayed upright, tugged by unnatural forces, but fighting against them as she loaded the RPG.

"Only one shot," Drake said.

Alicia snorted. "Yeah, I figured that unless you got another rocket down the front of your pants."

"You're *not* having that one." Laughing, Drake coaxed more speed out of the Ducati, his sudden increase in velocity leaving the seaplane behind. When Alicia tapped his shoulder, indicating she was ready, he applied the brakes and spun the bike.

Facing their oncoming friends, Alicia raised the RPG and took aim.

She also saw the lights of pursuing vehicles: motorbikes, fast cars and jeeps, they spread out across the entire bridge behind them.

A bloody mobile army, she thought, then sighted in the seaplane.

"Sayonara, you son of a whore."

The plane was slow to react, but then probably hadn't expected an RPG being fired at it from the back of a motorbike. It dipped fast, severely, a bomb suddenly falling out of the skies. The maneuver was so quick Alicia found that she had to readjust.

"Pricks. Just stay still so I can shoot you."

But the seaplane's pilot had other ideas, dipping beneath the topmost horizontal cable suspended between towers so that it was now running in between the dozens of thick vertical lines that supported the roadway.

Alicia's mouth turned down in concentration as she tried to sight on the plane between cables. "Ya think that's gonna stop me, asshole? Not a chance."

Alicia depressed the firing button. The missile streaked away trailing smoke, shooting between the rows of support wires and straight toward the seaplane. What her aim lacked, the heat-seeking sensor made up for, arcing the warhead until it locked onto the aircraft's welcoming signature and, even though the plane dipped at the last minute in an evasive attempt, the missile struck true and detonated.

The seaplane exploded, wreckage curving away from the main body and down into the black seas. Alicia dumped the now useless weapon as Drake revved the Ducati again and aimed its front end for the far side of the bridge.

Engines roared at his back and the other three bikes flew past. But as he prepared to make his tires scream in pursuit still more engines announced their presence as they continued to give chase.

"Still coming," Drake said over the comms. "We're not out of this yet."

CHAPTER TWENTY EIGHT

The remainder of the night unfolded at a more reasonable pace as Drake and his teammates shot onto Awaji Island, cutting between high concrete reinforcements and then keeping the expanding sea view to their left. Their pursuers tried in vain to keep up, but Drake had chosen wisely with the four bikes. He half expected another seaplane to appear, or at least a chopper, but the Yakuza must not have been able to rustle anything up.

Probably all out moving their friggin' contraband . . . among other things.

He recognized the hotel to his left from pictures and peeled through the entrance, switching his lights off and coasting down a sharp, twisting incline toward a long, wooden dock.

Two speedboats sat tied up, bobbing gently in the undulating swell.

Drake ditched the bike, taking care to conceal it before hurrying over to a waiting figure.

"Cheers for doing this."

"No thanks required, man, so long as I get paid."

"This guy's our banker." Drake pointed at Dahl. "Or something like that."

The figure pulled a hood back to reveal young features set within a pockmarked, scarred face. He didn't reveal his hands. "Don't care how many of you there are. Pay up now or I start killing."

Drake coughed in surprise. "Okay, pal, calm down, calm down." He dug into his jacket, still sweating inside his mask and trying to adjust to life at less than one hundred and twenty miles per hour.

Mai squeezed past him. "Nice friend you got there."

Drake paid and ensured they were all secure before casting his eyes back along what he could see of the highway. "Better without your running lights," he told the youth. "At least for now."

"I know how to smuggle," came the reply. "You still aiming for HK?"

"Yep."

"Cool. Get in."

Drake noticed the only space left was one between Hibiki, Mai and Chika. Unconsciously, he winced. Outwardly, he gave the others an aggrieved stare. This was all he needed. What he actually wanted was to hold Mai, to share his relief and sheer pleasure at saving her life, but this sure as hell wasn't the time. Not even close. Gingerly, he picked his way aboard the speedboat and took a pew next to Hibiki.

The boat powered up, stealthy at first, nudging out of the cover of the dock and over the rolling waves. The horizon opened up ahead, black and empty, and a sea breeze ruffled their clothing. Slowly, both speedboats ventured further out.

Drake gripped Hibiki's shoulder. "Great job back there, pal. You guys really owned that lobby for a while."

"I'm just happy everyone made it out alive," Hibiki said, staring between Chika and Mai. "How's the gunshot wound?"

Mai glared over. "Hurts like a bitch. How's the face?"

Hibiki blinked, not understanding. "Okay, thanks. I didn't—"

Mai leaned over and slapped him hard. "How about now?"

"Shit!" Drake couldn't help himself. "We came here for you. *Everyone's* here for you. Even bloody Alicia."

"Don't tempt me," Mai snapped at him. "You brought *Grace.*"

"She wanted to come." Drake knew the words were lame before he uttered them but his mouth ran away with itself. "To be fair the plan was that she stay back at the hotel."

Mai shook her head, saying nothing and staring at the dark horizon. Chika chose that moment to smile at Hibiki, the gesture achingly sad through all the blood, cuts and bruises that covered her face.

Drake stared the other way as Hibiki and Chika embraced, whispering their gratitude and love for each other, alone now in the full boat. His eyes locked onto those of Alicia, who stared over at him.

Even the sprightly Englishwoman looked sad.

CHAPTER TWENTY NINE

Drake relaxed for the first time in many hours as the team finally sprawled out around the safe house that a collaboration of Interpol and CIA agents had procured for them. Here in Hong Kong every agency in the world was active, and the SPEAR team hadn't been willing to trust the local police, despite having concealed their identities. In truth, the safe house was a little drafty and noisy, since it was in actuality a converted warehouse and not exactly Victoria Peak. The team took it in their stride, but Drake could tell nobody was particularly comfortable with their surrounds. He trusted Argento at Interpol and he trusted his team's abilities to be wary of their perimeter. For now, Honk Kong was far enough away from Japan and safe enough to hide in whilst others tried to collect Intel from the Yakuza HQ.

He tried to take their mind off it by jabbing the speakerphone open and calling Hayden in Washington. Now that they had Mai back they could all concentrate on and be useful in solving this lost kingdom problem; maybe even in apprehending Dudley and his cohorts. And it would keep Mai from tearing his and Hibiki's heads off.

Hopefully.

But first they needed to know where Hayden was at.

Their boss answered on the fourth ring. "Hey guys, how's it going?"

Drake gave her the summarized version, leaving out the

lobby scene, the subsequent chase, and Mai's exasperation.

But Hayden's voice was still hesitant as she asked, "And how's Mai?"

Drake glanced over at her but she lay lengthwise on the only sofa, tending her own wound with Grace kneeling beside her and pulling faces. "Good. Good. She'll heal." He didn't have to add: *I hope.*

"You're safe there in Hong Kong?"

"Safe and sound." It came out "seyf and sooond" with his Yorkshire drawl.

The American pushed on, "You've missed one hell of a lot, guys, but I'll try to keep it brief. The lost kingdom of Mu, a kind of precursor to Atlantis and the human race, is almost certainly real and submerged at the bottom of the sea between China and Taiwan."

Dahl raised his voice immediately. "How can you be so sure?"

"Well, we aren't but the Pythians seem to think it's real and that's what really matters. Castle walls have been found down there, other fortifications with perfect, genuine mortar joints, ancient structures and the Yonaguni Monument, stone circles—you name it. Real evidence exists, circumstantial or not. The find raises numerous problems, the potential worst of which is the location of the damn place."

"You think there'll be a squabble?" Alicia said drily.

"Shit, it could be outright war if someone lights the tinder the right way."

"For a place that's been missing for so long," Dahl said. "It seems to have been found awful fast."

"Once the right clues come to the surface it's only a matter of how fast you work," Kinimaka rumbled across the airwaves. "We found the tombs in Hawaii and Germany pretty quickly once the Icelandic one came to light."

"What clues?"

Hayden butted in. "We'll explain later. But the Americans have been searching for Mu since the 1940s so don't think this is a lightning find. They've sunk ships, stolen treasure and hidden artefacts to do it."

"Where does Dudley fit in?" Drake wondered.

"Working for the Pythians, he's over in your—how do you say it?" Kinimaka pondered. " 'Neck of the woods' right now."

"Not bad, Mano, we'll make an honorary Yorkshireman of you yet." Drake ignored the Hawaiian's snort. "Dudley's in Asia?"

"Him and his inner circle of jerks. They call themselves the 27-Club and there's seven of them."

"Yeah, stay alert, man," Smyth said. "They're bug-fuck crazy, worse even than Myles."

Alicia glanced over from her perch beside a makeshift bar, but didn't deign to comment. Chances were high she hadn't actually heard the entire sentence as Dai Hibiki was talking into his own cellphone beside her, liaising with his police office back in Tokyo. Hayden filled the silence. "Dudley has been seen in Taiwan, in the vicinity of where Mu is believed to lie. We're still working on the language to give us an exact location. He could be overseeing operations there."

"Interesting." Drake keenly wanted to end the man's

involvement in world affairs once and for all. "We could always pay him a visit."

"Sit tight for now," Hayden continued. "All that's old news. We're struggling with something new at present. You see, if the Pythians *have* found Mu what do they intend to do with that knowledge?"

"Or rather—who do they intend to hurt?" Karin put in with a resigned sigh.

"Any ideas?" Drake asked.

"Yes," Hayden said. "Unfortunately we do. Our friends in the Pentagon and others in the CIA report that the Chinese government is being *ransomed* for something, but we don't know what."

"The Pythians are ransoming Mu?" Drake said, feeling more than a little skepticism. "Its location maybe? That doesn't sound right at all."

"Not for them," Smyth agreed. "Too tame."

"And how're they gonna stop the Chinese from getting to it?" Dahl said. "No, it's something else."

"Well, that's what *we* think," Karin said. "Trouble is, it's the Chinese inner circle who are being ransomed and—to quote the great William Goldman—'nobody knows anything'."

"I may have something." At that moment Hibiki pocketed his phone and walked over to Drake. "Since you're already knee-deep in this Mu thing and I'm right here with you I've been asked to act as liaison between our *insiders* in Beijing and Tokyo. Nothing risky or serious," he said in response to a look from Chika. "Just collating the facts that trickle out of China's capital."

"You're their first contact?" Karin asked.

"I am now."

"So what do you know?" Drake slid the cellphone closer to him.

"There's an emergency meeting of the inner circle of the Chinese government scheduled for later today. Something's wrong with Mu, and the men of power aren't happy."

"*What* is wrong?"

"Like you said—nobody knows. But there's not one scrap of elation over the sudden discovery of Mu. Not an ounce of celebration. This kingdom is their ancestry, part of not only *their* beginnings but the creation of the human race, and all we hear coming out of Beijing are these sneaky connivings . . . and fear."

"The Pythians are up to something," Drake affirmed.

"Yeah," Hayden drawled. "But what?"

Mai lay back, struggling with the bizarre dilemma of occupying a room with so many people she loved and wanting to hurt most of them. Even Chika should have known better than to infiltrate the Yakuza. It was only going to end one way.

So she side-tracked herself with Grace. The young girl was none the worse for wear after her Kobe adventure; even more bubbly than usual because the constant activity had helped distract her mind. Even so, Mai saw dangerous storm clouds sweeping through the girl's eyes.

"There's something new," Mai said, sitting up a little, wincing as pain from the bullet wound and new aches began to pulse. "I can tell. Another memory?"

"Having the Japanese mob chasing me isn't enough?"

"No."

A sigh. "I just wanna be part of the team, you know? If I can't be a fighter let me be a geek. Like Karin. Drake said it'd be okay."

"Did he?" Mai wasn't entirely sure the Yorkshireman would have agreed.

"Well, he didn't say *no.* So that's a yes. Right?"

Mai read the flippant way Grace tossed the situation away and decided to dig a little deeper. The barriers were up. Maybe a little heartfelt admission would help. "Look, I'm grateful all these amazing friends came to help me. I really am. But I'm also really mad at them right now for endangering so many lives, including their own! I'm not a heartless bitch, Grace, I'm a *caring* one and that's why I'm furious."

"Even at Drake?"

"Especially at Drake."

Grace sniffed. "I like him. I'll take him off your hands."

Mai did a quick double take. The girl wasn't joking. "All right, all right, let's get real. You're sixteen going on thirty, I get that. But Grace, you need your *own* life. The fourteen years between now and then are the years that are going to shape you, make you, and heal you. Believe it—when we get back to the States it's straight to school for you, young lady."

Grace pouted. Mai had intended the statement to be part fact, part joke, but the huge implications of it suddenly weighed heavy upon her. *Could she ever go back? Could Chika?* The Yakuza would hunt them forever. They would have to be in hiding for the rest of their desperate lives.

She studied Grace closely. "Is that it? Nothing else?"

"Whilst Drake was out sorting the bikes and the cash yesterday," Grace spoke her mind out of the blue. "I got a call from the investigator, Hardy. He told me . . ." the seventeen-year-old paused, the words caught in her throat.

Mai reached out, sensing her distress.

"He told me that my real parents have been traced and that they're dead. They blamed themselves for losing me, couldn't cope, and fell apart. They just . . . gave up."

Mai saw tears in Grace's eyes and grabbed hold of her, hugging her close and cursing silently at the world. It couldn't even give this girl a break. Grace was trying her heart out, struggling to overcome her past, and Mai wished she could just get one fucking break.

"I'll train you," she said abruptly, out of nowhere.

Grace sniffed and pulled away. "Eh? You'll what?"

"I don't know." Mai's head was mush, full of doubt, uncertainty, anger and even fear.

"You said you'd *train* me. I heard you."

Drake heard and came right over. "Mai's a great teacher," he said with an idiotic smile that Mai wanted to slap right off. "You couldn't do better."

Grace looked even happier. "I'd *love* that. I really would. I'm already fast, maybe half-trained after . . . well, you know. See, I remember *that*. Oh, this is great. Let's start now!"

Mai could have slapped herself for blurting out such thoughtless words. To train somebody was to consciously place them in harm's way. It was not a passive act, not even a defensive one—not the way she did it. If she trained Grace it would be to turn her into a weapon.

And, after that, what came next?

Where do we go from here?

CHAPTER THIRTY

Hayden entered the home she shared with Mano, mulling over all the fragmentary pieces that comprised the Pythians' latest plan. This mastermind, this leader she had already met called Tyler Webb, seemed to have gathered a veritable mental institution together—an institution of like-minded, ultra-wealthy, powerful, repressed and psychopathic individuals. If aerosolizing bubonic plague wasn't enough, then how about ransoming and threatening the world's most formidable emerging superpower?

Probably not.

Memories of other Pythian projects filtered through her mind as she closed and locked the door. Galleons and Tesla and what was the big one? Saint Germain? One day she would have to hit serious research mode to see if some clues to the future were already emerging. Maybe it would help to advance Webb's incarceration date.

For they would get him, dead or alive. Of that she had no doubt.

Kinimaka headed for the kitchen, already rubbing his hands together and no doubt imagining up a grand feast. The couch shuddered as his left hip rammed into it. No matter. The Hawaiian was a substantial amount of incredible things but he was never going to be her dance partner.

Hayden headed for the shower, taking her cellphone with her. They were still very much on call, waiting for developments to emerge from China and Taiwan, but the little side trips like this were what kept them human, and on top of their game. The water was hot and refreshing, pounding down onto her shoulders and spine. She lingered a while and then wrapped the big soft towel around herself and stepped into their bedroom, casting around for fresh clothes.

Her phone rang. It was the hospital calling. Hayden's antennae rose instantly and then stayed on high alert as the head of security spoke for several minutes.

"Nothing was taken," he finished. "Nobody was harmed. It all seems whacky to me. Just this letter P drawn on the wall."

Hayden found her gaze transfixed on something as she listened. "Where was it drawn on the wall?"

"Umm, next to Miss Fox's head."

Hayden tried to drag her eyes away from something but couldn't. "And that's it? No damage? No . . . letter or anything? Nothing else that shouldn't be there?"

"Not that we can make out. Do you know what's going on here, Agent Jaye?"

"It's not *Agent*—" she began and then a hand fell on her shoulder, almost making her scream. Twisting away, letting the towel and the cellphone fall, reaching for her gun, she stared into the eyes of her attacker.

It was Mano, now transfixed and distracted by the sight of her body.

"Put your tongue back in." She reached down and picked up the phone. "Listen," she said. "We're on our way. Don't touch anything."

"We're going *now?*" Mano's puppy-dog eyes almost made her smile.

But then she remembered.

She turned, eyes again drawn to the far side of the room where a high chest of drawers sat in the corner. "What do you see, Mano? What do you see?"

"Only the greatest ass in the known universe," he said. "How did I get so lucky?"

"*There!*" Hayden jabbed her finger forward, catching his attention. "What do you see over there?"

"A chest of drawers," he said a little hesitantly. "A cordless phone. An alarm clock, not my favorite since its set so high I have to get out of bed to switch the damn thing off. A spare mag. Whoops."

Hayden gave up and climbed over the bed, gesturing at the drawers. "I didn't leave my underwear hanging over the side of this open drawer. I didn't leave it bunched up inside." She scooped every item out onto the carpet.

Kinimaka looked over her shoulder. "Crap."

"And I certainly didn't write that fucking letter P on the bottom of the drawer."

Hayden rose fast, suddenly shivering, suddenly feeling exposed. Quickly she grabbed the towel and sent her eyes roving over every corner of the room, searching every nook and cranny and light fitting and lamp.

"We're being watched, Mano," she said. "Now I'm sure. The Pythians are watching us."

CHAPTER THIRTY ONE

Matt Drake arrived in Hsinchu City, Taiwan, with limited Intel and no genuine idea of what to expect. Hayden had briefed them during the journey, their leader trying to prepare them as best she knew how but, as he knew, mission expectations and subsequent reality were often poles apart. Since the Pythians had discovered the supposed lost kingdom of Mu buried somewhere beneath the silty waters of the Taiwan Strait that separated China and Taiwan, close to the place where the *Awa Maru* had been torpedoed over half a century ago, very little had leaked out.

At first, Drake thought it unlikely that a handful of mercs working alone might locate such a thing, but soon understood it was all down to satellites, GPS and computer systems. Log a coordinate in America somewhere and even a baboon would be able to follow it to the ends of the earth. *And a good job,* Drake thought. He'd met some of the mercs the Pythians employed.

Next up, Hayden explained how certain members of the Chinese government had been sent reeling, and were now firmly entangled in some kind of power meeting. The Pythians were pulling many strings, and not in a nice Thunderbirds kind of way. Taiwan was highly suspicious but still mostly in the dark. Tensions between the two countries were rising yet again. Hayden had previously reported that she was pulling together a specialist dive team; now Drake and his colleagues were about to meet them after being smuggled into the country.

Hayden's language expert, David Daccus, had translated several parts of the infamous Niven Tablets, and had sent the pages of text to Dahl's new tablet computer.

"The Naacal Tablets, or so-called Niven Tablets, originated in the land of Mu and were written by the ancient inhabitants of earth—the Naacal. In essence they are unusual andesite tablets with unrecognizable markings. They were never deciphered until they were *lost.* It appears now the that Americans did decipher them, and since the markings bear a lot in common with Scandinavian petroglyphs I, with the help of my Icelandic colleague, Olle Akerman, have posited a theory that makes sense of most of the symbols. From this we have confirmed that the likely location of Mu, or whatever this lost kingdom might be called, is indeed close to where the Japanese hospital ship went down."

Dahl, talking aloud as others docked the boat, paused for a moment. "Olle Akerman," he repeated. "I wonder how the old dog's doing?"

Drake knew little as to the whereabouts of Dudley, although it appeared likely the man was also in Asia, furthering the Pythians' plans. For now, it was up to them to confirm the position of the lost kingdom and report back, at the same time as scanning for any signs of the Pythians. Hayden hoped the dive team would be able to get the job done within a day, thus reporting back before the Chinese made any kind of unalterable decision. This operation had become much more that a treasure hunt or military op now—men as powerful as President Coburn were waiting on an answer to decide how best to strategize a response to whatever the Chinese might do. This mission might put the US, the UK and even the Japanese a step ahead.

With the small boat docked, the team surreptitiously made their way inland, relying on paid locals to deliver them to Hsinchu Fishing Harbor where Hayden's dive team waited. The journey didn't take long, less than an hour, and soon Drake was out of the minivan and stretching his legs, wary of the tropical weather and the light rain that swept across the exposed harbor. A strong wind greeted them, sweeping in and out to sea. The harbor itself was a simple construction of wide concrete gangways to which boats were tethered, bobbing in the water, and where cars and vans could easily be parked on top. Tied and sheeted cargos sat everywhere and also piles of tires. Exposed stairs led down to the water's edge.

A man wearing a flat cap walked up to greet them. "Team's ready, Mr. Drake," he said in an American accent.

"Mr. Drake's my dad," he said gruffly. "I'm Drake. What do we have here?"

"All right, Drake. I'm Kearns. Over here we have Thibodaux, or Thib for short, Gale and Sims. We'll be your dive team today."

"Seals?" Dahl looked across the bay.

"Frogmen."

"Seals then." Drake laughed. "Why don't you just say so?"

"Do you tell everyone you're part of team SPEAR?"

"I do!" Alicia blurted. "I have ID and everything."

The frogman shook his head wonderingly.

Alicia looked over the side of the gangway. "Hope you got a bigger boat."

Kearns smiled. "We only have the one, I'm afraid. Surely you're not *all* wanting to go down?"

Drake glance over the group. "I guess just three," he said, knowing Dahl would be up for it and Alicia would skewer him if he didn't ask. The rest, he decided, either weren't in the right place for exploration or too inexperienced.

"How deep are we going?"

"Roughly seventy meters. That's the depth of the Taiwan Strait. Maybe a little less depending on sediment build up."

"So we're talking decompression stops?" Drake started to shrug into a scuba diving suit.

"Yeah, but we're compensating for that." Kerns was checking the respirators. "Larger volumes of breathing gas." He tapped two tanks, one reading oxygen the other reading EAN50. "Strap 'em both on, backplate and wing set up. We're using rebreathers too. Remember, decompression is your most vital procedure today, your ally. When we come back up the ascent rate ain't there for fun, it's mandatory. Got it?"

Drake nodded. Alicia struggled to pull on her suit, complaining hard, but when a Seal innocently offered to help she gave him the dead eye. "You said breathing *gas*," she told them. "Don't you mean air?"

"Nah. We use Heliox since it's less narcotic. Don't want any of you landies getting the narcs now, do we?"

"Whatever." Alicia tugged at the neoprene suit. "Damn! Why can't they make these things out of *denim?* I can pull a pair of jeans on in about two seconds flat."

"About a quarter the speed you can pull 'em off," Drake observed drily.

Alicia ignored his comment, finally ready, and reached out for her air tanks. The group then spent another few minutes climbing into the Zodiac Hurricane RIB—rigid hull inflatable boat—and waiting for Kearns to make ready.

"All right," he said. "We're just taking a look here. Nothing too invasive. If this lost kingdom is down there we'll see the signs. If the enemy have beaten us to it we'll see the signs. Reconnaissance and verification mission only. Understood?"

Drake nodded for all of them, already staring out to sea. Dahl shouted to those that remained on the dock, ensuring Hibiki and Mai remained vigilant, but with everything that was happening between those two and Chika and Grace at the moment they barely registered his call. The Swede stared over at Drake with a worried expression.

"Sorry, mate, but all that shit between them? It needs sorting or we're going to be looking at casualties."

Drake bit back the snappy comeback. Dahl was right and he dreaded to imagine the effect of losing another member of the SPEAR team. "I'm open to suggestions," he said finally. "But with the four of them it's like picking through an SAS obstacle course loaded with mines. Naked."

Alicia caught the final word and looked over. "What?"

Drake shook his head. "Life used to be simpler than this didn't it?"

Dahl shrugged. "Simple usually means no ties, no family and no real love. I prefer complicated."

The Zodiac began to rumble as its engines started and

then powered forward through the slight swell. Its higher-than-normal sides protected the occupants from little of the spray and wind but the roomy interior was adequate for their gear. Spluttering from a faceful of spray, Drake remembered he hadn't dived seriously in many years and put his mind to recalling the basics. Kearns, at the front of the boat, used a satnav system to zero in on preinstalled coordinates.

As the docks grew smaller, the wind whipped up, and they neared their destination in the middle of the Taiwan Strait, Drake held on tight and caught the leader's attention.

"One thing bothers me," he shouted. "Well, more than one thing, but this the most. Something's down there. We all know that. But how can anyone be certain it's Mu?"

Kearns made a noise. "Shit, how the hell do I know? Miss Jaye, though, she explained a lot of this whilst we were waiting for you guys." He stressed the word "waiting" just a little. "First, like you say, *something's* down there. Second, they now have these ancient, once undecipherable tablets to back 'em up. Third, can anyone in government ever afford to be wrong?"

Dahl laughed knowingly.

"Nah, didn't think so. Fourth, let's tip their hand and see what gives. Fifth, they also have the Peking Man fossil on the table and that boy's as real as they come. It all adds to the credibility, see? Add to that the fact that these tricky bastards inside the Chinese government all seem to *want* to go to war with Taiwan then you can see why the US is worried. *Any excuse,* Miss Jaye said." He spread his hands. "And here we are."

"Reconnaissance and verification," Dahl said. "Nothing ventured nothing gained."

"Easy in, easy out. Nobody loses," Kearns said.

"Can we stop with the clichés?" Alicia moaned. "Friggin' Navy Seals."

"Pride of the Navy," one of the men—Sims—spoke up.

A sudden explosion shook the skies, making Drake almost tip out of the boat. When he looked up he saw a streak of silver flying overhead, a jet fighter with loaded missiles.

"What the hell?"

"That's a Taiwan military jet," Kearns said. "Now I don't believe in coincidence and they can't have spotted us, so I'm guessing the Taiwan government have figured something out. Maybe they were tipped off. But when they start doing flyovers like that—the Chinese see it as a threat and a challenge. We'd best make this quick, guys."

Drake sat up straighter as the boat slowed. A blue horizon stretched ahead, China so far away its coastline appeared only as a haze. Blue seas lay to all sides, empty of marine traffic and seemingly deserted. He assumed that would not actually be the case. If the Pythians were laying claim to this find they would be keeping it under a twenty-four-hour watch. Kearns was wasting no time, already strapping into his air tanks and readying his face mask. The Seals checked their rebreathers.

"We're using the buddy system," Kearns said. "We're all shipmates here, so Drake you'll be mine. Now pair off."

Moments later the group were tipping themselves into the water. Drake breathed through the mouth, employing a deep and slow breathing technique to help cope with the extra demands on his lungs. The divers limited their descent, allowing their ears and other senses to adjust as the underwater environment slowly darkened. Drake equalized his ears as the pressure built, seeing Dahl and Alicia do the same. He decided to check the comms unit.

"All well over there?"

Alicia's head turned in slow motion. "Be better once I get you outta my head. First in Kobe and now here."

"Not what you used to say," Drake reminisced.

"Don't slow the ascent," Kearns' voice interrupted.

Drake's flippered feet fell further, drifting down at negative buoyancy. The world around him was a brilliant blue and above the light was bright white and suffused. Descending was a truly different world. Bubbles rose all around his colleagues, racing each other toward the surface and certain expiration. A shoal of silver fish flicked past. Darkness beckoned below and Drake fell into the heart of it.

"We're dead on the coordinates." Kearns checked a waterproof device. "Passing forty meters."

Drake again equalized his ears, slowing his descent. This wasn't exactly a technical dive but nevertheless still had to be conducted by the book as they were exceeding the recommended scuba diving depth. The Seals, he noted, carried numerous bits of equipment around their waists, including torches, cameras, sediment-hoovers and weapons. None of them ever stopped checking equipment and observing their surroundings.

At last the darkness enveloped them and finally they reached their depth at seventy meters. Kearns' feet brushed the sediment at the bottom, not landing too fast, and Drake was soon to follow, feeling an odd sensation as he set foot on flat ground far below the surface of the sea.

Alicia wobbled, drifting before setting herself straight.

"Bit out of your depth, love?" Drake quipped with a laugh.

"Har, har, your one-liners used to be as good as DATY, now they're about as funny as VD."

"Oh aye? What the heck are you on about?"

"And you can stop your Yorkshire-ishness right there. It ain't cute. And you've never heard of Dining At The Y? No wonder Mai's become a frustrated bitch."

"Hey!"

Alicia kicked off the bottom and tilted, waving her flippered feet at his face. Kearns swam to the right and Drake followed. The Seal team leader spoke. "A few miles that way," he indicated China, "and you would reach the Yonaguni Monument, a popular tourist attraction for divers. Who'd have thought this would end up being so close to it?"

"Makes sense to me," Alicia muttered.

"Nothing to see yet," Drake observed.

"Then you're not looking." Kearns surprised him and slowed. He reached out a gloved hand, brushing at a slab-like, moss-covered object on the sea bottom. "See that? Now look here." He scissored his legs, swimming around the side of the slab.

Drake followed, now seeing the stone staircase cut into the black rock. Six risers high it rose, each descending step wider than the other, ending at the sea bed. Kearns swam lower and brushed at the accumulated sand and sediment.

Drake saw sharp little flakes drifting away.

"Goes deeper," Kearns said. "See?" As his fingers cleared the silt more of the staircase became apparent.

"How much sediment is there likely to be?" Drake asked.

"At the bottom of the sea? That's like asking if you'd like to live one, one-thousand-year life or ten one-hundred-year lives, but in a storm-tossed, windy environment like the one we have above it could be a meter a year, maybe more."

"And they reckon this place is about ten thousand years old."

"Big dig, eh?"

Drake began to understand now why the Pythians might be ransoming the lost kingdom to China. He didn't understand *how,* but the why was clear. The task of uncovering it was impossible, even the task of exploration practically unthinkable. Having said that, China *was* the world's most influential emerging superpower.

"Castle walls." Kearns swam even further. "See the red walls? An ancient castle already discovered in the 1980s. And yet—nobody knows. Did *you* know?"

Drake shook his head, then realized Kearns probably couldn't see the gesture behind his mask. "No. Why?"

"They're pretty much unexplainable. Six- to ten-thousand-year-old, mortar-laced castle walls under the South China Sea? Thirty to seventy meters deep? At least five discovered by sonar graph? According to Miss Jaye the sonar graphs also showed many protrusions near the walls, indicating alleys, staircases and other walls."

Drake saw where the man, through Hayden, was going. Back to the old "out of place" artefact impasse. Ten thousand years had passed since this place became submerged. But none of that mattered now.

Through the others they began to get a feel for the size of the area, the depth and width of the walls and what other objects lay in the vicinity. Kearns noticed that several silt piles had been recently built.

"Somebody else *has* been here," he said. "A short time ago. Either they were doing a recce, like us, or . . ."

Drake stopped what he was doing. "Or what?"

"Or they left something behind. What the *hell* is that?"

CHAPTER THIRTY TWO

Dudley grinned from ear to ear, a smile so wide it threatened to split open the corners of his mouth, turning him into an evil clown.

"Aye, aye," he cackled. "The gang is all here. Time to die, I tink."

His brother, Malachi, stood staunch as ever by his side. "You'd better ring yer Pythian mates first, Callan. Them boys gonna make us richer than the Queen of England."

Dudley nodded knowingly. "Aye they are," he said, taking out a slimline smartphone and pressing a speed dial preset. All seven members of the 27-Club stood around a window on the fourth floor of an apartment building half a mile away from Hsinchu Harbor, powerful binoculars either set to their eyes or resting at their chests. The Pythians' plan had always seemed masterful; now it was also proving inspired.

Dudley waited for the call to connect, imagining what he could do to the SPEAR team right at that very moment, then wishing he could watch the devastating real-time effects. His eyes flicked momentarily to the wireless device that sat on the otherwise bare, rickety table behind them.

An explosive daisy chain? Fuuuuuuuck! The thought made him want to dance for joy. Even more, it made him want to act on impulse.

Luckily, the call was answered on the next ring. "Yes?"

"I have me finger on the trigger. Are we a go?"

Tyler Webb's sharp intake of breath said not. "Wait, just wait. The Chinese agreed to the Peking Man ransom only an hour ago. I have men en route now to acquire the Z-boxes from them."

"Men?" Dudley repeated, looking around. "But we're all here."

"I do have other men," Webb said caustically. "I'm sure you understand that your methods, whilst they do bring me great joy, have their time and place. A twitchy, strained meeting between the Chinese Politburo's closest guard and the Pythians' armed representatives is not that place."

Dudley cackled. "We'd just blow 'em to hell and take the feckin' boxes."

"Quite. The good news though is *very* good news. The Peking Man has effectively *purchased* our Z-boxes. The Chinese have a healthy interest in Mu, but it's an interest trumped by their higher aspirations. I have to say it is as we all thought."

"Taiwan knows too?"

"They do now. But too late," Webb said with a smile in his voice. "And they won't be able to deny that they knew about Mu. Wait . . ." Webb sounded like he was taking another call.

Dudley stared impatiently at the handset, wondering if he should just throw it out the window and get down to using the wireless device. Then Malachi, reading his brother's mind, put a reassuring hand on his shoulder.

"Remember, brother. Our plan. Make sure them boxes are comin' here."

Dudley nodded, memory jogged. "The Z-boxes," he said

into the dormant speaker. "When will they be here?"

"Good news," Webb came back on the line, "my men have successfully exchanged the Z-boxes and are on their way to you now. Please get them here as soon as possible. And Mr. Dudley . . . ?"

"Aye?"

"You can detonate that device now."

CHAPTER THIRTY THREE

Drake swam over to Kearns, perturbed at the Seal team leader's obvious horror. The man appeared to be quite simply dumbstruck, not an emotion normally associated with any Special Forces soldier. Kicking his flippered feet he closed the gap in seconds, twisting his body to glide in.

"What ya got, mate?"

"Explosive device," Kearns said after a moment. "And it looks like it's been daisy chained."

Drake felt his blood run hotter. *"What?"*

Through the comms shouts of disbelief went up.

Kearns swam as close as he dared, Drake at his side. Together they peered at the small, black circular object, noting the blinking red light on its cover.

"The positioning." Kearns indicated the nearby underwater structures, mostly buried beneath the sea's accumulated sediment. He flicked his body sideways, following his own circuit and soon unearthed another device, its light also blinking. "The mad, crazy bastards have mined this entire area to explode and it'll take your lost kingdom with it."

Drake stared into the dark depths of the ocean. "I don't see how they can detonate. That thing's wireless and wireless signals don't work down here."

Kearns held up a hand. "You clearly haven't been keeping yourself up to date. Whilst it's true that radio waves carry the wireless signals and are sluggish in water, cutting edge research has developed a prototype that relies mostly on sound waves. A large underwater modem emits chirps that can carry almost a mile. That means—"

"All they need is a boat up top," Drake cut him off abruptly. "Oh crap, are those lights flashing faster?"

"Move! The good news is that those underwater modems are slower than the old dial-up systems. We have a few seconds."

"Seconds!"

Drake kicked out, angling his body away from the chain of devices. Was this what the Pythians wanted? To blow up the ancient civilization that they had just found? Had the Chinese refused their offer?

What was going on?

Alicia's black shape darted past, sleek as a seal. Dahl was already scissor-kicking upwards, bubbles streaking all around him. The Seal team ascended in their wake, but then Kearns drew them up short.

"Slow down, people. Ain't no quick escape here unless you want the decompression to kill you. Move sideways as fast as you can to escape the blast radius."

Drake quelled a surge of horror. Depending on the number of devices—and judging by the first two's distance apart they were going to add up to a *shitload*—it was unlikely that they would escape the blast radius.

"*Move!*" Kearns cried, already swimming for his life.

Hibiki took a phone call, the number revealing it was his contact within the Chinese Politburo. Heart thumping, he assumed this must be regarding the outcome of the special emergency meeting in Beijing.

"Guys," he said. "Sorry, I have to take this."

Only Yorgi acknowledged his words. Mai and Grace were nestled together in an intense heart to heart—which to Hibiki's light relief was now actually producing one or two genuine smiles—and Chika was perched on the edge of a tractor tire, staring out to sea.

A sharp voice came through the handset. "Hello?"

"Yes, I'm here. Sorry." Hibiki heard a sound like rolling thunder behind him and frowned at the skies. The clouds were white and the heavens were blue, not stormy and gray.

"You must act quickly or we're all doomed. My government . . . I am shocked by the arrogant greed of my government."

"What is it? What have they done?"

"Placed themselves before our history. Put avarice and desire before our citizens. Government is but a ravenous glutton, consuming the energies of its greatest natural resource—its public, its society. We are doomed."

"I don't understand." Hibiki almost ducked as thunder cracked again in the bright blue skies.

Mai glanced straight up from her tête-a-tête with Grace. "Oh no."

"Dai, listen closely to me. We don't have much time and but a small chance. The inner circle have decided they want Mu destroyed so that they finally have a clear-cut reason to go to war with Taiwan. It's happening now. They've wanted this for years and its finally happening." The man sounded like he wanted to cry.

"War? *War?* Why?"

"Check your history later, but for now use every resource you have to try to delay it. *Every resource!* If China attack Taiwan, imagine what the US will do in retaliation and then . . ."

Hibiki didn't need it explaining. The thunder cracked once more above his head and finally he saw its source—fighter planes bearing the flag of Taiwan. They were streaking toward the Taiwan Strait.

"Don't freak out on me, Dai. One more thing quickly—they also ransomed a historical item today. The Peking Man for something called a Z-box. I don't know what that is but you can bet your life it's hugely important."

Hibiki nodded to himself and ended the call. An upwelling of pure disbelief almost overwhelmed him. Was the world always so close to war?

Ridiculous question. He already knew the first thing he had to do—contact Hayden Jaye.

Mai finally saw the terror in his eyes and rose to confront him. "What is it?"

Hibiki shook his head and then turned his eyes toward the sea. "Mu is about to be destroyed by the Chinese or someone else. Drake's down there now. And China are starting a war with Taiwan. Business as usual in your world, I guess."

"It used to be," Mai said with a blank stare. "I'm not so sure anymore. I think I should talk to that girl, the one that survived the Yakuza attack. Emiko, her name was."

Hibiki stared at her, shocked to hear her talking this way after all that he had just said. "I forgot to tell you amidst all the latest craziness," he said. "Emiko walked out on her police protection, slipped away. She's gone, Mai."

The Japanese woman's gaze was far away. "Yes, I really think I need to talk to her."

Hibiki walked to the edge of the docks and studied the rolling waters. Yorgi came up beside him. "Is there problem?"

"I'm just praying for their safety, my friend. Their safety and my sanity."

Drake was reaching for the surface when the blast occurred. The percussive force was like nothing he had ever felt, pushing him through the thick water like a giant, unfriendly hand. Suddenly out of control, the shock wave hit him and sent his body barreling forward, arms and legs flailing to both sides. He was vaguely aware of other human shapes thrashing beside him, caught in a tide of madness. Decompression was no longer an issue as they shot toward the surface. Kearns had made them pause frequently even though the clock was ticking. Drake just hoped it had been enough. A pool of white light appeared above, diffused and rippling, and then he was breaking the surface as walls of white water exploded all around him.

The sea burst skyward, rising in plumes of white, forming a ring of destruction around the lost land that had existed beneath. Drake slapped down hard as saltwater swelled and heaved all around him, the sound of the detonation echoing from far shore to far shore. Ramparts of seawater rose up, mighty, stunning in their furious beauty. Quickly, glad only that he still retained his faculties, he dived again, not wanting to be caught underneath a great deluge as the water crashed back down. Again, black slippery shapes clawed at the water all around but the uncontainable chaos made it impossible to stick together.

He breathed deeply, grateful now that the rebreather still worked and that his air still functioned. At last there was a mighty smash from above as displaced gallons came back down. Drake twisted and remained buoyant, holding his position. His immediate worry was for his friends.

To his left, just visible, he saw Dahl, hanging in the water. The Swede was fine, just drifting motionless whilst waiting to ascend. Kearns wove his body quickly around all three of his men to determine their condition.

And then Drake saw Alicia.

Drifting down, head down, the Englishwoman was not moving voluntarily. He flipped over as fast as he could, catching her under the arms and lifting her head up.

"Are you okay?" he shouted. "Alicia! Are you okay?"

No response.

He tried harder. The Englishwoman's eyes were closed. Dahl came over, followed by Kearns.

"She went up higher than all of us." He motioned up top. "Let's go."

As a team they scissor-kicked their way to the still-seething surface, breaking free of the water and bobbing with the waves. Kearns ripped his mask off and unhooked Alicia's. Drake steadied her position.

"Well, she's still breathing," Kearns said. "Let her sleep it off. Can anyone spot the friggin' boat?"

"I know one thing that'll wake her up." Drake positioned her so that her arms looped over his shoulders. "Slap her ass. Always used to work back in the day."

Dahl's face blanched. "I really don't feel like risking that."

"And a bloody good job you didn't, Torsty," Alicia murmured as her eyes flickered open. "And you, Drake. My peachy bum is reserved for Frenchmen only at the moment."

Drake nodded at all the bobbing heads. "Not *frog*men."

"No. *French*men."

"All right then."

The Seals took some time to locate their boat as Drake turned his mind once more to their new predicament. "Ey up," he said as jets flew over. "That can't be good. And speaking of not good—does anyone wanna guess at what just happened down there?"

"Somebody blew up Mu," Alicia said matter-of-factly.

"I know that, but *why?*"

"Speaking of blowing up." Dahl removed a watertight case from his suit and then a cellphone. "Our friend Kearns spoke of a wireless signal transmitted underwater. One thing about wireless signals—they can be tracked."

Kearns finally located their Zodiac using his own tracker and informed the group they were in for a swim. Dahl finished his call to Karin and zipped his cell back up. Together, they set out strong, taking about twenty minutes to reach the upturned Zodiac. Five minutes of clever maneuvering later and they were on their way again, streaking back toward Hsinchu Harbor, its outline becoming more distinct by the second.

Drake called Hibiki. Dahl spoke to Karin. By the time they reached the dock they were all apprised of the new situation and its connotations. The SPEAR team stripped out of their suits and thanked the Seals for their efforts.

All the while Dahl spoke to Karin.

Finally, he hung up. "The wireless signal bounced off a transmitter on the seabed up to a boat—we think—on the surface and then overland to an apartment block—" he shaded his eyes, scanning the bay. "Right . . . there."

Drake followed his hand, saw the gray building standing tall a few miles distant. "Wait. You're saying the people who blew up the Lost Kingdom and are trying to start a war are in that building? Now?"

"I am. Top floor. End apartment."

"Then what the hell are we waiting for?"

CHAPTER THIRTY FOUR

Drake led the assault against the apartment block, Dahl, Alicia and Hibiki at his back. Mai was left as a guard for the others, not that the Seal team wouldn't have done that, but Drake and Dahl, and even Hibiki, were beginning to lose a little trust in her judgment. The team figured they'd lost about an hour since the explosion and hope was waning that the perpetrators would still be on site. The other downside was that the Taiwanese authorities had started arriving in their separate groups, though most of their attention was currently devoted to the site of the explosion.

Drake opened the door and entered the stairwell before drawing a weapon. The recriminations would be high if his US-based team were caught raiding a Hsinchu apartment block. The risers were steep, echoing concrete, pockmarked with age and littered with various forms of debris. Windows stood open at every level, cracked to allow at least some breeze to offset the tropical heat.

Karin had pinpointed the signal, using a US satellite, to an apartment on the top floor at the very end of the block. Only one room faced the sea. Drake approached it now, becoming more attentive with every step. The assumption had to be that the room was hostile.

"Ready?"

Three affirmations came back. Drake paused momentarily to the side of the door.

"Ain't gonna smash itself in, Drakey," Alicia whispered.

"You're right," Drake said. He'd been thinking about trying to gain entry more quietly but realized that just wasn't his way. "Fuck it."

With a boot aimed at the lock he leapt forward. The door crashed in, bursting off its hinges. Drake entered first, gun high, flanked by Dahl and Alicia. A bare room greeted them, its only occupants a flimsy looking table and seven surprised men ranged along the far wall.

"The feck do you want?"

Drake slowed in surprise, recognizing Dudley immediately and then grasping the significance of their confrontation. This was the entire 27-Club then, caught red-handed. It was about time their luck turned for the better.

"Down on your knees," he said. "Hands behind your head. Do it, now."

Dudley set eyes on Alicia. "I don't feckin' believe it. That's the bitch, boys. Right there. The bitch that bested me."

"*You* don't believe it?" Alicia repeated softly. "I never imagined I'd get to meet the seven fucking dwarves. Grumpy, Sleepy, Dopey, Twathead . . ."

"Down!" Drake snarled at them.

"Shut yer feckin' face, soldier boy. Me and me brother, Malachi, here, we been talking 'bout this moment ever since we got the club back together. Hey, pretty. How ya doin'?"

Dahl waved his rifle. "I'm good, thanks. Now get down."

"Seven against four. Yer sure yer don't wanna back outta that door?"

Alicia snorted. "You may be a bloody goofball, Dudley, but even you can't believe you're gonna get out of this in one piece."

Dudley made a wistful face and then looked once across the line, catching the gaze of all his men. "Been a pleasure, boys."

All hell broke loose. The Irishmen attacked with only their bare hands, five of them springing fast whilst Dudley and Malachi held back. Drake opened fire, felling the quickest. Dahl did the same. Alicia toppled another. Then the Irishmen were among them, pushing at their weapons and forcing them back. Hibiki sidestepped the melee, felling a third attacker with a shot to the ribs. Those who had fallen were only wounded and though tight-faced in their agony, continued to fight hard, using their legs as weapons. Drake found himself on his knees, having to punch a bleeding man in the face and then render him unconscious as he refused to go down. Dahl was pulled backward by a seated man, spun and smashed a hard elbow into his ear but that man seemed barely to feel it, the only sign of his pain the sudden tightening of his lips. The Swede was forced to bend down and smash his head into the floor. Alicia kicked and punched at another, sent reeling by a hard blow to the thigh even as her opponent bled out.

"Tough fucker," she said, forced to accelerate his passing.

Only two of the initial five now remained, and they were both scrappers, punching and kicking and forcing their opponents into disarray. Drake's gun was on the floor, along with Alicia's. Dahl tried to wade through arms and legs. Only Hibiki was free and his gun was trained toward the only window.

Dudley screamed at the top of his voice. "Yer killin' me

brothers. There's no feckin' place on earth you'll be safe from me now!"

Then he was gone, closely followed by his brother and two others, choosing to save his vengeance for another day it seemed. Hibiki's shot smashed only the frame. Drake untangled himself from one of the downed Irishmen, then fell headlong as the guy clung on, visibly refusing to die. Landing hard and twisting he found himself staring down the barrel of his own gun.

The Irishman sniggered. "Tell Satan Darragh Brannan says hi."

This time Hibiki's shot found its target, killing Brannan before he could pull Drake's trigger. The Yorkshireman took a second to evaluate the scene.

"Are they all dead? That was like wading through glue. With limbs."

Dahl staggered to the window. "Dudley, Malachi and two others escaped. Why do you think they were still here? Waiting for someone?"

"Aye, probably," Drake said. "We knew Dudley was over in Asia but *here?* Detonating the bomb? What else has the bastard been up to?"

"Scheming for the Pythians," Hibiki said. "My contact with the Chinese said that they'd ransomed something called a Z-box, probably in exchange for destroying Mu and regaining the Peking Man fossil. Didn't you say Dudley was the Pythians' Lord of War, or something? I bet he's been awaiting delivery of the Z-boxes."

"They're sure using him for their dirty work," Alicia said, having triple-checked that the downed Irishmen were out of action.

"What's a Z-box?" Drake asked. "First I've heard of them."

"We don't know," Hibiki said. "But whatever they are, they're worth starting a war, destroying a lost kingdom and losing an ancient fossil for, at least to the Pythians."

"Not good," Dahl mouthed the understatement of the year, at least in Drake's opinion. "And then we have Dudley and his men sacrificing themselves so stupidly."

"Guy's gonna be pissed." Drake joined him at the window. "As if we didn't have enough crazies to worry about. C'mon guys, it's time to regroup and rethink."

"And get the hell out of Taiwan," Dahl eyed the skies, "back to Hong Kong."

"We should liaise with Hayden on the way," Drake said. "This thing's spiraling out of control and if we don't get a grip on it . . ."

He didn't need to finish; the crashing waves of rolling thunder accompanying a flight of jets overhead spoke for him.

CHAPTER THIRTY FIVE

Placing a round-the-clock watch on Lauren Fox, Dahl's family and their own homes was one of the hardest things Hayden had ever had to do. A simple physical matter of placing a call—it was far more than that psychologically. It was an admission that one of the most effective teams on the planet weren't entirely safe in their own homes, that the old Blood Vendetta had been relatively ineffective compared to a megalomaniac and his nasty little hobby. It was—almost—admitting failure.

Soon though, the events of the day put Tyler Webb's personal intrigues on the backburner. Key events were occurring in the world at large. China had released a tentative but enthusiastic communiqué about the discovery of a lost civilization and that they were close to verifying the find. Their defenses had been ramped up, jets patrolling the land and sea borders. In response, as ever, Taiwan had scrambled their own jets and the US had made rumblings about the preparedness of its nearby carrier fleet. *Chain shaking,* she thought. *Dick measuring.* Her country did it well but the Taiwan issue was always going to be a loaded one. Since 2008 relations *had* considerably improved but the Chinese, disinclined to make any proposals that might appeal to democratic Taiwan, had been left with only two options. Give up on the twenty-three-million-strong country or take it by force.

According to Beijing, the cost of losing credibility ruled

out the former option, especially in light of the ever-growing power imbalance in the Taiwan Strait, and key members of the PLA believed that Taiwan had no fight in them. Hayden knew China had never actually ruled out the possibility of force, even when relations improved between the two countries. The problem was, given China's declared defense budget at more than a 12:1 ratio over Taiwan's, the outcome was never in real doubt. That left America, Taiwan's principal security partner, with much more than a headache. Of course an attack or even an invasion would not be a simple matter—Taiwan employed F-16s, attack choppers and destroyers in their armory, not to mention the anti-ship, supersonic cruise missile system, Hsiung Feng III—and American warships would only escalate the problem.

The trouble was, these days China was always willing to up the ante. The US had already forewarned its fleet and even such minor transmissions were seen as acts of provocation.

Kinimaka entered her eye line, breaking into her thoughts. "Guards have all been assigned. We're going high-profile to warn these people off, rather than low-key and risk missing something. Sound okay?"

"Yeah." Hayden was distracted, ruminating over China and the latest developments. "Mano, we have a far, far bigger problem."

The Hawaiian stopped so suddenly his shoes squeaked across the floor. "We do? What?"

"The Taiwan Strait just went up in a water bomb. China have wasted no time blaming it on Taiwan, attributing their earlier overflies to sighting flights and provocation. They're calling the explosion an act of war."

Kinimaka's mouth fell open. "And the Lost Kingdom?"

"Nobody knows. But take a look at this . . ." Hayden spun her laptop around and pressed a button, playing a recording of the Taiwan Strait event for him. As he watched she continued, "You can bet your ass the Lost Kingdom's a helluva mess. Once the dust has settled who knows? But the consequences of that explosion . . ." Hayden shook her head.

"What do we know?"

"Dudley pressed the button. Almost certainly he's working with the Pythians who ransomed the Peking Man to China earlier. In addition, the Chinese gave them three items called Z-boxes. We're still working to discover what they are, but the rumors are frankly terrifying. Our current situation is this—Drake and the team are in Hong Kong awaiting instructions."

Kinimaka waited for more, then said, "That's *it?*"

"We don't know Dudley's location. The Yakuza are still hunting for Mai and Chika with a vengeance. What do you want SPEAR to do? Take control of Beijing?"

"I bet they could do it."

"I don't doubt it." Hayden rubbed her tired eyes.

"Hey," Kinimaka walked forward and held her. "Let's focus. The war problem is out of our control. Stick with Dudley. These Z-boxes that he probably has. Let's work that."

Smyth entered the room then, fresh from his visit to the hospital. "Damn, you two just hack me off. Ya can't stand around hugging all friggin' day. We got work to do."

Hayden pulled away from Kinimaka. "Would you like to punch him first, or shall I?"

CHAPTER THIRTY SIX

Tyler Webb smashed a closed fist against the top of his desk, exultant as he heard the news. The feeling he experienced bordered on sexual, so arousing it almost settled on a par with the feelings he got whilst stalking other people's homes and rifling through their personal lives, but then he remembered who was on the end of the line.

"Dudley," he breathed a little lower than he really wanted to. "Good job, my fine Irish friend. Good job. You're actually holding all three Z-boxes now?"

"Yer men just delivered them to me. We're all standing around in a nice little circle."

Webb luxuriated in the feeling of accomplishment. From the plan's earliest gestation he had been unconvinced—such a convoluted idea with so many possible places for it to go wrong. Finding the fossil, translating the tablets, locating Mu and so on. But it had worked! Maybe its pure diversity gave it the legs to succeed. An interesting lesson and one he would take to his heart and soul when forming his future plans. Well done Bay-Dale, the smarmy, arrogant old bastard.

Job done, Webb thought. *What's next?*

Dudley waited patiently and Webb simply let him. His mind flicked over the various scenarios that had already been offered up—Le Brun's galleons or "ghost ships" sounded positively delicious, real dead-of-night, roaring campfire kind of storytelling stuff, God rest her foul, malevolent soul, whilst his own Tesla suggestion, and in particular a project one of the new guys—Julian Marsh—had come up with were all vying for first place on the new agenda.

"Are yer still there?" Dudley's voice broke in.

"Yes, yes." Webb sighed and looked up, greeted by a window full of blackness. It was almost midnight in DC, not that the passing ant-life below seemed to notice. "Bring the boxes home, Dudley. Bring them here to DC."

A pause and then: "Are yer feckin' kiddin' me?"

Webb started, snapped back to reality. *What did this toady just say to me?* "Is there a problem?"

"Of course there's a feckin' problem! This Drake twat and his team killed three of my boys. *Three!*" His thick brogue pronounced it as *tree!* "Did y'not hear me? We be the 27-Club for fifteen bloody years, man."

"Okay." Webb couldn't care less about Dudley's life—past, present or future. "We'll deal with Drake later. I hear the Yakuza are now chasing him down as well as Ramses. That team—their future is dismal at best."

And I have my own personal interest in seeing them live at least a little longer...

"Feck that." Dudley assaulted his ears, shocking him still further. "We're gonna kill that fecker and we're doin' it in Hong Kong."

Webb took a deep breath, counting to ten and thinking that his other team—the team that had initially taken delivery of the Z-boxes from the Chinese—were standing alongside the Irishman and his three colleagues. *Perhaps...*

"Bring me the Z-boxes. They're more important than you

can ever imagine. Even your life pales beneath their importance. Bring them to me and we'll talk about Drake et al."

"Me life?" Dudley repeated. "Me life? All I know is how t'kill and maim and torture. Drake's gonna learn that. Him and his mongrel crew. You, boy, you can have yer feckin' boxes and feck ya."

The line went dead. Webb sat holding the receiver in his hand for almost a minute, trying to remember the last time anyone had spoken to him in such a way. It was so unusual it felt almost refreshing. Standing up, he knew that he couldn't trust the Irishman and placed another call, this one to the leader of the other team.

The Z-boxes were of vital importance now, more so than any other thing. If Webb owned those, he owned more of the US military than the recently deceased General Stone could ever have given him.

There was an eye-opening, quite improbable but true story about how America had sent most of its nuclear weapons to Georgia at some time during the cold war. At that time, if Georgia had seceded from the United States it would instantly have become the third largest nuclear power in the world.

Funny story, Webb thought. *What then if I personally held the key to all of them? What would I become?*

CHAPTER THIRTY SEVEN

Late afternoon in Taiwan and Callan Dudley had murder on his mind. The last thirty minutes had equipped him with an absolute wealth of information, everything this pathetic second Pythian team knew and how much King feckin' Pythian had kept secret from him.

Blood pooled everywhere, its metallic aroma a healing salve to his distraught senses. From detonating the chain bomb to losing three members of the 27-Club in just a few minutes; to fleeing the battle; to meeting the Z-box team and understanding they were more trusted than he; to taking their legs and their arms in a matter of seconds and leaving them curled in absolute agony; his day had been grueling to say the least. Extracting information from the men had taken the edge off, allowed him to relax. Malachi kept him from tipping too far over the edge, reminding him that despite all their failings the Pythians were still extremely powerful and shouldn't be left feeling too pissed off at the end of all this.

So they left one of their men intact and gave him two Z-boxes. Sent him on his way.

Dudley's plan developed as the hours went on. He learned about the Yakuza, about Drake and his entire team, about Alicia Myles in particular. He learned all about the things that the Z-box could do—terrifying, apocalyptic things.

At one point he turned to Malachi. "Brother, tell me. Do we still have them bombs left?"

"Aye, we do. In the back of the car. And we now have access to a smuggler's boat. Where do you want to go?"

"How much did that cost us?"

"Ah, the pilot don't mind. Not where he is."

Dudley grinned. The other remaining members of the club—McLain and Byram—had been absent, securing the boat, for over two hours. "This Z-box thing," he nodded toward the packaged object. "Could be worth millions. Hundreds of millions to the right people, I guess."

"Worth more than avenging our boys' murders?"

"Nah. Course not. But we could cause a lot more damage with that sorta money now, couldn't we?"

Malachi thought about it for a minute, mind straining, then said, "Feck it. Let's just kill Drake."

"Knew you'd say that." Dudley's grin was wide.

"Yer thinking to use the Z-box in some way?"

"That I am. Drake's in Hong Kong. He wants us. We want him. The Yakuza want his bird, Kitano. I say a three-way meet."

Malachi blinked, apparently shocked. "Yer talkin' a three-way pitched battle in the streets, boy. Say what ya will, his team's no pushover. And the Yakuza?"

Dudley watched his brother shaking his head. "Yer wimping out?"

"Nah. Was just thinking how much fun it's gonna be when we dance a jig on their still-beating hearts."

Dudley kicked a man hard in the ribs. "All right, we know from this fecker that the Jap cop's some kinda liaison. They have his details from the Chinese. I say we contact him . . . arrange a meet, an exchange, and invite the wee gangsters to the party."

"Party?"

"Tomorrow night in Hong Kong, the Pythians have organized some kinda high-society get together. The posh knobs think they're donating to charity, really they're funding terrorism. Same old, same old. We arrange a Z-box handover to Drake there, he's more likely to believe it's legit."

"Ach, yer on top form t'day, Callan."

"Must be the stench of blood in the air." Dudley cackled. "The sound of them bones breaking."

"Problem," Malachi said. "When yer start talking they'll know it's you."

"Why? I sound feckin' Irish or something?"

"A little."

"So we get one of these feckers to do it." Dudley kicked out again. "Let 'em live or let 'em die quick. Whichever."

"And how do we contact the Yakuza?"

"They have a head office in Japan."

Malachi stared. "Feck off. Yer shitting me."

"Nope. It's there all right."

Leaving his brother aghast, Dudley walked over to the Z-box. It was safe to say they had severed links with the Pythians now, but the fact that he'd still let them have two boxes should ease the blow. Using this last box to avenge both the deaths of his friends and past insults felt more than fitting, it felt justified.

He turned around. "Let's get one of these feckers as close to normal as we can. The bleedin' phone calls ain't gonna make themselves."

Malachi looked down at the bloody mess. "I ain't stickin' no one's teeth back in."

Dudley grunted. "Me either. Maybe we could hire a tramp or something?"

"Aye. I like the sound of that."

"Then follow me brother. This is gonna be one hell of a lot of fightin' fun."

CHAPTER THIRTY EIGHT

When Drake saw Hibiki take the call he didn't immediately understand its magnitude but, as the Japanese cop talked and his voice grew unaccountably hoarse and hushed, the Yorkshireman knew something was afoot. Locking eyes with both Alicia and Dahl he drifted over.

"I understand," Hibiki was saying. "Tomorrow night, yes, but why all of us? Wouldn't a smaller unit be less conspicuous?"

The answer made him grimace. "Yes, I understand. How will we gain entry?"

Yorgi joined them, looking pensive. "Is this problem?"

"Nothing good happens after 1 a.m.," Drake said. "You should know that, Yorgi."

The Russian frowned. "But it is afternoon."

"Not in Yorkshire it ain't, and that's where my time clock's based."

Dahl groaned. "You're as nutty as a bag of pistachios."

"Oh, am I? Not as cracked as a piece of Swedish shelving?"

Hibiki ended his call then, quite abruptly, and stood staring at his cellphone as if it might be about to sprout legs.

"Problem, mate?" Drake asked.

"That has to be one of the oddest calls I've ever taken," Hibiki said. "But wait, I don't want to go through it all twice, and neither will you. Let's get Hayden and co on the line."

Dahl checked his watch. "Is it worth waking her in the middle of the night?"

"It's bigger than the Taiwan Strait exploding."

Drake waited whilst Dahl contacted Hayden and then managed to loop everyone else into the conference call. Alicia fidgeted and gave Hibiki the eye, mentioning that there was a time and a place for teasing and it better be worth her while. Drake was pleased to see Mai take an interest and with her came an increasingly assured Grace and a healing Chika. Maybe they could salvage something out of this crude rescue after all. *A return to normality?* That alone would be worth all the effort.

At last the call was ready. Hibiki spoke up. "I just received a call from a man, a Taiwanese man, who told me he'd managed to steal one of the Z-boxes from Callan Dudley and wants to give it to us."

Now Drake understood why Hibiki wanted everyone involved. "Bollocks," he said. "Stealing anything from Dudley would be beyond tough, but then giving it away for free?"

"Guy said he's loyal to the US, to SPEAR and to the Ninth Division. A friend, he said."

Drake pulled a face and glanced across at Alicia, his old compatriot in that secret unit. "How's he know about the Ninth? Did he give a name?"

"No names. He said he used to do business with Crouch. Mentioned the Pythians, the Lost Kingdom. Seemed pretty switched on."

"Plenty of people know Michael," Drake said. "What else did he say?"

"That the other two Z-boxes were on their way to the Pythians." Hibiki shrugged as if that information helped prove the man's good intent. "And that we should dread what they might do with them. That the Chinese had agreed to the destruction of Mu for the perfect excuse to invade Taiwan—"

"Invade?" Mai repeated. "You gotta be kidding me."

Hayden spoke up then. "The Politburo have long since known that despite their recent startling advances, an occupation of Taiwan would not be feasible without putting boots on the ground. Failing that, it all might go pear-shaped and become a humiliation."

Hibiki tried to continue. "This man also said he would only exchange the box if the entire team were present, stating that he may want something from any of you in the future and that he wants you to be able to recognize him on sight. But it's for *your* eyes only and no pictures, no covert surveillance, that's why he wants the meet to be at a stylish, swish party tomorrow night in HK. That, and safety from Dudley. You'll all need to be dressed for the part and be able to pass through reasonable security."

Hayden jumped in as he took a breath. "When you say the SPEAR team? Do you mean *all* of us?"

"I'm not sure," Hibiki admitted. "Can you make it?"

Hayden paused as the entire team did the calculation. "It gives us about twenty nine hours to get to you and make ready. Yeah, we can do that."

"Then I would say get started."

"Can we pause for a second?" Mai said. "And address the issue of these so-called Z-boxes. I mean—we know the

Chinese developed them and then just gave them away. Why are they so important?"

"The Pythians want them," Dahl said. "So they're not waffle makers."

"Actually," Hayden said. "I was waiting until morning to tell you guys, but we recently got the low down on the Z-boxes from our contacts inside the Politburo. A ten-year deep cover asset had to blow his ID and then be *pulled out* to attain this info so you can bet your sweet asses it's of the highest importance, presidential level. The Z-box is basically a hacking tool. A complex, intelligent machine that cracks codes." She paused. "Almost any code."

"You're talking US military access," Dahl said. "Monetary and energy grids. That kind of stuff."

"I'm not just talking US or military, but *anywhere* and everything. Every essential service's infrastructure. Schools. Government. Entertainment."

"How would they do that?" Smyth wondered.

Karin answered that one. "All common individual systems, whether they be offense oriented, defense oriented, hell, even used for gas and electric distribution, run off the same sort of structural design, much the same as one corporation's personnel records run on systems pretty similar to another's. They're all based on the same designs. Access one, you can access another and another. Once you have their source code it's relatively easy to find vulnerabilities in the whole system. For malware writers as much as terrorists and serious hackers such vulnerabilities are the Holy Grail, an unlocked window for these sneak-burglars to get into. Alternatively they could alter the code for their own means or leave a backdoor for later. Sell the backdoor's password to someone else. This box does all that and more, and it doesn't need a super-geek to operate it. It provides access."

Hayden took over without missing a beat. "The US has accused China of conducting a cyberwar and cyber espionage against its interests for many years. Congress called them 'the single greatest risk to the security of American technologies'." She sighed tiredly. "And here we are."

Mai coughed loudly. "So, to recap, the Chinese developed a code box and everyone wants it."

"They're all at it," Komodo said with a disbelieving grunt. "NSA. British Intelligence. The Mossad. You name it. China just got here first."

"And since they gave it away so easily they probably already have a superior design."

Komodo laughed. "Well you know what they say about your PlayStation and laptops. By the time you buy the latest one it's already out of date."

"What I'm thinking," Hayden said. "Is that if we gained possession of a device we'd be able to better understand how they work. Maybe even crack *their* code, make them obsolete. I'm pretty sure the Secretary will have the same idea. I'll call him now but do expect to be on the next Gulfstream out. ETA fourteen hours or so."

"We'll start gearing up." Drake said. "Working the op. Build it on a 'don't trust the source' basis and take it from there. At the very least Dudley will be trying to get the box back. We don't want any surprises."

Smyth's sarcastic grunt filtered down the wires. "That'd be a friggin' first."

Drake admitted he had a point. "All right, smart ass. Fewer surprises than normal. How's that?"

"Still clutching."

"And bring your stylist, Smyth," Alicia cracked. "This party—it sounds posh. You for one are gonna take an awful lot of tittifying up."

"What the hell does that mean? Is that rude?"

Drake was laughing. "Bloody hell, Alicia, you're one to talk." Even Mai had to hide a smirk.

Alicia swept up on to her feet, a swan in perfect flight. "Vogue's my middle name, didn't ya know? I'm the chic chick. A glamour puss with a large helping of added 'Y'. The swank that makes you—"

"We get it," Dahl said. "You think you can pull it off and maybe you can." He surveyed the group critically. "My guess—Drake's the problem."

"Balls. The last time I looked the height of Swedish fashion was Abba's Agnetha. What have you had since then? Boris Becker?"

"He was German, you damn, ignorant Yorkshire tw—"

"Well, there you go. Even Saab went bust."

"Guys," Hayden interrupted. "Guys. Just start making ready. We're on our way. Hopefully this will be a ten-minute cakewalk. But failing that—"

"*Big Trouble in Little China* gets a sequel," Drake stated. "But bigger. Much bigger."

"Be ready for anything."

"Always am, Hayden. Always am. Already I see a plan B forming . . ."

CHAPTER THIRTY NINE

Drake spent the fourteen hours before Hayden and the others arrived casing the luxurious hotel in question, which stood at the edge of Victoria Harbor, overlooking the bay and nearby Kowloon, resplendent by day and sparkling at night. The party would be held on the top floor, naturally off limits to all but the insolently rich. With that in mind Alicia led a shopping trip to the Pacific Place Mall, spending hours and countless HK dollars to guarantee the team were properly outfitted. At first, Drake wondered about the odd change in her—Alicia Myles didn't really care if she was dressed in denim or lace, leather or silk, or *anything* for that matter—but then he caught up. This was different, it was engaging, poles apart from her self-imposed normality, thus—it appealed. For now.

For today.

He returned from his surveillance with Dahl to find the spacious warehouse abuzz with activity. Yorgi in particular sat with his chin resting on the floor, amazed, and Drake personally didn't blame him. Alicia, Mai and even Chika—though she and Grace weren't going to be involved in the operation—stood around in various stages of undress, trying on different variations of clothes and colors.

Dahl stopped in his tracks. "So this is a little inappropriate. Should we wait outside?"

"Are you kidding? This is my dream."

Drake headed inside, whistling tunefully. Mai turned

toward him, dressed in a floor-length, split-to-the-thigh, midnight-colored gown. With her hair pinned up and styled she took his breath away, this softer version of her one he rarely saw. Her slight smile tugged at his chest and he remembered again why he'd loved her all these years.

Not only for the vision she presented but for the strong-hearted, headstrong, perfectly capable woman within. For the insecurities she could not hide. For the way she held a blade. For the way she kissed him, heart and soul. For the woman that she was.

Then Chika spun her away and the moment broke, a fragile thread trying to tether their stormy emotions. Now Alicia moved into his eye line.

Again, he gawped.

Draped in a knee-length dress, golden and glittering, Alicia's blonde hair hung free. *A wolf in sheep's clothing if ever I've seen one.*

Dahl grunted at his shoulder. "This just makes me worry about what they bought for us."

"Really? That's your only thought?"

"Well, I'm also wondering how Smyth will react when he sees the girls. He's not the subtlest of characters."

Drake shook his head and approached Yorgi. "So what they got you wearing? Burberry? I hope it's off the bloody shelf."

"It is and so is yours, my friend. Over there."

At that moment, Alicia came up and linked his arm, gliding him across the dusty floor toward a pile of bags. The touch of her skin sent a spark through his body. Life was becoming more confusing by the minute.

"Yours was the most obvious choice of all," she said and held up the plain two-button, double-vented, black jacket. "The two-button styling ensures that whilst the suit remains sharp enough to charm the knickers of an unsuspecting air stewardess, it still offers enough movement to scale the walls of a military compound. Can you say: 'Drake. Matt Drake'?"

He started to laugh, unable to help himself. Alicia was like a breath of air on a sunny day. "I can," he said. "But I like the way you say it better."

By the time Hayden arrived, the team had rested and were counting down the last ten hours. Sans reunion they briefed each other on the latest developments and then the newcomers were dispatched to the Pacific Place Mall. As the hour neared the full SPEAR team took a moment to stand back and look at themselves, all expensively attired for the first time together, looking sharp and feeling awkward.

"If the purpose of this is to make me unnerved," Kinimaka said, tugging at the point where the knot of his tie met the top button of his shirt. "It's working. If it was to render us weaponless. That's working too. Can't we get anything past security?"

"Not this fast," Hayden said. "And we can't risk revealing ourselves to the authorities, otherwise we won't come away with the box. Look at it this way, Mano—the 'no weapons' directive goes for everyone." The American smoothed out the front of her pure white dress, making it hug her curves even tighter and turned to Kinimaka. "How do I look?"

The Lost Kingdom

"Amazing."

"Hmm, good choice of words, I guess. I'd have enjoyed a few more though."

Kinimaka wiggled his tie. "At the first sign of trouble this tie's taking flight. And so is the jacket. One thing's for certain, my arms are splitting this crappy stitching tonight."

"What are you—the Hulk?" Alicia asked.

"No. Just a little ham-fisted."

"Coming from Hawaii, shouldn't that be *spam*-fisted?"

Kinimaka groaned, as did the entire team. Drake took a look at his crew, his extended family, and offered up a silent prayer for their safety. Couldn't hurt. Smyth appeared as awkward as Kinimaka in his black suit. Komodo wore his with surprising sharpness, citing a boyhood of attending his father's military lectures as the reason. Only Karin remained in civvies, ready to work now as ever on comms and op logistics, cuddling into Komodo's strong right arm as if it was for the last time.

Drake touched the bud buried deep in his ear. "They won't detect these?"

"Military grade. Should be completely invisible. I'll be with you the whole way, with eyes on blueprints of the hotel and all surrounding areas. Real-time. And by the way, Hayden, I've been thinking. If Tyler Webb is indeed stalking our homes, wouldn't it be a good idea to task a satellite over them, let him do his thing, and then follow *him* home?"

Hayden stared as Drake, Dahl and Alicia questioned, this being the first they had heard. Ignoring the others she said, "We'll see. It all comes down to money and operational priorities. Personally, we don't really have either."

"He *is* king of the Pythians."

"Sure. I'll check with Price when we get back. He's a little busy trying to stop a war right now."

Drake read Hayden's reactions, seeing that she really didn't want to talk about her stalking problems. Were they really that bad? Poor old Mai and Chika were dealing with much worse from the Yakuza. *And then there's this bloody Ramses bloke.* He shrugged it all off and checked his watch. "Time to go."

The team took stock for one more moment, content among friends; no terrible adversaries in this relaxed room. The camaraderie strengthened their unit, made them more than a whole. And it helped remind them of exactly what they were fighting for.

Alicia typically moved first. The rest followed.

CHAPTER FORTY

Drake paced across the hotel lobby, submitting to a pat down and showing his invite, happy to have Mai on his arm but feeling strange and detached from the whole thing. Surreal didn't do it justice. This wasn't his world, this high-society, posh-knob kind of stuff, and he wasn't the least bit unhappy about that. The elevator arrived, its polished gold, gleaming surface sliding open. He urged Mai inside, followed by most of the others. A tall, dark-skinned man dressed in hotel livery punched a button.

Alicia stage-whispered, "D'you think we should tip him? I never can remember the etiquette at a time like this."

Drake gave her a glare. "Google it."

"Oh, I seem to have left my Android in my other knickers."

Drake stared at her gilded purse. "So what do you have in there?"

"Are you kidding? Three hundred dollars and it'll barely fit a lipstick inside."

"I don't think it matters now," Hayden pointed out as the elevator arrived. The operator kept a straight face as they all filed out.

Drake stopped immediately, trying to collect his senses and focus. The room was large, circular and resplendent. First, he looked up because most people never did. A spherical light gantry hung over the room, spotlights rolling and flashing. A three-tier chandelier was suspended through its center and twinkled like fire and gold. At the center of the room stood a raised stage, also circular, a lighted palisade running around its circumference, interrupted in four places to allow entry. Tables stood everywhere, full of fresh flowers and plates of food whilst waiters were arranged around the outside of the room, serving champagne and canapés on silver trays. Drake turned to his group.

"Anyone spot our mark?"

Hibiki shook his head. "We're a little early. Shall we mingle?"

Drake grunted in protestation, but allowed himself to be dragged further into the room. Mai sashayed alongside, appearing to be enjoying this distraction and perfectly at home. Conversely, behind Drake came several uncomfortable-looking male individuals, all tugging at their collars. Only Dahl looked relaxed, commenting softly on the layout, entry and exit points and offering other salient observations. Drake turned his attention to the guests. Women were painstakingly coiffured, impeccably dressed and all able to offer that haughty yet appealing guise that defined their status in life. Men were more daring, some bearing stubble and pink, open shirts beneath dinner jackets and others so bronzed they might be mistaken for valuable statues. Most walked at a steady gait across the highly polished floor or stood around in groups, smiling carefully and remaining observant. Drake noticed a large easel set at the center of the stage and guessed it held details about the charity that was the purpose of tonight's event.

A waiter appeared to his left, offering Mai a glass of

champagne and then him. He waved it away. Behind, he heard Smyth choke at the very thought of bubbly.

"Got any Bud, bud?"

The waiter affected a slight smile. "I wish." He drifted away.

Drake surveyed the entire room again. "Hibiki," he said. "It's almost eight."

Mai tugged at his jacket. "He said center-stage. Let's go there."

Almost unconsciously, the team ranged out, knowing not to bunch together and cover the angles. Alicia took hold of Dahl's arm, the lights dazzling around her dress and hair. Mai was the opposite, a stunning shadow in the light. Hayden wore the white dress as if it were a second skin, attracting straying eyes as much as any glitterati. Drake climbed a short set of polished wooden steps to the stage; noting the intricate design set into its surface. As he arrived a sudden rush of ice water flooded his veins.

Trooping up the other side, all in a line, were Dudley and his three remaining comrades. The SPEAR team stopped and spread out, surprise to them only a fleeting thing. Dudley came to a halt and grinned, his men also fanning out.

"Gotcha," the Irishman said.

"Ya reckon?" Drake said thickly. "Then you're as dumb as you fucking look."

Dudley's eyes flicked to the right, the grin never leaving his face. Drake didn't take the bait but when Mai gasped he glanced over.

Hibiki couldn't hold in a nasty profanity, then said,

"What do we do now?"

Drake saw twelve Yakuza warriors coming up onto the stage. Their leader, Hikaru, fixed Mai with a seething stare as the rest flexed their muscles, taut beneath sheer shirts. For a moment there was utter silence as dinner jackets were discarded.

The party melted away, the chatter and the clink of glasses and the scraping of cutlery all receded into the background. Time stretched on a taut wire, as delicate as a shop full of fine china.

All they needed was a bull to start the destruction.

Alicia Myles pointed to the easel. "So? You guys gonna donate or what?"

Drake moved before she finished speaking, targeting the harshest thorn in their side—Dudley. Mai skipped away behind, heading for the Yakuza. Hibiki and Smyth went with her. All Drake knew was that Dahl and Alicia were at his back and then he was in the middle of a pitched battle. Shrill screams rose amidst yells of warning and outrage. Dudley slipped through his grasp, leaping to the side. Drake kicked him full in the chest, sending him crashing backwards through the ornate palisade, timbers shattering to all sides. A man came in from the left, facial characteristics revealing him to be Dudley's brother, but Dahl slid in to intercept. Malachi swung a haymaker which Dahl caught, twisted, and then used to lift the offender off his feet. A second later Malachi was airborne, slamming down into a table full of flowers, half-empty champagne glasses and side plates. Malachi groaned as the whole mess tipped over him.

Drake raced after Dudley as Alicia clashed with the

Irishman's other two comrades, Komodo also in attendance. Dudley came up swinging, his blows hard and true, almost bone-bruising. Drake covered well, constantly moving, leading Dudley away from his backup.

"Do you think they even have a box?" Alicia asked at one point as she skidded by.

"Maybe. He described it pretty well."

Dahl caught up with Malachi, the Irishman grabbing a passing waiter and hurling him toward the Swede. Dahl caught the waiter in one hand, steadied him and brushed him down with the other.

"Exit's over there."

Then Malachi attacked, and Dahl shrugged out of his suit jacket, using it as a weapon to lash his opponents head. Malachi became more angry than hurt as the thick material thudded around his cheeks and skull, eventually dipping his head and charging like a maddened bull. Dahl threw the jacket over his head and then brought a knee up. The crunch of broken bone was loud even with the sound deadening afforded by the jacket.

Across at the other end of the stage an even larger battle was underway. Mai engaged Hikaru but then found her way blocked by three more Yakuza.

"Sakurai! Eto! Kiharu! Get her!"

Mai threw herself into battle. The gunshot wound pulsed sharply but she ignored it. Reality was, if she didn't survive this battle the wound wouldn't matter. A jab to the throat sent Eto reeling, another to the midriff stunned Kiharu. Only Sakurai plowed through her bombardment, taking the pain and using it to fuel an angry fusillade of his own. Mai utilized the split in her dress to use her legs without restriction; Hayden had no such luxury. Form fitting, her dress only hampered her movements. First, she kicked off the heels, glad she'd worn stockings not tights. Then she flung her empty purse at one man's face and jabbed another. Kinimaka barged them aside to her right, flinging two straight over the top of the palisade where they became entangled with tables and chairs. Smyth growled angrily as if expecting his attitude would make them bow down, and when they didn't he grew even madder. Hibiki held back a little, helping to cover Yorgi, but soon the extra Yakuza numbers forced both of them to join the battle.

Punches flew, blows to the head and chest and groin slammed home hard, bones shattered. The stage was a wild melee, a brawl, the center of a ruckus that quickly began to expand around the room. Waiters protested and then, seeing the gravity of it all, rushed to the exits. Security guards tried to get involved and were thrown to the ground. Drake smashed Dudley on the bridge of the nose and received a stunning cheekbone blow in return. Dahl pulled his jacket away from Malachi's face, saw the pouring blood there and then reeled as the dripping face launched in his direction. Alicia split the hem of her dress whilst kicking McLain in the throat just as Komodo went down under a hail of blows from Byram. Alicia used the time she'd made to drag the soldier free, slamming Byram in the haunches so that he flew head first out of the stage area like a human cannonball.

"Fly, ya evil little leprechaun, fly."

She held the hem of her skirt up. "Look at this. A

The Lost Kingdom

thousand quid just ruined. Beau woulda loved it."

"Thanks for the save," Komodo said, panting a little.

"Any time, my friend."

"And the dress? I doubt it would have stayed on long," Komodo commented.

"Oh yeah? Well, that's not the point is it?"

Komodo turned as Byram came in hard again, the seasoned 27-Club member not looking in the least daunted by his recent unexpected flight. This time, though, the soldier was ready, hitting hard from the beginning and making every blow hurt in imitation of the Irishman.

Drake broke away from Dudley and quickly evaluated the scene. Hayden was already relaying their unfolding situation through the comms but it was always better to get eyeballs on it.

"If we knew he didn't have a Z-box we could let the authorities deal with him and slip away." Hayden was saying. "But . . ."

Drake knew they couldn't risk losing a box. He saw Mai picking the Yakuza warriors apart. Those boys were no slouches, he knew, but were hand-picked and deadly, yet Mai's skill and fury overwhelmed all. The palisades were shattered, standing like broken toothpicks; the tables and chairs were wrecked; those guests who still remained crouched or crawled through the debris. He ducked as Dudley threw a heavy champagne bottle at him.

"Do you even have the box, ya bloody madman?"

"Mebbe," came the drawl. "Mebbe not. What do yer think?"

Drake thought that he did. "Where is it?"

"Petition me. I'll get back to yer."

Drake lunged. Dudley slipped away, firing out a jab at the last minute. Drake felt its power across his lower jaw.

"Walked into that one didn't yer, soldier boy?"

Drake tried hard not to get into a slanging match. It would only destroy his focus. Dudley threw a glass at him, then a coat, grinning all the while. The entire room still glittered with golden light as if too superior to notice the plebeians ruining its ambiance. Drake sidestepped within range, dodged a jab and a cross punch, then struck hard, staggering his opponent. Dudley folded. Drake stepped up to finish the job but was hit from behind by a solid object. He turned, feeling a trickle of blood starting to flow. Malachi stood grinning crazily at him.

"The other side of the mirror."

Dahl grabbed the Irishman, glancing apologetically toward Drake. "Slipped away for a moment."

Drake couldn't help but laugh. "Don't let it happen again."

As he closed in on Dudley and the rest of the Irish gang started to falter, the other free-for-all swept closer. A Yakuza collapsed in front of Dudley, receiving a heavy swat for his trouble. Kinimaka stumbled over a broken chair, neck suddenly exposed. Drake swooped down to help, blocking a Yakuza strike and helping the Hawaiian up in just a few seconds.

"Mahalo."

Drake found the Yakuza tussle spreading among them. Dudley drifted away. A gravel-faced Asian aimed multiple hits at his face and chest, grunting with the effort. Drake blocked them all, then kicked out, but his expensive black shoe was deflected. Standing back, he straightened his jacket and cleared his throat. A man dived in from the right but Drake, unruffled, looped an arm around his neck and twisted. The man fell. Drake unfastened his tie, used its knot to whip another Yakuza hard in the face, striking his eyeball. He glanced down, nonchalantly straightening his cuffs.

Alicia's raucous shout broke his concentration. "Get on with it, Drakey. This ain't Pinewood fucking Studios!"

Dudley and his cohorts suddenly made a break for it, all moving as a unit as if it had been pre-planned. An open door beckoned, the red sign above it reading *STAIRCASE*.

Hayden's voice broke through the comms. "Back left. Target's escaping. *We can't let them get away!*"

Drake recognized the fear and desperation in her voice, knowing how imperative and vital recovering a Z-box was to the world at large. Nothing could be more important. He smashed a Yakuza body aside, seeing Kinimaka do the same, and gave chase. He counted at least five Yakuza were down. Alicia and Dahl fell in alongside and then, as he looked back, it seemed the entire room was streaming after him. First came Hibiki and Yorgi and then Mai and the others, all running headlong for the staircase and chasing the madman, Dudley.

Life and death and the future of everything they held dear hung in the balance.

CHAPTER FORTY ONE

The staircase twisted acutely at first, thickly and lushly carpeted so that Drake's Valentinos sank into the pile. Again the weirdness of the evening hit him; running on the carpet was like running on a mattress. The last Irishman—McLain—was right in front of him. Drake reached out but the staircase turned unexpectedly and he overshot. Alicia took the lead, leaping two steps at a time and clearly gathering herself to jump and land on the back of one of their fleeing enemies.

"Too risky!" Drake cried.

But too late. Alicia jumped, missed her mark, and tumbled head over heels, striking a wall with her spine and emitting a low groan.

"Fuck."

Dahl bounded into the lead. Drake grinned as he passed the complaining Englishwoman. "Gazelle." He pointed at himself. "Donkey." He pointed at her.

Dahl gained on Dudley's men as Drake took a chance and looked back up the stairwell. The sight was incredulous: dozens of battle-hardened figures chasing down riser after riser, some turning to exchange punches as they ran, others actually tussling. The massive Kinimaka ran with a Yakuza warrior gripped tightly to his chest, reminding Drake of a boy and his teddy; then Mano hurled his charge at a wall at a switchback level, shattering the image. Komodo used his combat skills to help protect Yorgi as they ran together, the soldier purposely slowing for the thief.

Ahead, Byram and McLain turned as the Irish descended yet another level, then stopped. Dahl hit one of them in midflight. A window smashed. Dudley quickly jumped onto a PVC frame, disappearing through. Malachi followed. Drake elbowed Byram in the face, pulling up sharp and then realizing the powerful impetus of what was coming behind him.

"Oh, shit."

He slammed his body against the wall, flattening fast. Alicia joined him as Byram and McLain leapt desperately for the window, barely scrambling through. Dahl tried to follow but was barreled over by an unstoppable Kinimaka. Yakuza fell at his feet and rebounded from his decelerating frame. Hayden grabbed hold of him; Yorgi tumbled head over heels, Komodo right beside him.

All the while the Irish gang were escaping.

Drake grabbed hold of the window ledge, wondering what visions would greet him outside. They'd descended so many levels they couldn't even be all that high any more. He hoisted himself up, spurred on by Alicia's hand in the middle of his ass. Once balanced, he took stock of the scene outside. This window stood about three floors up, situated on the west side of the hotel, directly opposite a cramped row of slightly lower buildings. The rooftops were mostly in darkness but Drake quickly made out the escaping Irishmen.

"Damn it!" he yelled.

"Fucksake, Drake," Alicia murmured, so close he started a little. "Either you're James Bond or Jack Bauer. Make your bloody mind up."

"You're like a chatty little parrot, sat on its perch, y'know that?"

Alicia pouted. Drake measured the distance and drop between the window ledge and the first rooftop and then made the leap, hitting the roof hard and rolling. From there he was up, casting a quick glance in Alicia's direction then remembering to look away for the sake of her own decency as she jumped.

His eyes found four fleeing shadows, their deep brogue audible even this far away as they cackled and bulled each other up. Drake started in hot pursuit, trusting his team to make the jump. Alicia was at his side in seconds. Together they crossed the first roof and gauged the leap to the second—only about six feet—and hurdled it together. A filthy alley passed below, dark and silent in the dead of night but not likely empty.

They landed lightly and kept running. Their quarry was two rooftops ahead. Dahl shouted to their rear and Drake whirled just in time to see the big Swede, already on the rooftop, catch a following Yakuza in mid-flight and launch him back off the edge. This seem to deter those trying to follow, allowing the SPEAR team to fight their way through.

"Eyes forward," Alicia reminded him.

Drake, still running, turned just in time to see the next gap approaching. This one was wider, probably eight feet and a challenge. Drake sprinted hard, then jumped up and out, swinging his arms back, and then forward as he leaped. He applied every muscle in his body to the effort, focusing next on where he wanted to land. Knees up from the halfway point he straightened them aggressively, landing on the balls of his feet, then going down into a diagonal roll from one shoulder to the opposite hip.

Using the momentum from his roll he continued his sprint, Alicia but an instant behind. The Irish were just up ahead now, having taken longer to complete their leap.

Behind there came a cry. Hayden had tumbled, restricted by her dress, and Mai stopped to help, refusing to allow the Yakuza to hurt any of her friends. One of the Asian men had picked up a length of metal tubing and swung it at Mai's head. Before it connected Komodo stepped up and plucked it out of the air, reversing it and jamming its end against the attacker's skull. Blood flowed. Hayden was pulled up by Kinimaka and another scuffle broke out. Yorgi and Dahl caught up to Drake, both fleet of foot.

"They'll be fine. Come on!"

Another gap in the rooftops and another eight feet to clear. Drake almost managed to grab Dudley's jacket as he landed, his fingers brushing the material, but then stumbled and lost valuable ground.

"Yer time's comin', soldier boy."

Drake gritted his teeth. They were on the final rooftop now. Behind him, Kinimaka, Smyth and Komodo ran hard as they simultaneously battled the last six remaining Yakuza warriors. The soldiers were matched blow for blow, the survivors seemingly the toughest of the gang, barely acknowledging the damage they took. Hayden ran with a slowing Mai. Drake could only imagine the pain his girlfriend must be in—the bullet wound hadn't fully healed. Ahead, Dudley and his boys were reaching the end of the last roof.

This chase certainly couldn't go on forever. It was coming to do-or-die time.

Drake glanced back as Yorgi gave a yell, stumbling and sprawling head-first. The Yorkshireman was surprised—he'd thought Yorgi the most likely to embrace all this running and jumping shit—but the Russian recovered fast and was soon swallowed by Hayden's pack.

"Where are those aresholes going to go now?" Dahl panted, eyes forward.

Dudley skidded to a halt as the roof ended, then without a second's pause simply jumped. Drake felt his breath catch, but refused to pass judgment. He'd seen a lot of strange things in this world but a vanishing act still remained on his "less likely" list. This theory was tested as all three remaining Irishmen also leaped into mid-air.

Alicia turned to Dahl. "Had to open your big mouth, didn't ya?"

Dahl started to protest, but it was a weak effort, probably because he agreed with her. Drake slowed as he approached the edge, unsure what to expect.

He peered over the side, taking it in, mindful that their quarry might have secreted a weapons cache along their escape route earlier.

"There you go," Alicia grunted.

Drake checked their rear. The following pack were taking flight, crossing over to the last roof, battling on the way. Thinking fast, he spoke into his comms.

"Do we have time to stop and get rid of the Yakuza?" The running fight could be ended in minutes, he was sure.

"No!" came back Hayden's instant, highly-stressed reply.

"The Z-boxes are crucial to the safety of the world. Somehow, one of us has to take it away from Dudley!"

"It'd be bloody easier if—"

"No!" Hayden said again, cutting him off for what seemed like the first time ever, so abruptly he winced. "At all costs! The boxes are all that matter."

Drake bit his lip until the blood flowed. "I don't like this." Below, Dudley and friends had jumped down to the top platform of a fire escape and were even now clattering down its metal skeleton. His gut told him taking five minutes to stop the Yakuza was the correct thing to do—but Hayden was their established and readily accepted boss, and the Z-boxes were apocalyptic dynamite.

"C'mon," Alicia said by his side. "Let's just go. Orders are orders, right?"

Drake nodded abruptly, shaking the indecision and accepting the greater good. Alicia, Dahl and then Hibiki hopped over to the fire escape. Drake followed.

Damn you, Dudley. Where's that box?

Hayden approached the last gap between roofs with a sense of utter relief. The white dress she'd chosen for tonight's occasion, as well as being totally ruined, was simply too tight. Flecks of blood and streaks of dirt stained it like exclamation marks of horror. From the pitched battle inside the hotel to the chase down the stairs to the leaps across to the rooftops, Hayden had fought gamely, taking some Yakuza out and slowing many others, saving Komodo's life once in the process. The big soldier hadn't needed to thank her, it was what they did for each other every single day.

Karin's constant updates filtered through her comms, warning them about hazards ahead and the status of the Hong Kong police and potential hiding places for Dudley. The English girl was clearly following their every move, knowing when they were approaching leaps.

Hayden hitched her skirt as she ran, making the last jump with an inch to spare, throwing everything in to it. One thing she knew, Mai Kitano was having a much worse time of it. The brawling, the running and hard jumping—the roll at the end—would be aggravating if not reopening her bullet wound. Not only that, she was a constant target of Hikaru and the remaining Yakuza and no matter what Hayden and the others did to deter the gangsters they always came back to zero in on Mai.

Now her dress tore down the side; not a bad thing since it helped free up her limbs a little more. Sakurai—she knew their names by now thanks to the constant shouting—sprawled beside her, the rough surface of the roof scoring his palms. Hayden kicked him in the side of the head. Sakurai rolled away and came up fighting, blocking Kinimaka's path now and trading blows. Hayden struggled to her feet and helped Komodo tear Mai from the hands of Hikaru and Eto. Smyth bloodied their faces and then, at Hayden's urging, they were off again, trying to stay on Drake's heels, to keep sight of Dudley and locate that Z-box.

The edge of the roof came up fast. Hayden already knew what to expect; Drake had shouted it through the comms. She slowed and then jumped once more, arms tucked in and knees high, hitting the top of the fire escape and letting the balls of her feet take the force of the impact. The flimsy structure shuddered, not from her landing but from the amount of people already scurrying down it. Dudley's crew were near the bottom, pulling up in surprise as they realized the steps ended ten feet off the ground. Drake, Dahl and Alicia were a minute behind them. Hayden started to descend as the fire escape swayed away from the wall, making its moorings squeal.

Bad omen, there's some heavy artillery about to hit this thing! She was thinking about Komodo and Smyth and, in particular, Kinimaka. Mano would never forgive himself if he accidentally took an entire fire escape down.

Karin's voice burst through the comms. "The alley below you leads across Gloucester Road and then Hung Hing Road. Then there are causeways, slipways and part of the harbor. Dudley could be trying to reach a boat."

Drake came back instantly. "Then why the hell did he lure us out in the first place?"

"Just saying." Karin sounded affronted.

"Possibly hoped the Yakuza would kill us off," Hayden said as she descended. "Or—"

"Or he has a surprise waiting. Dig in, guys. This is gonna get even hairier."

Hayden kept her eyes below and on the guardrails as Dudley made the first leap to the ground, hitting lightly and rolling. Luck was not on their side as the Irishman jumped up unhurt, drawling and shouting at his pals to move. As one the next three leaped into space, shouting at the tops of their voices and whooping it up.

All three landed undamaged.

Hayden concentrated on her descent. Above, the entire structure groaned as everyone jumped on. Komodo ran last, now guarding Mai from the Yakuza pack, and took a moment to grab a leaping gangster by the scruff of his neck just at the moment he landed.

"Morino, isn't it?" Komodo growled. "Why don't you people just fuck off?" And he launched the man over the side of the fire escape, waiting to give a limping Mai chance to begin her descent. The following Yakuza also waited, milling like a wolf pack waiting for their kill to weaken.

Drake's bunch leaped off the fire escape, hitting the concrete and rolling to safety. Hayden arrived at the base next, the ten foot drop below suddenly looking much more daunting than it had on the way down.

Kinimaka puffed hard behind her. "Just go. The jump will give us a breather."

She smiled as the frontrunners chased up the alley toward the wide road and glaringly bright lights at its end. Then she leaped, keeping her balance as she flew, concentrating on the landing. A hard impact, a roll, a few scrapes, and she was up, backing away from the spot she thought Mano might land. Above her the entire metal structure was now pulling away from the brick wall, twisting and grinding, minutes away from destruction.

Nevertheless, at the top, the Yakuza jumped on and started to descend at a senseless, reckless pace.

Hayden waited, not wanting to leave any of her team behind. Kinimaka landed like an asteroid, cracking concrete; then came Yorgi making it look easy and Smyth grumbling even in mid-flight. Only Mai and Komodo were left up there, with the Yakuza closing fast.

Mai jumped first, and Hayden saw instantly that she was in trouble. Her balance was off. Coming down hard she twisted as she landed, smashing down on her injured side, screaming. Komodo fell beside her and Hayden rushed forward to help.

Shouts of bloodlust and victory came from above.

The Yakuza fell among them.

CHAPTER FORTY TWO

Hayden fought for her life and for the lives of her family.

Five Yakuza warriors jumped down, one hitting Komodo hard, another striking Smyth a full blow in the face, the momentum added by the long drop staggering the snappish soldier, sending him to his knees. Hikaru landed close to Mai, grinning at her pain. Hayden ran to help her. Yorgi was already sprinting away from them but pulled up with a skid, quickly seeing their predicament.

Hikaru had found a heavy piece of rock, its edges jagged and hard, and now held it above the kneeling, groaning Mai. Hayden could see the blood seeping from her recent wound and how she held it, eyes shut tight in agony.

"This is how it ends for you, Mai Kitano," Hikaru said with something like relief on his face. "You kill us, we kill you. The Yakuza will be avenged."

Hayden put everything she had into a last lunge, a headlong dive, grabbing his waist and forcing him off his feet. Together they slid a few feet and the rock rolled away. Then Hikaru was up, quicker than her, striking down at her exposed face with lightning fast hands. A sharp kick to the ribs knocked her off balance.

And suddenly he was past her, scooping up the rock again and approaching Mai from behind. Yorgi arrived and hit out at Eto. Kinimaka struggled with Tanji, the smaller man dealing out painful hits and moving faster than the big man. Smyth tried to rise, still dazed from the crushing blow.

The Yakuza's star was rising, reaching its absolute zenith.

And the SPEAR team's world, their family, would never be the same.

With Drake, Alicia and Dahl long gone, Hayden knew there were no miracle rescues about to happen. She made a despairing lunge for Hikaru, fingertips tapping his shoes but barely touching him. Her fleeting gaze saw Smyth go down again, battered by the powerful Sakurai who also held a weapon—a piece of sharp, copper tubing.

Mai managed to turn her face upward, features distorted in pain, the midnight-black dress falling around her like Death's harbinger. For so long now she had been haunted by her actions.

"End it, Hikaru. Just do it."

The Japanese woman sat in agony, her life flashing before her; all the hopes and dreams and small regrets coming back.

Finally it all made sense.

I shouldn't be living in a world of suffering and guilt. I made my choice that day. The only people I hurt by not moving on are the very people I love.

The rock came down hard, bone-crushingly hard. Mai found her will, and at the last moment tried to move, but the reopened bullet wound sent debilitating waves of pain crashing through her.

Hayden screamed, again reaching for Hikaru's feet.

Mai saw the rock, its huge jagged edges and unyielding surface. She saw Hikaru's face, a mask of bloodlust and hatred and triumph. She waited to die.

Someone else came between them. A large bulky figure. The rock struck him instead, full in the face, sending him lifelessly down to the floor. Mai froze in horror. Hikaru screamed as he was thwarted once more and fell atop the fallen figure, smashing the rock again and again into the man's skull, making sure that he was dead.

Hayden was screaming too as she scrambled up, taking Hikaru's legs from under him. The Yakuza boss landed an inch from Mai, his face suddenly scared.

Without a moment's hesitation she elbowed him in the throat, jabbed at his eyes, his throat again, and then his ribs until his larynx was totally unprotected.

Then she crushed it.

Hikaru died before her, choking. Mai didn't have the will or strength to watch. Instead she looked to the fallen figure, to Hayden's grief-stricken, wide-eyed face, to Yorgi who stopped fighting with his opponent; both men taking a step back.

To Sakurai and Eto and Tanji—the only remaining Yakuza warriors, who became suddenly inert. Affected by the death of their boss, they now bowed slightly toward Mai.

Hayden grabbed the fallen man, took hold of his big shoulders, and rolled him over, instantly knowing he was already dead.

Karin's screams filled her ears. "Komodo! Komodo! T-vor. Is he okay? Oh, no. Please no! *Pleeeeaase—*"

A heavy silence descended over the alley, broken only by the sound of Karin's sobbing and Hayden's choked, emotion-filled tones. "I . . . I'm sorry. I—"

Kinimaka came over and held her, falling to his knees beside the lost soldier, tears streaming from his own eyes. In the gentlest gesture Hayden had even seen the big Hawaiian make, he leaned over and hugged his friend for the final time. Smyth too dropped beside Komodo, resting a shaking hand against the man's head and holding it there.

Mai staggered to her feet, hand across her wound, blood dripping through her fingers. "We should kill all of you murdering bastards."

Sakurai didn't move a muscle. "We're all warriors here. Believe me, we have earned our place."

Mai did not doubt it. "We're not trying to avenge a mere insult any more. We're trying to prevent a disaster from which even the Yakuza would be affected."

"I have orders from my *Kumicho*. This death," he indicated the fallen soldier, "cannot be altered and neither can the deaths of our fellow warriors. But it may be enough."

"Enough? Is it? You mean if we let you walk away?"

Sakurai looked to his fellow combatants. "In war there is always death. Hikaru is gone, but we have been avenged. We will not keep fighting without our leader. On my honor I will take this to the *Kumicho*. It may be enough."

Mai waved them away, thankful that Karin hadn't been able to hear their words. Unable to remain upright any longer, she too fell in the dirt and the dust, sitting alongside Komodo's body with her friends; guardians, sentinels to the memory of their lost companion; protecting him in death where they had not been able to do so in life.

*

Karin Blake threw the comms device across the room, standing, fists clenching, fighting every instinct in her body that made her want to destroy and crush and even kill. She pounded her fists on the table, struck the concrete wall until bloody imprints remained. The monitor before her never changed—stuck with an image she would never, ever forget.

The site of her fallen, unmoving boyfriend and the team sat around him, heads down, hands touching, custodians in shared loss.

Chika sat rigid, unable to process the death. Only Grace could console Karin and the young girl crept over now, crying herself, encircling Karin's body with caring arms and hugging her close.

"I'm so sorry. I don't know what to say. I'm just so sorry."

All Karin could do was hold on.

CHAPTER FORTY THREE

Drake ran straight across Gloucester Road, leaping over the iron railing that separated the carriageways without touching it. Dahl tracked him, sliding over the front of a parked car, staying hard on Dudley's tail. The Irishmen veered right around a hoarding and suddenly a stretch of water was in sight beyond a row of white stone pillars and a locked gate. Yellow cranes and rigs sat just beyond, reaching for the skies. Dudley dashed through a confluence of roads, finally hitting what Karin had called Hung Hing road, its expanse full of flashing yellow lights and traffic cones—roadworks. A gleaming white yacht passed to the left, sat high on a frame, its keel exposed so men could work freely. Around a blind corner and Dudley ran through a wide entrance. Drake, gaining slowly, read the name of the place on a narrow, white, polished sign.

"The Royal Hong Kong Yacht Club."

"Seems that he is heading for a boat," Dahl commented.

"It's not right," Drake panted. "He's leading us into something."

Alicia snorted. "Duh."

As they passed the spotlessly white entrance building, leaping the red and white barriers, as they pounded beneath overhanging trees, as they dashed through an empty car park, now bathed in the club's bright lights, Karin's heart-wrenching scream cut across the airwaves. Drake stumbled and slowed, Dahl imitating him. Alicia took a breath that lasted almost half a minute.

Their world quaked.

Dahl brought his hands up to his scalp, scratching furiously. Drake saw it as a gesture of terrible stress and forced his own attention back to their situation.

"Let's finish up here," he said quietly. "And then go see our friend."

Hibiki had caught up to them. He raced on, face set, as they crossed the car park and turned toward the doors to an inner sanctum that held a heart-shaped pool, a bar and other luxuries. Dudley smashed through an obviously already unlocked door and disappeared. Drake powered after him, close now, spurred on by the heartbreaking news and the Irishmen's own smirking faces.

Skirting the pool, they hurdled a fence and were then running along a causeway, alongside the water and a line of bobbing yachts, the open sea right in front of them at the causeway's end.

More boats were moored there.

"Stop and fight you cowardly arseholes!" Dahl cried at the top of his voice.

"Oh yeah, dude, that'll do it." Alicia sighed.

But the four Irishmen then leaped unaccountably to their right. At first Drake thought they were jumping into the calm waters but then their boots came down on the deck of a yacht and they set off running again.

"Balls," he said. "Not another freakin' obstacle course."

From deck to deck, prow to prow, Dudley ran and jumped. The yachts were set relatively close together, making progress easier, but the row stretched for as far as he could see ahead, maybe twenty to thirty vessels. *What is this guy's plan?*

"Twat it," he shouted. "When in Rome."

He jumped to the side, both feet slamming onto a yacht's deck and then continued to run. Similar noises at his back attested to the other three doing the same. His expensive shoes didn't afford him the best grip, but he wasn't about to go barefoot. He vaulted a ship's rail, bridging a wide gap where water churned below, and hit the deck of the next yacht at full speed. Alicia yelped as she skidded behind, but quickly righted herself. Another polished white deck and another leap and then another until only a dozen remained.

Ahead, Dudley turned around, hand held high.

"Now, soldier boy. Now it's time to die."

There was no time to think, no time to adjust their course or even slow down. Drake spied a black object in Dudley's hand, possibly a cellphone or transmitter and, for better or worse, was instantly reminded of the man's role in the destruction of Mu.

Daisy chain bombs. Oh shit!

Dudley pressed a button. The roar of an explosion shook the night. Drake staggered as the very *deck* of the yacht he was crossing heaved up and splintered. Timber blew apart beneath his feet. Spars shifted and exploded. Metal, carbon fiber and glass convulsed under intense pressure.

But he did not stop running, and neither did his teammates. Their pace took them beyond the bomb's initial range of damage and then they were jumping high, airborne as debris swirled at their back, and then landing again at full sprint onto the next yacht.

Which exploded.

The deck shattered, the sound of the bomb filling their

world. Solid ground fell away before Drake's shoes. A blast furnace shot through the air at their backs. Mustering every ration of speed, he sprinted on, not seeing them but *knowing* his team sped along beside him, still alive, still fighting with every ounce of their being. Again they cleared the destroyed vessel, pushed toward the next by a not so gentle hand, the blast hot on their heels. Another landing and another explosion, the whole row of yachts daisy chained by bombs and blasting apart in rapid succession.

Dudley landed on the far causeway when Drake still had four yachts to go.

Dahl reached his shoulder, urging him with competitiveness, with sheer spirit. Alicia panted a string of curses at his back. Hibiki was head down, his clothes spiked by debris. All around the sprinters a blizzard of shattering fragments raged; decks heaving, hulls reeling and prows sinking. The one thing that saved them was that the bombs had been secured inside the yacht's cabins, not where they ran. Still, a flurry of lethal carbon fiber shards pursued them, nicking at their necks and faces. An intact steering wheel whickered by at incredible speed, passing inches in front of Drake, an object that might have taken his head from his shoulders. Dahl glanced across as they leaped to another deck, the mad Swede's eyes alight with exhilaration. Another lurch and another blast, Drake almost stumbling to his death. With only two yachts to go the explosions were coming quicker, timed to take them all out at the end, but the SPEAR team would never give in.

As Alicia tripped—a guard-rail rapping her shins—Dahl reached down in mid-sprint, yanked at her arm and dragged her along through the continuing detonations, moving so fast she couldn't quite regain her feet. Drake bounded and soared, bouncing from one point to the next until the causeway lay dead ahead and if it had been any narrower he would have hurdled right off the far end.

Still, he hit hard, tumbling across the concrete and tearing most of his clothes, smashing his head against the ground. Blood flowed but it was a mere trickle, a graze across his forehead. Hibiki came down in front of him; Dahl and Alicia behind, the Englishwoman forced to cry out as her knees struck first.

Dahl remained standing.

Faced off by four angry Irishmen. Dudley stepped forward as Drake struggled upright. Malachi crouched as Dahl grinned. McLain and Byram gave surly acknowledgements to Alicia's obvious pain. Hibiki pulled a splinter the size of a dagger from his arm.

A strong sea breeze cooled their skin for one moment as the dying echoes of the final explosion rang across the bay and clouds of exploded debris floated down from the skies, gliding and spinning, hanging and twisting all around them.

"This is the last of the 27-Club," Dudley growled like a hurt but terribly dangerous lion. "Givin' yer some payback."

Then Dudley ran in, bounding through a cloud of swirling debris and draped in sharp slivers and shards. Alicia stepped before Drake, in the same cloud, taking on the leader of the 27-Club as she had done once before, determined to defeat him again. Drake faced off with Malachi. Dahl and Hibiki shared McLain and Byram. The combatants came together, trading blows, knuckles finding flesh and boots striking bone, foreheads smashing down into noses.

Drake glanced behind Dudley at the fast-looking motor launch at anchor. Chances were the Z-box was hidden in there. Now that Dudley's explosive plan with the yachts had failed, he was defending it. When Malachi lunged at him he gave the man a double blow to the side of the head. Anyone else would have fallen, reeling, but this man danced back up, clearly agonized but grinning through bloodied teeth.

"Feckin' pussy man," he grated. "How 'bout throwing a real punch?"

A haymaker missed Drake by millimeters. Drake caught the arm and bent it until it snapped. The expected scream didn't come, only a hiss like steam venting and then a new attack. Malachi swung around with his good hand, a shard of timber clasped between thumb and first finger. Drake saw it coming, threw an arm up to block and felt it rip through his jacket, shirt and skin. The point sank deep enough so that the improvised weapon stuck. Malachi fell away, good hands scrabbling for another deadly fragment. Drake plucked the timber away then threw himself at Malachi's chest, feet first. The blow smashed the air from him. Gasping, he threw gathered debris at Drake, temporarily blinding him, then plucked a bouncing trash can from the air. Catching it he swung it at Drake's head and though it was plastic the Yorkshireman still saw stars.

Stepping away, taking stock, still squinting through drifting particles of demolished yacht, he eyed Malachi.

"Never been good at givin' up." The Irishman inhaled deeply. "Not us. We'll die and then take yer to Hell with us."

"Been there," Drake said. "Done it. Even got the bloody T-shirt, Hawaiian print. Didn't like it."

When his opponent scooped up another, even more-wicked looking splinter, Drake jumped in, launching several incapacitating blows, but still Malachi fought and tried to rise despite wrenching his broken arm still further. The Yorkshireman then snapped the other one. What these guys lacked in skill they sure made up for in madness and tenacity. Lifting his foot, he brought a polished Valentino down on Malachi's neck, ending the fight.

Alicia jabbed and punched at Dudley, allowing him to speak before striking, watching his moves and awaiting her moment. She could tell he was wary, having lost to her before.

"Damn it, bitch. When are yer gonna lie down and die?"

"Not whilst I've got legs and can keep moving 'em forward, boy. Not whilst there's a horizon in front of me."

"Then I'll take it away. I'll feckin' kill yer."

Alicia sidestepped his lunge, delivering a heavy blow to his temple. "Not a chance. It's easy to take you down, Dudley. Just takes a slap to the nutsack."

She feigned a kick, following it in with a body barge, slamming her elbow as hard as she could into his chin. Dudley shook it off, a rabies-infested mad dog, and tried to bite her. Alicia spun him around and threw him over the fallen body of his brother, Malachi. Dudley hit the causeway, head cracking against the concrete. To his right lay a thick timber spar. He snapped back to his feet in a single movement, waving the spar around his head and screaming. Alicia ducked it twice, jabbing hard both times, then broke it in half. Still the remaining piece looked deadly and hurt when Dudley breached her defenses and smashed it against her ribs. Alicia flinched, but never stopped moving.

Dudley riled and insulted her, dropping the spar and plucking a floating wooden dagger out of the air. He took a moment to wipe his brow, fragments and shavings falling from his hair. Alicia felt yacht ruins landing on her own head and shoulders, clinging to her spoiled golden dress, and brushed what she could away. She found a dagger of her own and when Dudley lunged with his she deflected it away and came up under his belly with the three-inch shard, burying it deep.

The Irishman flinched, eyes suddenly wide as he fell away. Staggering, he caught himself, back to snarling already and ignored the wound. Alicia sidestepped to his right.

She heard Dahl telling Hibiki he looked tired out and to take a break as he dealt with McLain and Byram. Somewhere along the journey Dahl had heard that McLain liked to hurt security guards and that knowledge was now taking a heavy toll on McLain's limbs. The last of the 27-Club were falling to pieces.

"You wanna die at twenty seven?" Alicia asked the straining Dudley. "I'd be happy to oblige."

The Irishman came at her, snarling, all in for the last skirmish. He caught her around the waist, lifted and carried her backward several feet before her elbows jabbed down hard into his shoulders, staggering him still further. She skipped away, careful not to fall off the causeway and into the rolling harbor waters. He leaned over, swaying, blood pouring from many wounds, but he would not go down.

"Yer gonna have to kill me, bitch."

"Y'know what?" She eyed him dangerously. "That just ain't a problem for me."

He lunged, stance wrong, arms swinging, and she jabbed at his eyes and throat, then his ribs, finishing him with a sharp kick to the nose. Prone on the floor, he coughed blood, still jabbering, still crazy.

Alicia turned away, ignoring the blather.

As the last vestiges of the explosion floated down to earth his scrabbling hands found one that had landed earlier. A thick piece of metal railing, it was heavy, long and jagged—a deadly spear. Without thinking for one moment, the Irishman summoned every last ounce of strength, twisted his broken body and stabbed upward toward her lower spine.

Alicia never saw it coming. Her eyes were on Drake, fixed, perhaps even already wondering where she might go next. The fatal spear punched through the air, powered by the last strength of a madman. Alicia saw Drake react, then reach around her . . .

He grabbed the spear with his hand and arrested its thrust only a centimeter from her body.

Dudley screamed and wrenched at the weapon, but to no avail. Drake held on, gripping it tightly and holding Dudley's eyes with his own. After a few seconds he pulled it free, then reversed it and plunged it down into the man's chest.

The Irishman breathed his last.

Alicia stared at Drake, knowing full well how close she

had come. "Y'know what?" she said. "Here's a slogan for you—no guns were used in the harming of these murderers."

"Aye, love. I know."

"Thank you for my life."

"Any time. You know you're worth it."

Dahl sauntered up. "Nice workout." He nodded the way they'd come, all the way to the shadow of the hotel where they'd started.

"Komodo," Alicia breathed, a break in her voice.

The pall of misery redressed them. The blackest of shadows hung back there, a dark, endless gloom that would never be pierced.

Drake had never been more aware of a silent comms.

CHAPTER FORTY FOUR

In the aftermath, Drake found the Z-box in the motor launch whilst Dahl and the others trussed up the surviving Irishmen, an insane, spirited gift for the Hong Kong authorities. It was true the 27-Club had crimes to answer for back in the States, but the team were realistic enough to know they would never get them out of the country—or even away from the yacht club—unseen. It was a quick job, they had to be out of the area before the police arrived, and their legs were aching as if they'd all run a marathon, but slipping along in the shadows had never been a problem for a Special Forces team. No words were exchanged as they retraced their steps back to the alleyway where their comrade had fallen.

And met their friends, gathered around the body.

"He goes home," Hayden said. "Whatever the cost."

Drake took his turn beside the body, remembering all that Komodo had gone through and what he'd done not only for his country and the team, but for Karin and himself too. They'd first met the man back when the Blood King was discovering the gates of hell, such a long time ago now. And though they faced danger every day, ate it for breakfast and then went even harder into lunch, the loss of a true comrade was always surprising, always soul-destroying and never simple.

Drake finally looked up to see Mai kneeling beside him. "The Yakuza?"

"We allowed the three survivors to leave. They're soldiers, just like us. Hikaru got his just desserts. Honor was maintained. There is a chance they may call the debt paid."

"Somebody had to die?" Dahl breathed. "As my sleeping friend here would say—life sucks."

Alicia found herself thinking of her kids—Russo, Healey and Caitlyn, Crouch too—and hoping they were safe and secure. The losses she experienced in her life never prepared her for the next. Her eyes found Drake's in the semi-darkness and she wondered if one of them would be next.

One life, she thought. *Live it.*

"Do you have the box?" Hayden pressed gently after a while.

Drake handed it over.

"There's something else you guys need to know."

As they waited for transport, just minutes away, she explained more of Tyler Webb's little venture—the stalking of Lauren and the invasion of their house, other small, psychologically scarring incidents that had occurred. Drake stared down at Komodo as he listened, taking it in but unable to get the thought of poor Karin out of his head.

First Ben and her parents. Now this. How will she cope . . . ?

Dahl picked up immediately on the personal side of it all. "This bastard has been stalking my wife? My girls?"

"No clear evidence on your side," Hayden admitted. "But we believe so."

Mai took hold of Drake's arm and motioned that they should move away from the group. Drake sensed trouble. Already the lights of their transport van were visible at the end of the alley, approaching slowly.

"What is it?"

Mai moved easier now that Kinimaka had bandaged her up. "I have to return to Japan for a while," she said. "With Grace. Her parents died there. We have to find them. And with Chika and Hibiki. There's a lot to talk about. And also I have to come to terms with what I did to Hayami, how I killed him just to locate my parents."

Drake imagined that she was absolutely right. Grace's sojourn went without saying, and Mai would be the best one to accompany her. The relationship between Chika and Hibiki and Mai had also been tested beyond natural limits during this exploit—much of it would need repairing. He also knew that the Yakuza had murdered all of Hayami's family with the exception of one young girl—Emiko.

"Take as much time as you need," he said.

The Japanese woman hugged him long and hard, and to Drake it felt like the hug of companions together for the very last time. "It's not goodbye," she said.

It bloody well feels that way. "I know, Mai. We'll see each other again soon."

In another life, if not this one.

They were all merely flesh and blood, prone to dying and leaving loved ones behind. As good as the SPEAR team were they could never change fate.

By now the transport had parked up. Kinimaka, Smyth and Dahl lifted Komodo and carefully placed his body inside the black van. Then they hopped up. Everyone followed, and soon there was nobody left in the dark, lonely alley.

Just the ghost of a great man, the last deeds of his life, and the remnants of the fallen tears of his very best friends.

THE END

Please read on for more information on the future of the Matt Drake world

With Drake and the team taking a well-deserved break, it's back to Alicia's 'Gold' adventures next. Her new crew will be treasure-hunting and causing much general mayhem in Istanbul, Vienna, Paris and London around August time in *Crusader Gold*. And even though the SPEAR team are kicking back, I'm already researching Drake's next adventure which is shaping up nicely. Not entirely sure yet when I'm going to fit in the final part of the Chosen trilogy—but it will happen! What would *you* prefer after Alicia 2? Matt Drake 11, Alicia 3 or the final part of Chosen? Have your say! Let me know . . .

As always, e-mails are welcomed and replied to within a few days. If you have any questions just drop me a line.

Please check my website for all the latest news and updates—www.davidleadbeater.com

Word of mouth is essential for any author to succeed. If you enjoyed the book, please consider leaving a review at Amazon, even if it's only a line or two; it makes all the difference and would be hugely appreciated!

Printed in Great Britain
by Amazon